THE
Assignment

PENELOPE WARD

Editing: Jessica Royer Ocken
Proofreading and Formatting: Elaine York, www.allusionpublishing.com
Proofreading: Julia Griffis
Cover Photographer: Scott Hoover
Cover Model: Jay Byars, Instagram: @iamjaybyars
Cover Design: Letitia Hasser, RBA Designs

THE Assignment

Chapter One

Aspyn

"What's up?" I asked my supervisor, Laura Rowlings, who'd just called me into her office.

"Remember last weekend when Louie Serrano went missing?"

I worked at Horizons, a home for the elderly, as the activities coordinator. Mr. Serrano was one of the residents. Last week, his adult grandson had gotten a slap on the wrist for violating facility rules.

"Yeah. I wasn't working that day. But I heard it was a circus. The grandson broke him out of here?"

"Yup." Laura nodded. "Took him for a joyride without clearing it with management. We thought Louie had wandered away somehow. Then the grandson brings him back here like it was nothing. He knew about the policy. Didn't even pretend like he didn't. And it was the second time he's pulled something like this."

While I didn't personally understand why it was such a big deal if someone took a family member out for a bit, I did know the facility had a strict rule about getting clearance first. Mr. Serrano's grandson absolutely should've gotten permission, but people around here were treating this like he'd broken the old man out of prison. More often than not, the people who lived here had no family members visiting at all. So it seemed strange to vilify someone for paying attention to their loved one. I thought the whole scenario was kind of cute, to be honest.

"Does that situation have something to do with why you called me in here?" I asked.

Laura sighed. "Yeah. Apparently, this grandson has moved back to Meadowbrook from Seattle to look after the grandfather in his father's absence. The man's dad— Mr. Serrano's son—is traveling around Europe for a few months. This guy insists his grandfather needs to get out on a more regular schedule. He's now got permission from Nancy to take him out twice a week at designated times without having to clear it first, so long as he brings him back by a certain time."

"The way she was ranting about what he did..." I shook my head. "I'm surprised Nancy accommodated his request."

"Well, she was mad until he came in the next day and formally apologized. This guy is quite the looker, and pretty persistent—cocky but charming. I saw him when he went in to talk to her. I think Nancy fell for him a little."

I rolled my eyes. "Okay."

"But because he can't be trusted to stick to the rules, given his past behavior, Nancy said she would only allow the regular outings if we sent along a chaperone from the facility who can make sure Mr. Serrano is safely returned on time."

It suddenly hit me where this was going. "Let me guess...I'm the one who gets to babysit the bonehead grandson?"

"There's no one else we can assign. You're the only nonessential staff. You'll just ride with them and stay in the background."

"When does this start?"

"2 PM this afternoon."

What? I looked at the time on my phone. "Not much of a warning. That's in ten minutes."

"I know. I'm sorry. She forgot to let me know about it until a little while ago. I've already canceled the singalong you were supposed to do in the dining room at three."

I looked down at myself. Even though I wasn't medical staff, the center wanted me to come to work in the same garb the nurses here wore. Scrubs weren't an essential clothing choice for an activities director, but I liked the fact that I didn't have to choose an outfit for work—kind of like school uniforms back in the day, except much more comfortable. However, it also meant that today I'd be venturing around town in a pair of scrubs covered in the Disney character Goofy.

The one consolation in all of this, I supposed, was that Mr. Serrano was one of my favorites. He was incredibly friendly and had a sharp and speedy wit. I wouldn't mind spending time with him.

I dashed to the bathroom and ran a comb through my straight, light brown hair. I hadn't gotten a haircut in more than two years, so my tresses fell to just above my butt.

After freshening up, I made my way down the hall. I had no idea where we'd be going and found myself a little nervous to meet this grandson who'd supposedly charmed our tough-as-nails facility director.

When I walked into Mr. Serrano's room at 2 PM sharp, I was surprised to find him alone.

"Hey, Mr. Serrano."

He was sitting in his wheelchair, ready to go. "I heard you're gonna be my chaperone today, Aspyn."

I chuckled. "Well, I think it's your grandson I'm technically chaperoning."

"He's a good kid. Well, not a kid anymore. He's twenty-nine and a professional. Makes more money than I ever did. But I still see him like a boy. He's a good guy. And if it sounds like I'm trying to sell you on him, you'd be right." He winked.

"Anyway..." Mr. Serrano continued after I didn't respond. "He didn't mean anything by sneaking me out of here."

"I know that, but it's our job to keep you safe, so we need to know where you are at all times." I opened the shades to let more sun into his room. "And apparently, this has happened more than once?"

"Yeah. The first time, I wanted to watch the Mets. This place has cheap cable, so I couldn't watch the game here. The second time I was craving an ice cream from McDonald's. If he brings it for me, it's too melty by the time he gets here."

I couldn't help but smile. "Well, they didn't want the third time to be the charm. So now you're stuck with me."

"There are worse people to be stuck with." He grinned.

He's such a flirt.

Then a deep voice startled me. "Goofy is the one joining us?"

I turned around to find a very tall, handsome man with a gorgeous mane of brown hair scrutinizing me. I now wished I'd worn anything but the Goofy scrubs today.

"Aspyn, this is my grandson, Troy."

Troy.

I squinted. *Those eyes.* This was no first-time meeting.

No.

It's him.

This is a nightmare.

Troy Serrano.

Good God.

Troy.

Serrano.

Somehow I'd never connected Mr. Serrano's last name to *that* guy from high school. It had been eleven years, which was why I hadn't immediately recognized him. His hair was a bit longer. But not only had Troy Serrano been one of the most popular guys at Meadowbrook High, he was also the ex-boyfriend of my best friend senior year. He'd cheated on her, and let's just say I...went a little apeshit on him. And after that, we became enemies.

This was *not* good.

He looked me up and down. "Aspyn Dumont. I almost didn't recognize you."

Mr. Serrano looked between us. "You know the lovely Aspyn?"

Troy's eyes narrowed. "Lovely? That's not exactly how I remember her."

Mr. Serrano smiled, seeming amused. "How do you two know each other?"

I cleared my throat. "We went to high school together."

"Get out of town!" Mr. Serrano smacked his hand on the arm of his wheelchair.

I *wished* I could have. This very second. *Far* out of town.

Troy flashed a smug grin. "Yeah. We go way back. But we didn't exactly get along." His eyes met mine. "Isn't that right, Aspyn?"

Without even knowing the extent of my misbehavior, his poor grandfather tried to defend me. "How is that possible? Aspyn is a sweetheart."

"A sweetheart who keyed my car and put laxatives in my team's donuts," Troy scoffed.

"Not the *entire* team's donuts," I clarified. "Just the Boston cream one we knew you'd take."

He glared. "Oh, right. Forgive me. You only tried to kill *me*."

Mortification washed over me. If only I could sink into the floor and disappear. I cleared my throat. "It was a very immature thing to do. And I'm not proud of it. But at the time, I felt you deserved it for hurting my friend." I let out a long breath. "Anyway, it's been over a decade. No sense dwelling on something that happened forever ago when we were practically kids."

"What did he do to deserve it?" Mr. Serrano asked.

"I cheated on my high school girlfriend," Troy answered.

"Well, then she's right. You *did* deserve it."

Love you, Mr. Serrano. My stomach twisted. "Like I said, it's ancient history. I'd ask management to assign someone else to chaperone your outings, but we don't have the staff to accommodate an alternate."

"Are we taking separate cars?" Troy asked.

"No, I was told to ride with you."

"They don't trust me?"

I raised my brow. "Should they?"

"You don't have any keys on you, do you? If so, I'm not letting you anywhere near my car."

I rolled my eyes. "Okay, I deserved that. And my keys are staying behind."

"I guess you can come, then." He smirked.

Troy wheeled Mr. Serrano out of the room. I followed to start what would undoubtedly be the longest two hours of my life.

I focused on Troy's broad shoulders. He'd always been attractive, with an incredible body despite his ugly personality. But now he was like the boy I remembered, only better-looking—a full-grown man. I could only imagine the damage he'd done to poor, unsuspecting women over the past decade.

The August sun was nearly blinding as we walked through the parking lot. Troy drove a black Range Rover. Clearly he was doing well for himself. That didn't surprise me. Men with the arrogant confidence he'd always exhibited typically went on to become successful—probably because they walked all over people to get there.

I helped Mr. Serrano into the passenger side before Troy collapsed the wheelchair and placed it in his trunk. I then situated myself in the back while Troy got into the driver's seat.

The car reeked of his cologne. It was overbearing, just like him. His striking, bluish-green eyes locked with mine for a moment through the rearview mirror. I immediately looked away.

Troy turned to his grandfather. "Where do you want to go, Nonno?"

Nonno. Italian for grandfather.

"McDonald's."

"I can take you literally anywhere, and you always choose the same place. Let's change it up."

"I like their ice cream. Sue me. And it's where your grandmother and I used to go on Sundays after church. It reminds me of her."

Who can argue with that?

Troy sighed. "Okay, old man. Whatever you want." He turned down the road toward the plaza where the McDonald's was located.

A bit of awkward silence passed before Troy put on some music. Frank Sinatra's "Come Fly with Me" started playing.

"Well, at least you have good taste in music," I said.

"Sinatra is cool..." He pointed his thumb toward his grandfather. "I play it for this guy."

I smiled, leaning toward the front seat. "You like Sinatra, Mr. Serrano?"

"What's not to like? He was the best. Nobody better than Old Blue Eyes."

"I agree. They don't make 'em like that anymore."

When we pulled up to the drive-thru, Mr. Serrano hollered back at me. "You want a frosty, Aspyn?"

Frosty? I had to think for a second. He must have meant ice cream cone. "No, thank you."

"She's frosty enough," Troy quipped, flashing me a mischievous grin through the rearview mirror.

Damn that smile. As evil as I'd always thought him to be, he was annoyingly handsome, even more so now than in high school.

Troy ordered an ice cream for his grandfather and a large fry for himself. Of course, he could eat whatever the hell he wanted and still look that good.

"You sure you don't want anything?" Troy asked. "My treat."

As of the last fifteen minutes or so, I had a splitting headache. Some caffeine would really hit the spot. I decided to take advantage of his offer.

"Actually, I'll have a black coffee, but I can pay for it myself."

His brow lifted. "No cream or sugar?"

"No."

"Figures."

My eyes narrowed as he ordered me a coffee.

As he drove around, I said, "What was that supposed to mean...*figures*?"

"You seem like a black-coffee type of person."

After he stopped at the pay window, I asked, "How so?"

"You know...plain, bitter. But a lot of time's passed since high school, so maybe you've changed. If you'd like to prove me wrong, I'm open to that."

"You don't know crap about me—then or now," I said, anger heating my face. "You're basing your judgment on things I did in defense of my friend. Things I did because of *your* actions." I shoved three dollars in his face, but he wouldn't take it.

He placed his hand briefly around mine and pushed it back. "Put your money away. You're here because of me. You shouldn't have to pay for anything."

I crossed my arms and huffed in the back seat as Troy paid the cashier.

He pulled up to the pick-up window and a few seconds later passed a soft-serve cone to his grandfather. He placed the fries in his lap, and grabbed my coffee from the attendant.

Troy turned and handed it to me. "Are you seriously still mad because of something I did in high school?" he asked. "We're pushing thirty. There are worse things to worry about in the world, you know?"

I shrugged. "You're giving *me* an attitude and calling me plain and bitter. Sounds like you're the one who needs to get over it."

"Well, maybe I've been on defense because you've been looking at me like you want to kill me from the moment you recognized me."

"I'm sorry. I wasn't aware it was that obvious."

He flashed his sparkling white teeth. "So, you *do* want to kill me..."

"No. That's not what I meant. I just..." I let out a breath and stopped talking.

He pulled into a spot and put the car in park. Then he popped a fry into his mouth before turning to me and holding out his hand. "Let's have a truce, okay? Might as well, since we have to spend four hours a week together."

God. That sounded like a lot of time to have to deal with him. But I could certainly *pretend* to be cordial for my sweet client's sake. I would do it for Mr. Serrano.

I finally took Troy's hand and shook on it. "Fine."

My traitorous body enjoyed the warm touch of his skin, and that made me disappointed in myself. It proved how instinctual physical attraction could be. Troy Serrano's sex appeal had never been up for debate. Not then and not now. It was his soul that was questionable.

I was ashamed to admit that before Jasmine had started dating him, I'd actually had quite a crush on Troy. He was the quintessential popular football player. And I was exactly the type of girl who was invisible to guys like that. My head was stuck in the books, not up the asses of jocks. I never wore makeup or flaunted myself in skimpy clothes like Jasmine and many of the other girls did. But I still had eyes, and I was only human. When Jasmine talked about what it was like to be with him, I remember the ache of wondering what that might feel like. Then he hurt her and became Enemy Number One to me.

After a few minutes, Troy started the car again and drove down the road as Frank Sinatra continued to play. The smooth music was a stark contrast to my heightened nerves. The next song was "Under My Skin," which I found to be terribly ironic, considering Troy had definitely managed to get under mine today.

I could see Mr. Serrano's face in the sideview mirror. He looked so content eating his ice cream and listening to his favorite music. If only life were that simple for all of us.

"Where are we going now?" I asked.

"The mall," Troy answered.

"What's there?"

"Stores," he deadpanned.

"I know." I gritted my teeth. "But is there a specific place we're going?"

"Nonno just likes to browse," he said, observing me through the mirror. "Why the long face? They have a Disney store. I can drop you off there if you want, Goofy."

"And this truce of yours has lasted all of what? Three minutes?" I blew on my coffee.

"It's still on. I just like messing with you. I mean, come on, you're wearing freaking Goofy scrubs. That's like asking for ridicule."

I rolled my eyes, even though he was right.

When we got to the Meadowbrook Mall, Troy parked and got Mr. Serrano's wheelchair out of the trunk. Once Mr. Serrano was settled, the three of us walked together from the lot to the main entrance, which was right by the food court.

Inside, Mr. Serrano decided he wanted cinnamon pretzel bites, so we ventured over to the Auntie Anne's kiosk and waited in line.

My eyes landed on Troy's expensive-looking watch, then traveled up to his muscular forearm and the veins lining it. A waft of his scent momentarily overpowered the smell of the cinnamon.

"You want some?" Troy asked.

"Hmm?"

Want. Some?

Oh.

The pretzels. Right.

"No." I shook my head. "I don't eat sugar."

His eyes widened. "You don't eat sugar at all? What's there to live for, then?"

"4 PM," I said.

He grinned. "Ah. It took me a second. 4 PM. The time after which you no longer have to grace me with your presence."

"You got it."

Several seconds passed. "How did you end up working at Horizons anyway?"

The truthful answer was not something I'd get into with him. This job had never been my dream, by any means. But I felt lucky to have it after several years of feeling lost about my career path. Working at Horizons was the career I'd settled for after many lost opportunities.

"I sort of...fell into it," I said.

"What exactly do you do there—besides babysit men you hate on mall trips?"

"I'm the activities coordinator."

"What does that entail?"

"Booking field trips, arranging transportation, and leading in-house activities, among other things."

"Sounds kind of fun."

"I've grown to like it." I shrugged. "Anyway, you... seem to be doing well for yourself. What is it that you do?"

"I'm a financial advisor—creating personalized financial plans, executing trades in the market, and coming up with tax strategies, that kind of thing. My firm is based in Seattle, where I live, but I can work from anywhere, which is why I'm able to be here temporarily. They started transitioning everyone to mostly remote a couple of years ago."

"When did you come back to Meadowbrook?"

"I've only been here a month. Not my choice, really. But someone needed to keep an eye on my grandfather.

My dad just retired early from the fire department and planned a trip to Europe with his girlfriend. He needed peace of mind while he was gone. He felt guilty about leaving Nonno, so I told him I'd move here for a while and hold down the fort so he didn't have to worry."

"Well, that's...commendable."

He smirked. "It pained you to say that, didn't it?"

"A little. How could you tell?"

"You had this look on your face like you were constipated when the words came out. Your disdain for me doesn't take a break, even when you're giving me a compliment."

"I'm sorry if I can't hide my reaction to you. When someone hurts my friends, they hurt me."

"Okay, but you got me back, didn't you? All that crap you pulled? Keying my car?"

"There's no comparison between hurting a person and hurting a car."

"Don't forget about the donuts. You could've *easily* hurt me if I'd shit myself to death."

I fought laughter. "What do you want me to do? Look, I told you I wasn't proud of my actions back then. They were extremely immature. We've agreed to a truce, but that doesn't mean I can just instantly forget about the bad blood of the past. That will take time—more than the half hour we've been together. Yes, it was forever ago, but somehow it still seems like yesterday."

"It seems like yesterday because you're stuck in a time warp."

I crossed my arms. "What are you talking about?"

"I bet you've never left Meadowbrook, right?"

"Why would you assume that?"

"Wild guess?"

"What does staying in Meadowbrook have anything?"

"This place hasn't changed a single bit. Look at this mall. Everything is the same. You should've left by now, experienced some of the world. Maybe you wouldn't be so damn sensitive about shit that happened in high school if you'd lived out of this bubble."

Feeling my blood start to boil, I immediately went on the defensive. "There's nothing wrong with Meadowbrook. And not everyone has the luxury of just picking up and leaving."

Of course I might've wanted to explore other places, but this jerk knew nothing about my life or the circumstances behind my decisions.

He searched my eyes, seeming to have read through my words. "Why couldn't you leave?"

"I have my reasons. I'm not gonna get into them with you right now in a line for pretzels."

"Why not?"

"It's not the appropriate place."

"Says who? Auntie Anne?"

"Shut up." I laughed.

"Watch your mouth, Goofy." He winked. "You don't want Mickey to hear you."

Mr. Serrano chimed in. "Boy, you two don't stop, do ya?"

We turned to him in unison.

Thankfully, it was our turn in line, which gave me a break from having to talk to Troy. Mr. Serrano was happier

15

ɪan a clam once he got his bag of cinnamon goodness. Even though I'd given up sugar, I still loved the sweet aroma of anything freshly baked. My stomach growled—a little too loudly.

Of course, Troy didn't miss a beat.

"Your stomach is begging you for mercy, Dumont," he said.

"No, actually. It was just complaining about having to spend time with you."

"Good one," he said as he chewed.

We lingered just to the side of the kiosk as Mr. Serrano enjoyed his snack.

Then Troy interrupted my reprieve. "How's Jasmine doing these days? I saw she has a baby."

It surprised me that he knew that. "Yeah. A little girl who's a year and a half now. How did you know?"

"She friended me on Facebook."

"Jasmine friended you?"

"Yup," he said with his mouth full.

"When?"

"About a year ago, maybe?"

"Hmm," I muttered, finding that a bit strange.

"Even Jasmine can forgive me," he said. "But you can't seem to let shit go."

The fact that Jasmine would initiate contact with him perplexed me. She was happily married now to a guy she'd met in college. They'd moved to a town in Pennsylvania that was only an hour drive from where we were in New Jersey. I found it peculiar that she would randomly friend Troy when she'd talked so much smack about him. Jasmine had been obsessed with him while they were dating. All she ever talked about was how good he was in bed and how big his dick was. He'd been the best thing since sliced bread until she caught him red-handed at the movies with another member of the cheerleading squad.

"You guys still thick as thieves?" he asked.

"We don't see each other all that often anymore since she got married and had a baby. But I visit her from time to time. She lives in New Hope now."

"Nice."

"Yeah. That was a nice place to settle."

"The word *settle* sounds so depressing." He laughed.

"That doesn't surprise me, coming from you."

"When I think of settle, I think of my coffin *settling* into the ground."

"I take it you have no plans of settling down, then."

"Not anytime soon."

"I figured."

"Maybe someday, though." Troy sighed, wiping cinnamon off the side of his mouth. "Look, I was a dick for cheating on Jasmine. But for fuck's sake, I was barely eighteen. I didn't know my ass from my elbow, least of all how to be a boyfriend. I get that it pissed you off, but hurting women isn't something I make a habit of now."

"How exactly do you manage to avoid it?" I asked, genuinely curious. I found it hard to believe he'd changed all that much, given his looks and attitude.

"I don't lead anyone on. Being with more than one person is not cheating if you're never committed to anyone in the first place."

"Ah." I crossed my arms. "A commitment-phobe."

He looked down at my hand. "I don't see a ring on your finger."

"I'm not currently involved with anyone, but I'm not afraid of commitment. I look forward to being able to find my soulmate when the time is right."

"God forbid he crosses you," Troy cracked. Then his eyes went wide. "Where the hell is my grandfather?"

My head jerked toward where Mr. Serrano had been sitting. He'd disappeared.

My heartbeat accelerated. "What the hell?"

"You had one job, Goofy. So much for chaperoning."

Ignoring his asinine comment, I looked around. "Has he ever left your side before?"

Troy shook his head. "Nope."

My heart began to race. "Should we stay here in case he comes back or go looking for him?" My lack of experience in guarding people came into sharp focus.

Troy let out a breath. "You hang out here. I'm gonna take a walk around."

A few minutes passed, and Mr. Serrano never showed.

Troy came walking back toward me, holding out his hand. "Give me your phone."

"Why?"

"I'll enter my number so we can keep each other informed. I'll take this side of the mall." He pointed. "You head in the other direction."

I handed it to him, and he put his number into my contacts before we separated.

As I marched through the mall, I felt so disappointed in myself. How had I managed to lose poor Mr. Serrano on the first day of this task? Damn Troy had distracted me. But ultimately, this was my fault. I was supposed to be the responsible one. That was the very reason I was here in the first place.

About five minutes passed before my phone chimed. It was a text from Troy.

Troy: Anything?

I typed.

Aspyn: No.

Troy: Shit.

Aspyn: Where the hell could he have gone?

Troy: Fuck if I know. I tried the tobacco shop, but nothing.

Aspyn: Tobacco? He smokes?

Troy: He likes a good cigar.

Aspyn: Gross.

Troy: Not if it's the right one. You never tasted a cigar?

Aspyn: Can you stop texting me and look for your grandfather, please?

Troy: I'm using voice to text. Still looking while I talk.

Aspyn: Anywhere else he likes to go?

The dots on the screen moved around.

Troy: Victoria's Secret.

Aspyn: Cut the shit.

Troy: LOL. I'm serious. That just came to me. He could have gone there.

Aspyn: Why in God's name would he be in a lingerie store?

Troy: My grandmother used to wear this body spray from there.

Oh. My heart clenched.

Aspyn: He still buys it?

Troy: Sprays it on his sheets.

Aspyn: Oh my God. That's the fruity scent I always smell in his room.

Troy: Yep.

I stopped at the mall directory to check where Victoria's Secret was located.

Aspyn: That's on my side of the mall. Heading over there now.

Troy: Okay. I'll keep looking on this end.

As I entered the store, I accidentally sideswiped a pile of colorful, clearance underwear, causing them to fall to the ground. I picked them up and dropped them on the table in a messy pile before rushing to the register.

"Excuse me. Can you tell me if an elderly man in a wheelchair was in here by any chance?" I asked the cashier.

To my surprise, she nodded. "Yes, actually. He left about a minute ago. He bought a bottle of Love Spell body mist."

"Did you happen to catch which direction he went?"

"No, I'm sorry. I wasn't watching."

Damn it.

I texted Troy as I walked out of the store.

Aspyn: They said your grandfather was in here buying the spray! He left just before I got here. I'm still looking.

Troy: Did you leave with any new underwear?

Aspyn: Very funny.

Troy: Because your panties have been in a bunch all day. You could use some new ones.

Aspyn: Don't text me again until you've found your grandfather.

Swearing under my breath, I shoved my phone in my clutch.

After wandering my side of the mall for another twenty minutes, I came up empty-handed.

Suddenly, I noticed Troy walking toward me. Looking frustrated, he held his hands up in defeat.

He stopped when he reached me and ran his hand through his hair. "I need to get him a damn phone."

"He doesn't have one?"

"He's got an old flip phone, but he never takes it with him."

"We'll find him." I sighed, noticing genuine concern in his eyes.

This is all my fault.

I swallowed. "I mean, he's got to be somewhere in here, right? He wouldn't have left." Then a lightbulb went off in my head. "Let's ask mall security to page him."

He snapped his fingers. "That's a fucking great idea. Why the hell didn't I think of that?"

"Because you're not very bright?"

He glared, and we took off together in search of help. But before we had a chance to find anyone, Troy tapped my arm and stopped walking. He pointed to a flower shop.

Through the glass, I spotted Mr. Serrano, sniffing a large bouquet of flowers the attendant had just handed him.

Troy rushed through the doors as I followed.

"Why the hell did you take off?" he yelled. "We've been worried sick."

Mr. Serrano didn't even flinch as he continued to smell the yellow roses. "I figured I'd leave you two to go on with your arguing."

Troy tightened his jaw. "You could've told us you were leaving."

"Did my leaving help you two stop bickering?"

Troy sighed. "Well, yeah, but..."

"Then mission accomplished."

"You nearly gave us a heart attack in the process, Mr. Serrano."

"How far do you think I could've possibly traveled in this chair?"

"Anything can happen in a place like this," I said. "You could've been robbed or taken advantage of very easily."

His expression softened. "I'm sorry to upset you, pretty lady."

"Why are you buying flowers anyway?" Troy asked.

"These were your grandmother's favorite—yellow roses. But they're not for me. They're for you."

Troy's eyes narrowed. "For *me*?"

"Yeah. For you to give to Aspyn and apologize for being such a knucklehead."

I held up my palm. "That's really not necessary."

"Sure, it is," Mr. Serrano insisted before handing the bouquet to his grandson.

Troy reluctantly took the roses before offering them to me. "Goofy, will you accept these roses?" He flashed an impish grin as he batted his lashes, which seemed insanely long for a man.

"While I'd love to throw them back in your face, I'll accept them on behalf of your sweet grandfather who meant well." I took them and turned to the old man. "Thank you, Mr. Serrano."

The three of us left the flower shop, and I thought we might be leaving the mall until Troy stopped in front of the mattress store.

"Hey, can we go in here for a second?" Troy went inside without waiting for a response.

"I'm in no rush to head back," Mr. Serrano said as we followed.

Troy began walking around, pushing on various mattresses.

"Is it really necessary for you to go mattress shopping today?" I asked.

"Actually, it is, because I've been sleeping like crap," he said as he bounced on one of them. "The bed my dad put in the room I sleep in at his house is hard as a rock. Pretty sure it's his old mattress. I want to get a nice memory foam one."

"Memory foam!" Mr. Serrano shouted. "I could use some of that. Will it help me remember shit?"

I laughed and sat down on the bed across from Troy.

He lay all the way back and spread his arms out. "Ahh, this one is nice. So damn comfortable." His shirt rode up a little, and I pretended not to notice the glimpse of his rock-hard abs.

I got up and sat down on the edge of the one he was raving about. It was firmer than I like. "This one is nothing compared to the one I was just sitting on."

Troy lifted himself off the bed and moved over to the other one. After bouncing a few times, he said, "Oh, no way. The other one is better."

"I disagree."

A sales rep walked over. "You know you're not gonna win this argument, right?" she said to him. "The wife always gets her way in the end."

Troy snorted. "Goofy? She's not my wife. She's just a girl who tried to poison me in high school."

"Oh. I'm sorry. Can I help you with anything?"

"I'll let you know."

"He's noncommittal. Don't waste your time," I chided.

Sure enough, fifteen minutes later, Troy walked out without placing a mattress order.

The rest of my afternoon with the Serrano men was pretty uneventful. Before leaving the mall, we accompanied Mr. Serrano to the smoke shop, where he purchased a cigar, which Troy promised to let him enjoy when he had more time during the next outing, seeing as though Horizons didn't allow smoking on the premises. When we passed the Disney Store on the way out, Troy had a field day, of course, suggesting I go in and buy something on his dime—like a stuffed Goofy. I ignored him, despite being tempted to take advantage of his offer and get something for my niece. No way I'd give him that satisfaction, though.

After we returned Mr. Serrano to his room at the facility, I was on my way to clock out for the day when Troy stopped me in the hallway.

"Hey, Aspyn..."

I turned to face him. "Yeah?"

"Thank you for today—helping me look for him. The situation freaked me out. Having you there made it easier."

"Yeah, well, he wouldn't have left if we weren't arguing in the first place."

"It's crazy how this whole thing happened, huh?"

"What are you referring to specifically?"

"You and me having to spend time together. What are the chances? Terrible luck on your part."

"I'd have to agree."

Troy snickered. "It's a small world after all."

It took me a few seconds. *"It's a Small World After All." The Disney song.* I rolled my eyes. "Stop with the Disney jokes."

"Stop with Disney clothes, and I'll stop with the Disney jokes." He winked before walking away.

The fresh air that hit me as I went out to the parking lot helped clear my mind and mood a little, but the events of the day ran through my head the entire ride home. I couldn't stop thinking about how easily Troy still got to me after all these years.

Since I was stopping at my parents' on the way to my house, I thought I'd give my mom the flowers Mr. Serrano had bought.

I parked in front of my parents' place and reached over to the passenger side for the Vera Bradley clutch where I kept my money and phone. I patted the seat. *Where is it?*

I couldn't remember bringing it back into Horizons with me. My heart dropped.

I left it in Troy Serrano's car.

Chapter Two

Troy

On the way home from Nonno's, I stopped at the home improvement store to pick up a shoe rack for the closet in my room. When I opened the back of my Range Rover to place the flat box on the seat, I noticed something: a wallet made of flowery fabric with a thin strap. It was on the side of the seat where Aspyn had been sitting. I picked it up.

Shit. I was just about to text her when I realized her phone was tucked into the front flap. *Damn it.*

I opened the wallet and looked inside for her license. Her photo featured the same resting bitch face she'd aimed at me most of today. The address listed wasn't all that far from where I lived, and even if it were, I needed to get this back to her tonight. Returning to the driver's seat, I popped the address into my GPS and took off down the road.

On the ride over, I thought about today. Aspyn had seemed to soften a little by the end, but overall she'd been really on edge around me. Was I that much of an asshole in high school? Deep down, I knew the answer was yes.

I always remembered her as an odd duck. Back in the day, she'd tag along with Jasmine and me but not really say much. I liked her enough—until she went batshit crazy. She'd given me every reason to dislike her after that. I thought I'd long moved on from anything that happened back then, but it was clear *she* hadn't. I respected her for sticking up for her friend, even if she'd fucked me over to do it. But at the time, I'd taken her actions as a personal attack.

I have to say, Aspyn was definitely cuter than I remembered. She'd really grown into herself over the past decade. Her long, sand-colored hair was beautiful—straight and voluminous, practically down to her butt. Her ass looked pretty nice in those Goofy pants, too. They fit like a glove. She was tall, curvy, and jiggled in all the right places. Scrubs don't lie. No, I definitely wouldn't throw Aspyn Dumont out of the bedroom, although she'd probably cut my dick off in the middle of the night.

When I pulled up to the house, I double-checked to make sure the number on the mailbox matched the one in my GPS. I grabbed the wallet from my passenger side and headed toward the door.

After knocking, I waited.

About thirty seconds went by before I knocked again.

There was no answer, but through the window, I could see the television was on. There seemed to be a kid's show playing. I knew she liked Disney, but damn.

I rapped on the door a third time and called out, "Hey! Aspyn, are you home?"

"Go away!" A child's voice came from behind the door. It sounded like a little girl.

"Uh…" I blinked. "Who am I talking to?"

"Are you crazy?" she said. "I'm not telling you my name!"

"Why?"

"Stranger danger!"

"I promise I'm not a dangerous person. My name is Troy. I just need to get Aspyn her wallet and phone. She left them in my car today." After she didn't respond, I said, "How about this…if you open the door a crack, I can just stick it through. You won't even have to see me."

"Open the door just enough so you can shoot? How do I know you don't have a gun?"

"Technically, I could shoot through the door if I had a gun. But I *don't* have a gun, and I promise you I'm totally legit."

I could hear muffled talking and then the door suddenly opened. Aspyn stood there with her hair dripping wet, looking like she'd just gotten out of the shower. She seemed out of breath.

Before I could even utter a word, I looked down to find the pint-sized girl with a gigantic water gun aimed at me. I held up my hands, but not before she began to shoot. A deluge of water came at me. Because of her height, the line of fire was aimed straight at my dick.

Shit!

Bursts of water continued to pummel me.

"Kiki, stop!" Aspyn finally shouted.

It took her long enough.

"What the hell?" I said, looking down at my drenched pants.

The girl's chest heaved as she withdrew her weapon. "You shouldn't have opened the door!" she told Aspyn.

"He's not a stranger. I know him." Aspyn turned to me, a hint of amusement on her face. "I'm really sorry."

My brow lifted. "Are you?"

"Kiki, go to your room, and please put that away," she ordered.

The little girl shot daggers at me before she marched off.

I held out the purse, which somehow managed to stay mostly dry. "You left your wallet thingy and phone in my car."

Her eyes fell momentarily to the gigantic water spot on my crotch before she looked back up at me. "I know. I tried to get in touch with your grandfather for your number, but they said he was asleep. And for some reason the office staff couldn't locate your contact information. Nancy was gone for the day, and they couldn't reach her. I was going to look you up on Facebook to try to message you as soon as I got out of the shower. You just beat me to it. Thank you for bringing it by. Sorry about the attack just now."

"I'm surprised you told her to stop shooting."

"Yeah, well, you were nice enough to drive here with my purse, so..."

I looked beyond her shoulders. "Is she...your daughter?"

Aspyn hesitated. "My niece."

"Ah. You don't have kids then..."

"No."

"Babysitting?"

She looked down at her feet. "Not exactly."

"She lives with you?"

Aspyn looked up at me. "My sister...died. So, my niece divides her time between my place and my parents' house."

Shit. I swallowed. "I'm so sorry. I didn't know."

"You don't have to feel sorry for me. I can see that look in your eyes again." She mocked, "Poor little Aspyn stuck in Meadowbrook."

My heart sank, regretting the stupid shit I'd said earlier. "That's not what I was thinking at all. Not in the least."

The sad look in her eyes hit me hard. I wanted to hug her, which was weird, considering how much I knew she disliked me.

Droplets of water dripped down her T-shirt as she blew out a breath. "Anyway...thank you for dropping this by. I really appreciate it."

"Yeah." I slipped my hands into my pockets. "No problem."

I lingered for a few seconds until she grabbed the door handle. I took that as my cue to leave. Nodding my head, I made my way out the door, and she wasted no time closing it behind me.

Aspyn couldn't get rid of me fast enough.

• • •

Because I'd had to drop off the wallet, I was ten minutes late meeting my buddy Eric for dinner at a local bar and grill. Eric had gone to high school with us, and this would be my third time hanging out with him since arriving back in Meadowbrook.

He was already seated in a booth when I got to Boone's Pub, where the air always smelled like a mix of burned meat and alcohol.

Eric immediately looked down at my wet spot. "What the hell, man? Did you piss yourself?"

"No." I took a seat across from him. "I got shot at with a Super Soaker. I didn't have time to head home and change."

"What the fuck?"

"Yeah...this little girl—long story. I'll explain later." I grabbed a menu. "Let's just order. I'm starving."

After we put in for our food, I asked him the question that had been weighing on me the entire ride over. "You ever take one look at someone or something from the past, and it just brings back all this shit you've tried to forget? Makes you realize all these feelings you thought were gone never really went away?"

Eric nodded. "That's how I feel when I look at Stoli vodka. Reminds me of the time I puked all over Christy Hemingway in tenth grade."

Aspyn was like my very own pile of vomit.

"You remember Aspyn Dumont from high school?"

He ripped apart a piece of bread. "Yeah, sure."

"She works at the place my grandfather's at."

"Really? Wasn't she psycho?" he asked as he reached for the butter.

His use of the word *psycho* jarred me a little, mainly because I knew he'd gotten that idea about her from *me*. That had been my usual nickname for her after the incidents in high school. But even if I'd thought she was a little *psycho* back then, I should've chosen the words I'd spoken aloud more carefully. I felt like shit right now.

"She had her moments, yeah. We pretty much hated each other, talked shit about each other. But a lot of it was my fault."

While we continued waiting for our food, I caught Eric up on the situation with Aspyn and explained why she'd been assigned to chaperone the outings. I also reminded him of the reason behind some of the crap she pulled on me in high school.

I sipped my beer and stared down at the bottle. "Anyway, I don't know why I'm even talking about her..."

"What does she look like now?" he asked.

The waitress came by with our food, and that gave me a minute before responding. I thought about Aspyn's physical appearance. Her sand-colored hair was so long, almost down to her voluptuous ass. Without a drop of makeup, her skin was smooth and flawless. She was naturally beautiful, even more so somehow when she got mad at me. I'd been taken aback by the fact that I found myself very attracted to her, someone I used to have nothing but disdain for. That was a contradiction I hadn't experienced before. Maybe somehow her hatred made her more appealing in a twisted way?

I downplayed it. "She's not a knockout or anything, but she's...pretty. Nice ass and tits. It was hard to see past the look of hatred on her face, though."

"Well, sounds like you're gonna have other opportunities to change her mind about you if you're stuck with her twice a week."

"Not sure I should bother trying to change her mind. She seems really hung up on the past."

He chewed a sweet potato fry. "How long are you staying in Meadowbrook anyway?"

"For as long as my dad's away. Probably a few more months max. He hasn't bought his return ticket, because they're sort of winging the whole trip."

"What's he doing again?"

"Touring Europe with his girlfriend."

"Damn. Nice life."

"Yeah, well, he earned it." I opened the ketchup and poured some onto my plate. "I'm staying at the house, making sure everything's kosher while he's gone."

My father had busted his ass raising me as a single father. We never took vacations, and he rarely did anything for himself. A couple of years ago, he met a woman he really connected with. It was the first real relationship I could ever remember him having. He turned fifty this year and became eligible to retire early from the fire department. So that's what he did. He and Sheryl decided to tour Europe. He almost didn't go, because he felt guilty about leaving my grandfather. We didn't have any other family locally. But I assured him I'd handle everything. It was the least I could do for a man who'd devoted his entire life to raising me. And I wasn't easy. Despite my dad's best efforts, I'd acted out a lot as a kid. Even though my grades were good and I excelled at sports, I gave him a run for his money, constantly getting into fights and stirring up trouble. I owed him a lot.

That night, after I returned home from dinner with Eric, I kicked my feet up on the couch and decided to Google *Aspyn Dumont*. The first thing to come up in my search was her sister's obituary from eight years ago. While it didn't list a cause of death, it said she'd left behind a six-month-old daughter. That made my chest hurt. Ashlyn

Dumont was only twenty-four when she died. *Ashlyn and Aspyn.* They must have been close. I was an only child, but I couldn't imagine losing a sibling. My chest tightened. I felt guilty once again for taunting Aspyn about staying in Meadowbrook now that I knew she'd been helping to care for her niece. That wasn't an easy life.

I couldn't change how I'd treated Aspyn in high school or the nasty things I'd said about her behind her back. But I *could* at least try to show her I'd changed. The big question was: *had I* changed? Or was I still that same selfish asshole?

That question gave me pause, and I honestly didn't know the answer. All I knew was that being back in Meadowbrook sure as hell made me *feel* like the bad guy again. I wanted to be a better person, and somehow, it mattered to me to show her I was. But why?

Aspyn felt like the personification of all my past mistakes, so maybe getting her to like me would absolve me of my sins.

• • •

On Thursday afternoon, when my second outing of the week with Nonno rolled around, Aspyn looked happy as always to see me when she met us in his room. *Not.*

"Are those donuts on your scrubs?" I asked.

"I wore them in honor of you." She flashed a genuine smile.

Figures. The first real smile I get from her is related to trying to poison me.

"Did you buy those just for me?"

"Believe it or not, I already had them."

"I do believe it, actually."

"My scrubs are conversation pieces around here."

"Then I think you should tell everyone what the donuts represent. Or might you be too ashamed to admit that you almost shit me to death?" I laughed, noticing she did the same. "I like that you're finding your sense of humor, though."

"It took me a while to dust it off. But it was in there, after all."

When she smiled again, I noticed slight creases around her eyes. My stare might have lingered a bit too long.

"Ready to go?" she asked, interrupting my gaze.

I cleared my throat. "Yup."

"Let's roll," my grandfather said as he wheeled himself to the door.

Since it was a dry, summer day, I thought it would be nice to spend our time outdoors. I'd promised Nonno I'd bring the cigar we'd bought at the mall on Tuesday so he could smoke it.

The three of us packed into my car and drove to a nearby park. Once I pulled into a parking spot, I removed a large Ziploc bag with the cigars I'd brought from my glove compartment.

We picked a spot under a shady tree. I took my grandfather's cigar out of the bag and handed it to him. "Here's your Macanudo, Nonno."

After he placed it between his teeth, I lit a match and held it to the tip.

"Thank you, good sir." He puffed on the stogie and flashed a huge smile. "This is the life."

I chuckled. It certainly didn't take much to please him. I hoped I could be that easily satisfied someday.

I took another cigar out of the bag and handed it to Aspyn.

"What are you doing?" She took a few steps back, as if I were trying to hand her my dick or something.

I held up the Tatiana Classic. "This is for you. We're gonna smoke, too."

She shook her head. "Oh, no, no, no. I don't smoke."

"You don't have to inhale it. Just enjoy the flavor. Yours is infused with vanilla. As far as I know there's no sugar in it. So, I think you're good."

"I've never smoked a cigar, and I don't plan to start today."

"I'm gonna pop your cherry. Literally."

Aspyn squinted. "Excuse me?"

I pointed to the tip. "The lit part is known as the cherry, by the way."

Her frown lessened. "Oh."

"Just try it. If you don't like it, you can throw it down and stomp on it."

To my surprise, she gave in, taking the cigar from me. She held it wrong, like a cigarette.

I intervened. "Rest it on your middle finger—you're good at using that one—then curl your index finger around it."

She did as I said, and then hesitantly placed the cigar between her lips. Something about that was damn sexy. I felt my mind venturing toward the gutter.

I lit a match and reached it out to her. "Puff gently as I light it."

Aspyn inhaled and immediately started coughing.

"What part of *puff gently* did you not understand?"

"I inhaled it," she coughed out.

"Yeah, I got that. I told you not to do that. Just suck a little into your mouth and taste it."

My mind was *definitely* fully in the gutter now.

"It's all about technique," I said. "Watch and learn." I lit my own and demonstrated. "First thing," I said as I took a little of the smoke in. "You can't neglect the cherry." I pointed to the tip. "You've got to keep it lit. At the same time, you have to find a happy medium between smoking too fast and not fast enough."

She mimicked what I did, puffing lightly this time.

"That's it. Draw it into your mouth—never your lungs. Not too fast and not too slow. If you suck too hard, you'll fuck it all up." I couldn't help myself. "Probably the only time I've ever said that."

She coughed. "I'm sure." Aspyn took another puff. "I can actually taste the vanilla."

"There are no chemicals in these. So you should be good with whatever diet you're on."

"If you think this is healthy, Troy, you're kidding yourself."

"One won't kill you." I wriggled my brows. "You should try *everything* at least once."

"I beg to differ. There are some things best kept away from *entirely*."

Pretty sure I got that message loud and clear. I watched her for a bit and noticed she was taking the smoke in too frequently.

"Wait about thirty seconds between puffs, then gently allow the smoke to fall out of your mouth," I directed. "The beauty of this is that it's supposed to force you to relax. Perfect for high-strung people like yourself to practice chilling out."

"I need something a bit stronger rolled into this paper to deal with you, Serrano."

"That can be arranged next time." I winked.

"Please don't bring weed to the next day trip."

"Why not? I'm already in trouble with those fuckers at Horizons," I joked. Then she flicked the ash. "Don't do that! You need that ash at the tip to help control the temperature."

"You're so bossy," she said as she flicked the ash again just to spite me. Some of it landed on my shoe.

"It'll overburn if you keep doing that," I scolded. "Leave it on, and let it do its thing. Then give it a small roll every once in a while if you have to get rid of the excess." I smirked. "Unlike you, the cigar is delicate."

"Who says I'm not delicate?" She flashed an amused look.

"You are no delicate flower, Aspyn Dumont. I know that. And that's not an insult, by the way. Just stating a fact. You're strong, and you know it. And that's attractive."

She narrowed her eyes. "What are you trying to pull?"

"I'm sorry my complimenting you somehow comes off as offensive."

"Every time you say anything nice, I feel like I'm getting punked."

"Wow." My jaw dropped. "It's like that, then."

"I'm sorry."

"It's okay. You're being honest."

Her tone softened as she took a deep breath. "Okay, I get it. I'm supposed to slow down and enjoy this. I'll try."

"As you get to the bottom, the flavor will change a bit. There's a certain point where the cigar won't taste as good. That's when you know to stop. Usually, I ditch it and move on to another one."

"Kind of like your love life?"

"Very funny, Dumont." *Is it wrong that I want to smack her ass right now?*

I looked over at the spot where my grandfather had been just a second ago. Or was it several minutes ago? *Fuck!* I'd been so into Aspyn smoking that fucking cigar like it was my dick that I'd lost track.

"Where the fuck is Nonno?" I shouted.

"Oh no." Her face turned red as she frantically looked around. "Not again."

I gritted my teeth. "He's doing this on purpose."

"Shit, Troy. How could we have let this happen a second time?"

We tossed our cigars.

"You go that direction." I pointed behind me. "I'll take that end."

As I went in search of my grandfather, I somehow ended up caught in a game of ring-around-the-rosy, with a group of girls dancing in a circle around me. I managed to escape and proceeded to run across the park.

After about five minutes passed, I took out my phone and texted Aspyn.

Troy: Any luck?

Aspyn: Nope.

A few minutes later, though, she texted.

Aspyn: Found him!

Thank God.

Troy: Where is he?

Aspyn: He's chatting up this lady on a bench.

Troy: Where?

Aspyn: We're behind the public restroom building.

Troy: For fuck's sake. Thank you.

My original plan was to ream Nonno out—until I noticed him smiling and talking to the woman, who was laughing at everything he said. Not wanting to embarrass him, I decided to wait until we left the park to scold him. Technically, it wasn't only his fault. We'd let this happen—again. But I also knew my grandfather, and he was playing games, getting a kick out of Aspyn and me having to stop our bickering long enough to unify in search of a missing old man.

Aspyn stood off to the side, watching my grandfather talk to his new friend. Her eyes locked with mine, and we shared a smile. Neither one of us had the heart to be mad at him.

After we returned Nonno to Horizons that afternoon, I saw Aspyn in the parking lot.

Jogging toward her car, I shouted, "Wait up."

"What's up?" she asked.

"You left so fast. I just wanted to say goodbye."

Her mouth curved downward as she hung her head.

"What's wrong?" I asked.

"I'm mad at myself," she admitted. "I almost feel like reporting myself to management. I deserve to be fired."

"Whoa." I stopped walking for a moment. "No, you don't. He's pulling this shit on purpose, so how could it be your fault?"

"Well, I let myself be distracted by your...cigar."

We stopped in front of her car.

"Aspyn, don't be so hard on yourself. You deserve a break."

She crossed her arms. "How do you know what I deserve?"

"It's obvious. You work hard at your job. Nonno told me all of the staff loves you. Then, on top of everything, you take care of your niece. That's not an easy life. Unlike mine—I have no responsibilities. So what if you got a little distracted? I say, it's about damn time."

She looked out toward the highway in the distance, then turned back to me. "You don't need to feel bad for me. My life isn't miserable, if that's what you're insinuating."

Damn. I really couldn't win with her. She twisted every compliment I tried to give.

"I wasn't insinuating that your life is miserable, Aspyn. Just acknowledging that you have a lot on your plate and you shouldn't feel guilty for anything that happened today." I sighed. "What do you do for fun?"

She bit her bottom lip, seeming to struggle to come up with an answer. "I..."

"That wasn't a trick question, you know."

"I just...have to think about it."

"You have to think about it, or you can't remember the last time you let loose?" I shook my head. "Fuck, you're really wound up tight, aren't you?"

"Keep your impressions of me to yourself. You don't need to be concerned with how much fun I have."

"All work and no play is no way to live."

She blew out a frustrated breath. "Okay, then I have a proposition for you. Why don't you come over tonight and help Kiki with her homework while I go out on the town?"

"I would totally do that, if you'd let me."

The funny thing, I was dead serious.

She shook her head. "I was just making a point. I would never let you do that."

"If you trusted me, you would."

"That's right. I *don't* trust you."

Ouch. I nodded. "It's okay. I'd probably end up dead by water gun before I made it out of there." *"I don't trust you." Jeez. Tell me how you really feel, Aspyn.* I'd made light of things, but what she said bummed me out.

She cracked a smile. "That's probably true about the water gun."

That comment felt like a small victory.

"Well, see you later," she said.

I hadn't been ready to end this conversation, but she was clearly eager to be rid of me. Yet again.

"Have a good night," I said. "See you next Tuesday."

She was about to open her car door but paused. "Was that a hidden cunt joke?"

"What?"

"C-U-N-T? See you next Tuesday?"

"For the love of God, Aspyn. Give me one shred of credit."

She laughed as she got in her car.

I stood there and watched as she drove off.

Damn, she was a hard nut to crack.

$$\bullet \bullet \bullet$$

That night, I felt restless. My days here in Meadowbrook were nothing like my life in Seattle. Back there, I had a large social network, meeting friends a few times a week for drinks after work. I also went on at least one date a week. But I hadn't gone out with a woman here since arriving a month ago. Aside from visits to Nonno, I worked all day, then did pretty much nothing unless Eric was around. But he had a girlfriend who took up a good chunk of his time, so he wasn't always available when I felt like hanging out.

Stuck in my dad's house and bored, I decided to reactivate the dating app I'd used out in Seattle. I just reconfigured the preferred settings to New Jersey. Over the next half hour, I swiped left to reject almost every profile shown to me. I was a picky sonofabitch—I had no problem admitting that. If she didn't completely rock my world in the looks department and have an interesting write-up on top of that, it was an automatic no. But the pattern of rejections tonight came to an abrupt end when I stopped on one particular profile. It took several seconds before I even believed what I was seeing. Staring back at me, smiling, was none other than Aspyn Dumont.

Well, what do you know? She's not a complete hermit after all.

This was an Easter egg of epic proportions.

I gleefully perused her photos, feeling like I was getting away with murder. In one, she wore heavy makeup and a fancy dress, a far cry from Goofy scrubs. In another image, she wore a black halter top and looked to be out at a bar, based on the hanging drink glasses in the background. My eyes fixated on her cleavage, which I knew she wouldn't be caught dead willingly showing me. God, she had amazing tits. Perhaps I should tell her that and wait to get my ass handed to me. *Look at that smile.* No resting bitch face to be found in any of these photos.

When I looked down at the description in her profile, though, I cringed. It was filled with dating app clichés and might as well have been automatically generated by a robot.

Looking for someone with a heart as big as his sense of humor. I enjoy long walks on the bike path and nights in by the fire. Dishonest people need not apply.

Yawn. Come on, Aspyn. You can do better than that.

This generic mumbo jumbo didn't even begin to represent the spitfire she actually was. Passionate, loyal, *a little nuts.* I supposed pulling the word *crazy* in her bio wouldn't have been good, but at least it wasn't generic.

I kept staring at the photo of her in the black halter top. Her smile in that one seemed particularly genuine compared to the others. It wasn't a selfie. And that made me wonder who was on the other end of that camera. It was nice to see her looking happy, and I honestly couldn't take my eyes off her. The right thing to do would have been to swipe left to reject her as an option—but that would have been no fun at all.

No. Instead, I swiped right. In any case, I knew if Aspyn ever spotted me on here, she'd swipe left to reject me faster than she could blink.

Chapter Three

Aspyn

My old high school friend Jasmine lived in the beautiful town of New Hope, Pennsylvania, right near the Delaware River. Her house was close to the center of town, with lots of eclectic shops and restaurants nearby. It was about an hour's drive, and I almost always came out to visit her. Jasmine's husband, Cole, traveled a lot, and she never seemed to be able to find a sitter.

I'd called her two days ago when I got home from work after the second outing with Troy to tell her I'd like to come see her and the baby this weekend. One of the reasons for my trip was to tell her about the situation with Troy—her ex.

When I arrived, Jasmine had just put Hannah, her daughter, down for a nap. Holding a bottle of wine and two glasses, she plopped down on her mustard yellow, velour sofa. She'd always had unique style. There was a neon *No Vacancy* sign in the middle of the living room and modern artwork adorning the walls. The shoes she'd worn on her wedding day—Stuart Weitzman encrusted with Swarovski crystals—were proudly displayed in an illuminated glass case in the corner.

The wine glasses clanked as she placed them on the rustic coffee table, along with the bottle. "So, you mentioned you had something interesting to tell me?"

I rubbed my hands together. "Yeah, actually. But maybe you should pour us some wine first."

I'm definitely going to need it for this.

Jasmine poured us each a glass of rosé, and I began telling her the story—how the grandson of one of our seniors broke the old man out of the facility. I felt it was important to give her the background first before dropping the bomb.

"So, ready for the clincher?" I finally asked.

She leaned in. "What is it?"

"Turns out, the guy I'm chaperoning is...Troy Serrano."

Her eyes widened. "What?"

"Yup. How's that for bad luck?"

She put her glass down. "You're absolutely kidding me."

"I wish I were."

"What are the chances?"

"With my bad luck, apparently a hundred percent." I shrugged.

"What the hell is he even doing back in Meadowbrook?" she asked. "I thought he lived in Seattle."

"He came back to temporarily look after his grandfather. I think he's going back once his father returns from Europe."

She lifted her wine again and stared into her now nearly empty glass. "I can't believe it."

"Yeah, it's been quite the adventure. Both times we've taken his grandfather out, we've managed to lose the poor old man because we get caught up in an argument." I thought back to our time at the park. "Well, the last time wasn't technically an argument. Troy was trying to teach me how to smoke a cigar. And I was a bit resistant. Long story."

She shook her head and blinked. "Wait. Cigars? Losing the old man? You need to back up."

I chuckled. "We took him to the park so he could enjoy a cigar, since you can't smoke anywhere at Horizons. Troy brought cigars for everyone. He was teaching me how to smoke mine, and Mr. Serrano wandered away. He did the same thing the first time we took him to the mall. He strays while we're distracted. He totally does it on purpose and nearly gives us heart attacks."

"Where did you find him?"

"He was talking to a lady he'd found sitting on a bench."

She tilted her head. "What do you argue with Troy about?"

"Anything and everything. Stuff from high school. His assumptions about me. We've bickered over a lot of things. Old habits die hard, I guess."

"It's been over a decade, though, Aspyn."

"Tell that to him." I huffed, downing my remaining wine. "Pretty sure I've spoken to him more in the last week than I did the entire time we were in high school. He seems to think he has me figured out. He's so...annoying."

Is it hot in here or is it just me? I wiped my forehead.

"Yeah...you never did interact with him much," Jasmine said. "You'd come with us to the movies and stuff, but you were mostly the third wheel."

"Exactly. The most interaction I had with him was after he cheated on you and I went after his car—and the donut incident."

"You were batshit crazy to do that, girl."

"Or as Troy likes to call me, *psycho*."

"I do appreciate you looking out for me, though." She chuckled. "The funny thing is, Samantha is now married, and her husband knows Cole. Small world."

Samantha was the cheerleader Troy had cheated on Jasmine with. She was our archenemy back in the day.

"She didn't even date Troy that long, did she?"

"By the time he and I broke up, it was the middle of senior year. I know they went to different colleges, so it couldn't have lasted much longer than graduation. He probably dumped her before then, though."

I set my empty glass down and wiped my mouth with the back of my hand. "He mentioned that you friended him on Facebook like a year ago."

"Yeah." She shrugged. "I had a little too much wine one night after I put Hannah to bed. I was stalking his photos. He looks like he has quite the life back in Seattle. Anyway...my finger basically slipped, and I hit the add friend button. We messaged briefly after that. Just mundane crap—how are you doing, what are you up to these days—that kind of stuff. I refrained from bringing up the past. We never spoke again after that night, although I stalk his photos from time to time when I'm bored."

"So, you must not be that angry toward him anymore if you'd reach out like that. I thought you'd never been able to let go of the fact that he cheated on you."

As I waited for her response, I felt oddly vested in her answer.

Why does it matter what she thinks of him now?

Moreover, why is this man constantly on my mind?

She sighed. "It was high school. People do stupid shit. Is there some lingering resentment? Sure. Do I think he's to be trusted? No. I wouldn't date him again if I were single. Once a cheater, always a cheater. And if we were face to face, I probably wouldn't have been able to resist giving him a piece of my mind, just to let it out. But at some point I had to choose to move on. I mean, it's been over ten years."

Huh. That surprised me, but I nodded. "Okay. Good to know."

I'd thought we were done with the Troy conversation until she said, "God, he's even hotter now, isn't he?" She lowered her voice. "To this day, still the best sex I've ever had."

I swallowed, inexplicably uncomfortable with her admission and feeling a little offended on behalf of her husband. "Really? You still feel that way?" I whispered, though no one besides the baby was home. "Even over Cole?"

Jasmine's husband was a very handsome man who gave Troy a run for his money in the looks department. But more importantly, he was a good guy.

She leaned back against the couch. "It was just... different back then. I was young and everything was exciting. Troy was the first guy to really make me come. That's not something you forget." Jasmine leaned in and poured more wine. "And you know, I wasn't with him long enough to tire of him. It was still fresh and new when it ended."

My cheeks felt tingly. I didn't quite understand my reaction. Or maybe I did, and it was just upsetting me. What she'd said about Troy had me hot and bothered for some reason, and that was...disturbing.

"Don't get me wrong," she said. "I'm obviously happily married. But married sex...it's different. You get very comfortable with each other. It's no longer about achieving the best possible orgasm or trying new things. It's more like, *can we even sneak this in before the baby wakes up?*"

"Yeah, okay." I exhaled. "I can understand that."

Deep down, I would've given anything to have what Jasmine did. A gorgeous, loyal, hard-working man who seemed to worship the ground she walked on. I liked to think I could be happy being alone forever and didn't need anyone. But I longed to find someone to share my life with. The thought of being wrapped in the arms of a loving husband at night sounded more appealing to me than some sexual tryst in high school, that was for damn sure. Nothing could replace the security of knowing someone had your back.

"Well, at least Troy was good for something back in high school," I quipped. Then a random thought occurred to me. "Whatever happened to his mother?"

"She died when he was a baby. He never wanted to talk about it. Just said it happened before he could remember anything and left it at that. I never pried."

"That's sad."

"He seemed to be alone a lot. His dad was always working his firefighter job, and his grandparents owned that bakery on Banton Street where the line was always around the corner. There was never anyone home. I certainly didn't mind that, though, because at the time it meant we had his house to ourselves." She laughed. "But yeah, kind of a sad upbringing."

"That would be like if Kiki didn't have me or my parents around twenty-four-seven." I shook my head. "I can't imagine."

"How *is* Kiki doing?" she asked.

"She's good. Actually, funny story, the first time I had to accompany Troy and his grandfather, I left my wallet and phone in his car. He stopped by the house to drop it off, and Kiki blasted him in the nuts with her water gun."

Her mouth dropped. "What? Why?"

"I was in the shower when he knocked. She thought he was trying to break into the house or something. I don't know. She's very paranoid about everything—always making sure the doors are locked and stuff. I think it has to do with the fact that someone robbed my parents' house one night a year ago while everyone was sleeping. Very scary. She hasn't gotten over it. Anyway, I don't think she meant to get Troy in the nuts. He's just tall, and she's short, so..."

"Well, I'd say her aim was *perfect*." She laughed and took a sip of wine. "Anyway, maybe you should go for it, just for fun."

She snuck that last part in so fast, I nearly missed it.

I stopped mid-sip. "Go for what?"

Jasmine shrugged. "Go for Troy..."

She wants me to go for her ex-boyfriend? I blinked. "Are you kidding?"

"No. I mean, you two are hanging out regularly. And from the way you're describing it, there's this weird sexual tension. I'm getting a vibe from you. So, I just want you to know that if for some reason you feel like going for it, that would be okay with me."

I'm giving off a vibe? I snorted, so incredibly uncomfortable. "Sexual? That's *not* what's going on."

"If you say so..." She smirked.

But I couldn't seem to leave it at that. "Anyway, that really wouldn't bother you?"

She sighed. "I mean, it would be a little weird. But it was a long time ago. And I don't really have a right to be jealous. If you're bored, and you're both single, why not?"

"Um...because we don't *like* each other, for one."

"That might change."

Sweat prickled my forehead. "No. It won't. But more importantly, didn't you say 'once a cheater, always a cheater' earlier? That you'd never date him, if you were single? Why is he suddenly good enough for me?"

"I'm not suggesting you get *involved* with him, Aspyn. Just that you have some fun, if the opportunity presents itself." She shrugged. "He's good for that."

I laughed angrily. "No, thanks. I'll go get a root canal for some fun rather than subject myself to Troy Serrano."

"When was the last time you were with someone?" she asked.

Ugh. "It's been a while."

"Why?"

"I don't know. I just get caught up in the day-to-day stuff. I did recently reactivate the dating app. But the guys on there tend to want only one thing. I always cancel it soon after I join. One week is usually my limit. And even in that short time, I could make a huge collage of crazy-looking mug shots from the profiles they send me. And what the hell is it with the guys who post pictures of themselves with other women as their profile photo?"

She poured herself more wine. "They do that?"

"Yes! I don't get it. Is that supposed to make me want to date you? It's basically like putting up a sign that says: *I'm a player.* And oh my God, the worst ones are when they cut a woman out of the photo, but leave a little shred of her body in. That's just proof of laziness on top of everything else."

Jasmine crossed her legs and leaned back. "You never meet anyone at all worth your time?"

"Not anyone who isn't only after one thing."

"Well, sometimes a guy who only wants sex isn't the worst thing in the world, as long as you're safe. Less complicated."

Rubbing my temples, I said, "I'm getting too old for that."

I had fantasized about such a relationship. If I couldn't find "the one," then someone reliable to have sex with was the next best thing. But it took just as much effort to find the right person for that as it did to find someone worthy of more.

"What's the alternative?" she said. "You can't just stay celibate until you find your soulmate. What if you never do, or if it takes many years? You need to let loose." She took a gulp of her drink. "Do it for those of us who no longer can. Shake things up before you dry up."

"I may be past that point. I think I'm already dried up and currently in need of rehydration. And shaking things up sounds like a lot of work. I think I'm too tired for that."

"Yeah." She blew out a breath. "I do tend to forget how much you have on your plate. I guess if you were truly single, without responsibilities, you'd have more energy on the weekends."

"That's exactly it. It's so much work to weed through the mostly bad options out there. It's easier to just relax and chill at home when I have free time, rather than go on some futile hunt. I envy anyone who can just leave the house and meet their dream guy on some street corner, or by sharing a cab, like you see in the movies. That doesn't happen in real life. Not only that, but guys don't normally love it when you tell them you're basically a single mom during the week."

She nodded. "I hadn't thought about that, either. I'm sure that definitely makes it harder."

"It does. And Kiki isn't exactly an easy sell. She's not very trusting, and that only makes things more complicated. What's worse is when she actually gets used to the guy, and then we break up. That's yet another loss in her life." I sighed.

"Like with Holden." She nodded.

"Yep." I sighed again.

She kicked her feet up. "Okay, well, promise me something."

"What?"

"Promise me you'll stick with the app for longer than your usual week before you cancel it this time. You have to give it a chance," she said. "I never had to do online dating because I met Cole in college. So, I can't speak from experience, but they can't all be bad."

"No, they're not all bad. Some are bad and some are terrible." I chuckled.

Jasmine and I talked for another hour and finished off the wine. Then I waited until evening to drive home so I could sober up a bit before hitting the road.

On the ride home, I felt a mix of emotions. Her suggestion that I mess around with Troy? That was the weirdest thing that could have come out of her mouth. I couldn't imagine telling my friend to go for my ex. And it was almost like she wanted to relive her high school days vicariously through me. I felt like I needed a shower from the conversation alone. But it was also a relief to finally tell her I'd been spending time with Troy. If I'd waited too long, it would've seemed like I was hiding something.

• • •

It was around 8 PM when I finally got back to my house that Saturday night. Since it was the weekend, Kiki was with my parents. She went over there on Friday afternoons, and she'd stay with them until my mother dropped her back off at my house on Sunday evening. On weekdays, I got her from my parents after I got off work at four, and she slept at my house Sunday through Thursday. It worked out better that way since I was more equipped to help her with her homework. And her being with my parents on weekends allowed me a social life. Or the potential for one, I guess. The only problem was, lately I was in a bit of a rut.

Tonight, I decided to have an evening of self-care. After the week I'd had, it was badly needed. So I took a bath, put on a green face mask, and got into my comfy pajamas. I threw on my fuzzy robe, a recent late-night impulse buy after spending too much time watching one of those home shopping networks. Then, I brewed some green tea.

Despite my vow to relax, Troy Serrano was still filling way too much of my head tonight. I kept thinking about the conversation at Jasmine's, and then those thoughts moved on to what Troy had implied about me having no life. His comments the other day had been what motivated me to reactivate the dating app. I didn't want to admit his words affected me, but they'd given me the kick in the ass I needed.

I picked up my phone to scroll through that sea of mostly contaminated fish on the app again. This always felt like a side job I had no time for. Either I got to chatting with someone I got along with and then he ghosted me, or I'd meet guys who turned out to be unappealing in person compared to their online profile. It was mostly a huge waste of time.

It was time to try again, though. I hadn't gone out with a man in ages, and I needed to get back in the game before I shriveled up. I laughed to myself. *If only these dating app boys could see me in this mask and robe.*

I sipped my tea and began to alternate scrolling with shoveling unsweetened cacao nibs into my mouth.

After several minutes of swiping through, I suddenly stopped chewing at the sight of a familiar pair of pearly whites.

I know those teeth.

I know that man.

Oh God.

Staring me in the face was none other than Troy Serrano.

Holy crap.

Troy, 29

I tossed my phone as if it were infected with a contagious virus.

A few seconds later, I picked it back up and stared at his profile picture. I wouldn't have imagined Troy needed to use a dating app, but being new to town again, maybe he felt like it was the easiest way to meet people. Of course, the app had sent him my way in part because we were geographically close to each other. I wanted to block him, but I wasn't sure exactly how to do that. I'd never had to block anyone from seeing my profile before. But there was no way I wanted him to notice me on here. If he'd come up as an option for me, surely the app would present me to *him* at some point. My stomach sank. I'd figure out how to block him right after I thoroughly scrutinized his profile.

The photos he'd chosen were, of course, really good. But could he even take a bad photo with that face and fuck-me hair? In one, he wore a form-fitting black sweater and leaned up against a brick wall. In another, he held up a fish he'd caught, with his chiseled abs on display.

Then I scrolled down to the section where you were supposed to describe yourself. Whereas most men write a simple paragraph, Troy had written an obituary.

God, what the hell is this?

Financial advisor Troy S.'s love of life will live on through his many friends who will continue to honor his legacy by living their lives to the fullest.

Born in Meadowbrook, New Jersey, to a single father who broke his ass raising him, Troy learned firsthand what it meant to work hard. On his own, though, he figured out that working hard meant you should play harder.

Troy attended the University of Florida for both his undergraduate degree and Masters in Business Administration. (Go Gators!) After several years of partying it up, Troy decided to take life seriously for once as he embarked on a career as one of the premier financial advisors in the Pacific Northwest. Troy shared his passion for numbers with his many happy clients.

The simplest pleasures in life brought great joy to Troy. He was equally happy Netflix-and-chilling as he was ziplining in Costa Rica. On weekends, Troy often spent time teaching himself how to play the guitar. He loved to explore local hiking trails and struck up conversations with strangers in many of Seattle's coffee shops, charming people with his charisma and verve for life.

He had a remarkable ability to see the silver lining in everything. His positive personality was contagious to everyone he met. Troy is survived by his father, grandfather, and one needy cat.

Lucky for you, all of the above is mostly true except that Troy's not actually dead. He's very much alive and eager to see if you're a match.

Lordy.

My phone vibrated, scaring the living hell out of me. It was a text from Jasmine, making sure I'd gotten home okay. But then the screen changed. *Wait, what?* When my hand jerked, I'd accidentally swiped *right* on Troy's profile. I wouldn't have even realized this were it not for the words: *It's a match!*

What?

Oh no.

No. No. No.

If we matched, that meant one thing: Troy had previously swiped right on *me. Ugh*! How long had he known I was on here?

I threw the phone again, as if it were infected with yet another dangerous virus.

For about a minute, I just sat in a panic, my hands wrapped around my face.

Then I picked up the phone to try to undo the action. But before I could find the information, a notification popped up. Troy had sent me a direct message through the app.

My heart pounded in my chest. I clicked on it.

Troy: Well, well, well. What do we have here?

I couldn't type fast enough.

Aspyn: We have nothing here. I accidentally swiped right on your profile. This was a mistake.

My pulse raced as the little dots moved around.

Troy: Um, what now? How exactly does that happen? Accidentally swiping right?

I realized how ridiculous that sounded. But it was the damn truth! Figures the stupidest thing *ever* would happen to me, and I'd never be able to convince him it was true.

Aspyn: My phone vibrated and startled me. I happened to be looking at your profile at the time.

Troy: Oh, that explains it. Phones vibrating can be quite traumatic.

I blew a frustrated breath toward my forehead.

Aspyn: You don't have to believe me, but it's the truth.

Troy: Why were you looking at my profile?

Aspyn: Because this stupid app force fed it to me.

Troy: So, were you looking at my pictures, thinking: "Damn, he's a handsome sonofabitch. Too bad I hate him."

Aspyn: You got the last part right. ;-)

Troy: What did you think of my profile?

Aspyn: Honestly?

Troy: Yeah.

Aspyn: It's utterly obnoxious.

Troy: Why do you say that?

Aspyn: That fake obituary? LOL Do you expect people to take you seriously?

Troy: It was supposed to be FUNNY and clever. I thought you said you liked funny men, according to your boring-as-fuck bio.

Aspyn: If I'm so boring, why the hell did you swipe right on me?

Troy: Because I couldn't get myself to swipe left. I felt bad for you. Let's talk about your bio, though.

I looked up and screamed at the ceiling. My voice echoed throughout the house.

Aspyn: Let's not.

Troy: Boring. As. Fuck. First off, though, a compliment: You look really hot in those photos. I barely recognized you.

I refused to acknowledge the chill that ran down my spine at his backhanded compliment. Instead, I typed again.

Aspyn: Nothing like immediately following up an insult with a compliment and then another insult.

Troy: It's constructive criticism. I know you're better than that bio. It was as if you copied and pasted it from some other boring-as-fuck profile.

Aspyn: There's nothing wrong with it. It's simple and to the point. You're not supposed to write a dissertation—or an obituary.

Troy: But you're not selling who you actually are.

Aspyn: I didn't realize I was supposed to be "selling" myself. I have enough trouble on the app attracting losers without doing anything at all. Maybe I should intentionally remain boring to keep them away. Yeah, that's a better idea.

Troy: Well, your photos are the bomb. So you're gonna attract a fair share of men. But come on, put a little life into the other stuff.

Aspyn: I was embarrassed for you reading your profile.

Troy: Well, at least within my fake obituary lies the essence of who I am.

Aspyn: A buffoon? You're correct.

Troy: Let me help you rewrite your bio.

I cackled and typed.

Aspyn: No, thank you.

Troy: Give me a sec.

Oh, Lord. What is this man doing right now?

Aspyn: You're insufferable.

Several minutes passed with no response from Troy. I wasn't sure what I was wishing for at this point. Did I want him to come back on and continue this conversation, or did I want him to disappear? A part of me was enjoying this. I couldn't deny that. But I was annoyed at myself for sitting here like an idiot as I waited at the edge of my seat. So, I got up and made myself another pot of tea.

When I returned, nothing had come in. Yet still, like a dummy, I waited.

I immediately regretted not logging off when Troy's next message finally popped up.

Troy: Here's your new profile:
Aspyn, 29: I'm the girl who'll key your car if you hurt the ones I love. And be very afraid if I bring you donuts, particularly Boston cream. You should be scared of me, but you haven't stopped reading yet, have you? Because let's face it, those first couple of lines intrigued you. They kept your attention, so you stopped scrolling. The truth is, I'm passionate, complex, and far from the boring

cookie-cutter types you find yourself swiping left on. If you're looking for a challenge, someone who's not easily pleased, then I'm your girl. I run on black coffee and anything that tastes like dirt. Don't bother bringing me chocolates, because I'll throw them right back in your face. Here's the thing, though. I might be tough to please, but I'm unique. And I'm worth the effort of getting to know me. You've probably read this far because you couldn't take your eyes off my pictures. And the photos don't even show the best part. Let's just say they don't call me ASS-pyn for nothing— so bootylicious and jiggly that Goofy looks like he's laughing when I walk in my Disney scrubs at work. (All real, by the way.) No catfishing here. Hit me up and see if we match.

Several seconds passed as I sat with my jaw hanging open.

What in the ever-loving...

I finally typed.

Aspyn: I don't even know what to say to this.

Troy: It's better than yours, isn't it?

Aspyn: I would never date any man who swiped right after reading that.

Troy: I would TOTALLY swipe right on this.

Aspyn: My point exactly. You're deranged.

Troy: I hope you know I'm kidding!! Jesus Christ, I would never let you post that. I was just trying to be funny. Are you laughing at all? Even a little?

Aspyn: Maybe a TINY bit. But only because of how stupid it was.

Troy: Confession...

Aspyn: Do I really want to know?

Troy: I meant what I said about your butt. Hope that doesn't offend you.

Aspyn: Offend me? No. But you can be sure that you will never see those Goofy scrubs again, Serrano. I may just have to burn them now that I know Goofy looks like he's laughing when I walk. WTF?

Troy: Damn. I shouldn't have said anything. Totally messed that up for myself.

Aspyn: That's right, you did.

Troy: LOL. This is all in good fun. I don't want you to hate me, Aspyn.

Aspyn: I never said I hated you. You've assumed that this whole time. But I never said that.

There was a pause in our interactions for a few minutes. Then he sent another text. But this one was different.

> **Troy: For some reason, it's important to me to make things right with you. Like maybe you getting assigned to accompany me out with Nonno happened for a reason. It's my chance to do something I never would have had the opportunity to do—make amends with someone I hurt in the past.**

> **Aspyn: You owe me no charity, Troy. But I appreciate the sentiment.**

> **Troy: It's not charity. It's more like CLARITY. I can see more clearly now the wrongs of my past. And I want to show you who I really am. Or who I think I am.**

I sighed. We were both at fault for how we'd acted in high school.

> **Aspyn: Look, it took two to tango. I was no saint, either. So let's move past it.**

But he wouldn't let up.

> **Troy: In order for you to believe I've changed, I need to prove I'm a better person than I was back then.**

Aspyn: That's not necessary.

Troy: It's important to me.

Troy: Seriously. Let's be friends.

Aspyn: What does that entail?

Troy: We can hang out sometime. Like grab a drink after the outings with Nonno.

I needed to be friends with Troy like I needed a hole in the head. But the thought of grabbing a drink with him sent an odd wave of excitement through me. And that was *exactly* why I had to nip this right in the bud.

I typed the response out fast, before I could change my mind.

Aspyn: I don't think so.

Chapter Four

Troy

The interesting thing about this whole situation was how much I loved arguing with Aspyn Dumont. I couldn't remember a single thing I'd enjoyed more in recent years. She might not want anything to do with hanging out with me, but unfortunately for her, I could be very persistent.

Troy: I'm not above begging.

There was no response for the longest time. *Damn.* Had I lost her?

I sat there staring at the phone while my dad's cat, Patrick, climbed behind my neck and purred. *Well, I guess this little show is over.* I must have scared her away. Just when I was about to close out, she sent another message.

Game on again.

Aspyn: I tried my hand at redoing your bio as well. Here you go:
Troy, 29: Run! Don't walk. I might look like a

smiling, confident barrel of fun, but in fact, I wouldn't know how to keep my dick in my pants if my life depended on it. If you choose to continue because you're mesmerized by my annoyingly handsome face, you can expect me to be a judgmental asshole at times, always with a modicum of snark. I'm good for not only financial advisement (which is probably all wrong), but other unsolicited advice as well. Basically, if it's none of my business, you can expect to hear from me. I'll be the first to tell you to get a life. Meanwhile, I'm so trustworthy that I can't even take my grandfather out in public without losing him—twice.

After I stopped laughing, I typed out a response.

Troy: Damn.

Aspyn: LOL. I'm sorry. I couldn't help myself. Don't forget you declared this "all in good fun."

Troy: I love how you snuck that last part in about my grandfather even though you're just as much at fault.

Aspyn: I know. I debated leaving it out for that reason.

Troy: But wait...back up. Annoyingly handsome? I think I just got my first compliment from you. Let's talk about that.

Aspyn: Let's not.

Troy: I guess we're even now. You called me annoyingly handsome. And I said you have a nice ass.

Aspyn: Does that conclude this conversation, then?

Troy: You can't wait to get rid of me, can you? Just like that night I dropped off your phone. The door practically hit me on the way out.

Aspyn: Sorry. You caught me off guard that night.

Troy: YOU were caught off guard? My crotch got caught up in a tsunami.

Aspyn: LOL

Troy: I'm glad you find it funny. My friend thought I'd pissed myself when I met him for dinner after.

Troy: By the way, bring your sneakers on Tuesday.

Aspyn: Why?

Troy: You'll find out.

Aspyn: Should I be concerned?

Troy: Nah.

Aspyn: Give me a hint.

Troy: Pretty sure it will be the only time this week you'll have balls flying in your face.

I immediately regretted that joke. It might have been too much. But it was the first thing that came to mind. *Whoops.*

Aspyn: Seriously?

Troy: You asked for a hint! I gave it to you.

Aspyn and I continued our back-and-forth for the better part of an hour before she announced that she needed to go wash off some face mask. I asked her to send me a photo of herself with the mask on, and she told me to go to hell.

I grabbed my old Michael Myers mask and sent her a photo of myself in it. It was hard to tell, but I think she thought it was funny.

After we stopped texting, I was revved up. You would have thought I'd had a ton of caffeine or something. I couldn't sleep at all. Instead, I kept having imaginary arguments with her in my head. Not the usual way a woman kept me up.

• • •

The following Tuesday, Aspyn showed up to Nonno's room wearing solid black scrubs with no pattern. I couldn't help laughing. She must've picked the darkest, plainest scrubs she owned because of the laughing Goofy comment I'd made. This was a protest, and I heard it loud and clear. Lucky for me, though, the black scrubs still hugged her derriere quite beautifully.

"So, will you tell me where we're going now?" she asked.

Nonno beamed and answered before I had a chance. "We're going to play basketball!"

She grinned. "Oh. Cool. I didn't know you played basketball, Mr. Serrano."

"Well, Troy and I used to play back when I could walk around easily. I've missed it. It was his idea to try it again. We'll have to see."

She looked over at me. "I think this is a fantastic idea."

"I'm glad you think so." I gave her a once-over. "Nice scrubs, by the way."

"I'm mourning the loss of my dignity the other night," she said, low enough that my grandfather couldn't hear.

I bent my head back in laughter. "Come on. It was fun, and you know it."

Her cheeks turned red. *Hmm... Is she really still embarrassed?*

Before we went to the basketball court, I stopped at McDonald's. That pit stop kicked off every outing. I automatically ordered Aspyn a black coffee.

"Want anything else?" I turned to ask her.

"No. There's nothing here I can eat."

I wondered why she was so restrictive about her diet. My inclination was to tease her about it, but I didn't this time, reminding myself to tread a bit more lightly. It seemed like I'd made a little progress with her lately, and I didn't want to ruin it.

The basketball court was empty when we arrived. Once we began playing, it was obvious my grandfather was having a blast. This had been a good decision. Even though Nonno couldn't get the ball into the hoop from his chair, he enjoyed passing it to us and catching it. The fresh air was good for him, too. I threw the ball to him, he'd pass it to Aspyn, and she'd attempt to shoot. She kept missing until one time she didn't. I ran to her and offered a high five, which took her about thirty full seconds to accept. *Such a hardass.*

We stayed at the court for almost the entire two hours, which flew by faster than usual. We'd all been having fun.

After we returned my grandfather to Horizons, I again caught up with Aspyn in the parking lot as she was heading to her car to go home. I could tell she was trying to sneak out without saying goodbye.

"Did you have a good time?" I asked, walking alongside her.

"You know what?" She smiled. "It was really fun, yeah."

"Is this the first time you've had fun with me?"

She pretended to have to think about it as we stopped in front of her car. "Well, it's the first time we didn't lose your grandfather."

"This is true."

She searched for her keys. "Good on us for not being negligent for once."

"I think we should celebrate that." I decided to go out on a limb. "Have dinner with me tonight."

Aspyn stopped searching in her purse and chewed on her lip, looking like I'd just asked for her first-born child. "I can't. I have to get home to Kiki."

Shit. How did I not remember that? She'd told me she picked her niece up from her mom's after work every day.

"Of course. I'd forgotten that you have her on weeknights." I tilted my head. "When do you not have her?"

"Friday night."

"You want to get dinner Friday, then?"

She looked down at her feet a moment. "I...actually have a date Friday."

Feeling deflated, I swallowed. "Really? Good for you. Someone you met on the app?"

"Yeah."

"Where's he taking you?"

"Not sure yet. We're meeting for drinks, then deciding on dinner after."

"Okay, so you're busy Friday. How about we hang out Saturday?"

The silence was deafening.

Aspyn chewed her lip for several more seconds before she finally said, "I don't think so, Troy. I appreciate that you want to be friends. I really do. But I'm just not there yet."

So there was more to this than her just being busy. She really didn't want to hang out with me. I certainly wasn't going to be an ass and push it. I did have *some* pride. But this sucked.

"Okay. Fair enough." I took a couple of steps back, feeling like I had a giant letter L slapped across my face.

This girl had gotten to me lately. And I couldn't figure out why. Was it because of our past? Or was I just into her despite all that? Normally, I could let a rejection roll off my back. But it felt different this time.

She took her keys out. "Have a good night."

"You, too."

I stood in place, watching her drive away.

Instead of getting in my car and heading home, I decided to go back inside to hang out with Nonno while he ate his dinner in the dining room.

I found him and settled in next to him, but we didn't talk much while he dug into his meal.

Finally, my grandfather interrupted me in the middle of a daydream. "Why the long face?"

I grabbed a fork from a spare place setting next to him and took a bite of his pasta. "It's nothing."

"You and Miss Aspyn seemed to be getting along better today."

"Smoke and mirrors," I mumbled.

"What are you talking about?"

"We were doing great until she rejected me out in the parking lot. I asked her to go to dinner with me—not on a date, just as friends."

Nonno chuckled. "You expect me to believe that?"

"It's true. I know she wouldn't want to date me. I just want to make things right with her, maybe get to know her on a platonic level after all the shit in the past."

My grandfather cracked up.

I narrowed my eyes. "What?"

He wiped his mouth. "I'm old, but I'm not blind, kid. You like staring at her ass more than I like McDonald's ice cream and Sinatra."

"You think I like her? I'm not looking for anything more than just being her friend." I rubbed my temple. "Of course she's attractive. But that's not what this is about."

Nonno pointed his fork at me. "You kiddin' yourself or something? Of *course* you like her. She's a beautiful girl—in that natural way, too. And she's a decent, strong, independent woman. Very sweet. What's not to like? Even though you two have a history, that's in the past—has nothing to do with today."

Mindlessly twirling some more of the pasta around my fork, I said, "There is something more to it than just wanting to hang out with her. I have this nagging feeling that I need to prove I'm not a bad person. I'm not sure where it's coming from."

He nearly choked on his food from laughing. "It's coming from below the belt."

I rolled my eyes and dropped the fork. He wasn't going to believe me. I could understand why he doubted my intentions. Admittedly, I did like staring at Aspyn's ass, but I *wasn't* trying to get into her pants. Or her scrubs. Not to sound like a dick, but I had no problem getting laid, if I wanted to. I didn't need to resort to groveling over some woman who hated my guts in the hopes that she'd sleep with me.

That said, I had thought about what it would be like with Aspyn. I might have fantasized once or twice about how that energy between us would translate to the bedroom, what it would be like to make her lose her mind to the point that she no longer cared whether she hated me.

"The way you two go at it?" my grandfather said. "I wouldn't be surprised one bit if it all comes to a head one day. She's invested in you. It might not seem like she likes you, but you get to her. Usually if someone doesn't care, they're ambivalent. She might have told you no because she's afraid, not uninterested."

"Well, my ego is certainly happy to eat up that theory, Nonno."

He chewed. "So, she just told you flat-out no when you asked her?"

"Yeah." I leaned back in my chair and crossed my arms. "I really was just asking her to have dinner, nothing more. Maybe, like you, she didn't believe my intentions. But she'd rather go out with some guy she's never met than have dinner with me on Friday night."

"She's got a date?"

"Yeah. With some dude she met on a dating app."

"What's that?"

"Online dating. You know, that thing I showed you once on my phone when you asked me if I was looking for a mail-order bride?"

"What does she need to do that for?"

"It's how everyone meets people these days. There's no such thing as going out and meeting someone by chance anymore."

He frowned. "That's sad."

"Yeah, but by the same token, it's easier to meet people."

"It's too much," he said. "Like being a kid in a candy store. It conditions people to pass up something good because they keep thinking something better might come along on that conveyor belt. And they probably pass on someone every day who could've been the great love of their life. It takes more than just a quick look to know if someone's right."

I swallowed my water. "That's an interesting perspective. And I agree, it can be too much sometimes. I'm sure it was better when life was simpler. Unfortunately, we're not there anymore."

Nonno crumpled up his napkin. "Look, you're my only grandson. I want the best for you. And I can only hope you're lucky enough to meet a woman you love someday as much as I loved Nonna."

Deep down, I did want that. Just not right now. Or anytime soon. But someday? Sure. My grandfather had been in his mid-thirties when he met my grandmother. And my father's only serious girlfriend was his current one, whom he'd started dating in his late forties. That was proof that sometimes it takes a while for the right one to come along.

"I know how much you miss Nonna," I told him. "It breaks my heart."

"If everything you're saying to me is true, she'd be proud of you for trying to be a better person, Troy."

An image of my grandmother's face flashed through my mind. Her love and lessons didn't always come the easy way. "Well, her hitting me with that wooden spoon once or twice might have knocked a little sense into me, even if it took a decade to sink in."

• • •

On Friday night, Eric and I went to grab drinks in Meadowbrook Center after work before he was meeting his girlfriend there for dinner. Even though Meadowbrook was a suburb, it had a nice little town center with bars, restaurants, and an urban feel.

After leaving the bar, I got stuck in a long line of cars, stopped at a red light on the main road where a lot of the restaurants were located. I could hardly believe it when I looked to my right. I squinted to make sure, but it was her. Aspyn was sitting with some dude at an outdoor table just off the sidewalk. The guy's back was toward me, but I could make out her face clear as day. She didn't look all that comfortable, twirling her hair as she seemed to be listening to something he said. Her eyes wandered a bit.

Body language never lied. There was no way she was into this guy.

Spying on Aspyn's date while stuck in traffic was like accidentally coming upon a car wreck; I knew I shouldn't have been looking, but it was impossible to turn away. I got so into watching her that I hadn't noticed the light change to green. The car behind me beeped, and I instinctively put my foot on the gas in a knee-jerk reaction. The only problem was, the car in front of me hadn't moved yet. I crashed right into the back of it, rear-ending a poor, unsuspecting person—a person who now exited his vehicle with a look of rage on his face.

The man flailed his arms. "What the fuck is wrong with you?"

I got out and closed my door as cars began driving around us. "I'm sorry, man. There's no excuse for that. My head was somewhere else."

So far up Aspyn's ass, it's not even funny.

"I don't even have fucking insurance!" he screamed. "What the hell am I supposed to do?"

"No worries. It's obviously my fault." I pointed to the side of the road. "Let's move over there and exchange information."

With my hazards on, I pulled over, and he did the same. He was still pissed, but seemed to calm down once I assured him my insurance would cover the damage.

After I gave him all of my info, he drove away.

I was just about to get back into my Range Rover and drive off when I heard Aspyn's voice.

"What the hell is going on?" She rushed toward me. "You got into an accident?"

It surprised me that she'd left her dinner to come over.

"Just a little fender bender," I said.

She looked over at the front of my vehicle, which was dented. "Shit."

"I know. It sucks."

"You just happened to crash your car in front of where I was tonight?"

I realized how this looked, but offense is the best defense. "What are you getting at, Aspyn? That my being on this road wasn't a coincidence? It's the main road through town. You can't get anywhere without passing through here."

"No, I wasn't suggesting that. It's just weird that it happened right in front of where I was eating dinner. That's all."

Running my hand through my hair, I said, "Sorry to burst your bubble, but I wasn't stalking you."

I sure as fuck wasn't going to admit that she was the reason I was so distracted. This entire situation could've been avoided if it weren't for my...curiosity.

"You should go back to your date," I told her. "There's nothing more here to see." I immediately regretted my sharp tone.

Her mood softened. "I'm sorry if you thought I was insinuating that you were spying on me. That would, of course, be ridiculous. I was just surprised to see you, that's all."

Just then, Aspyn's date walked over. He was a tall, skinny guy, wearing a suit jacket that looked two sizes too big for him.

"What the hell is going on?" he spouted.

Right off the bat, I didn't like his attitude—at all. My fists tightened.

"I told you," she said. "This is a friend of mine. I was just checking to make sure he's okay."

It surprised me that she'd referred to me as a friend—considering how hard she'd tried not to accept my efforts in that regard. Maybe I'd made more progress than I realized. Anything was better than "that dude who made me miserable in high school."

"A friend?" The guy lifted his brow. "You looked like you were arguing."

"We weren't," she said.

He placed his hands on his hips. "Well, I think it's pretty rude to leave a date to go talk to another man."

Is this asshole serious?

"What the fuck is wrong with you?" I spat. "She just told you she was checking on a friend."

"He crashed his car," she added.

He looked between us. "Yeah, well, regardless, I think it's rude that you've been standing here chatting it up while I'm over there."

Aspyn looked around like she was readying herself to flee the scene. "I'm sorry you feel that way, but—"

"Don't apologize to this *psycho*," I said.

"You like that word, don't you?" She flashed me a sarcastic smile and turned to him. "I don't appreciate your attitude, Brian. You have no right to tell me what's right or wrong when we've only just met. Moreover, you have no right to raise your voice to me or my friend."

Second reference to friend. *Boo-yah.*

She reached into her purse. "Here's a twenty to cover my half of the drinks."

The loser actually took the money from her before shaking his head and walking away in a huff.

I couldn't help calling after him. "You should use that money toward a suit that actually fits, asshole. What, were you playing in your daddy's closet? Fucking loser."

"Jesus..." she muttered.

Aspyn and I stood in silence for a few moments.

"I'd ask you how your date went, but..."

She rolled her eyes as her hair blew in the breeze. "Very funny."

"Okay, you have to admit, this whole thing kind of *is* funny."

"Actually, you crashing your car in front of the restaurant was the best thing that happened. I was looking for a reason to escape that miserable date."

"Well, then I took one for the team. Maybe this is the first step toward me getting into your good graces."

"If a car accident is step one, I'd hate to see the next level."

"One might say I started the process...with a bang." I chuckled.

"Indeed." She laughed.

Damn, she has a pretty smile. And she looked so nice tonight, dressed in a green dress that hugged her curves in all the right places. Goofy scrubs be damned. *I think you have some competition.*

I sighed. "Seriously, though, what a loser."

"Yeah. His reaction to my coming over to talk to you wasn't the only red flag. He was getting all touchy-feely earlier when we were waiting in line for a table. To be honest, I should've just said I was feeling sick a while ago."

I swallowed my anger. "Well, if you had ditched him, this awesome spectacle wouldn't have occurred. Now I have an interesting story to tell my grandfather when I bring him breakfast tomorrow."

"He'll get a kick out of this for sure."

I cleared my throat exaggeratedly. "I noticed you used the *F* word to describe me."

She wrinkled her forehead. "I did?"

"Not the F word you usually use." I laughed. "You referred to me as a *friend.* Twice, actually." I shrugged. "Not that I was counting or anything."

"Ah. I suppose I did, didn't I?"

"Should I not get too excited about that?"

"Yeah. Don't go, you know, crashing your car or anything." She chuckled.

My eyes briefly traveled down to her cleavage. I felt my heart race. *Shit.* My grandfather was right. My intentions couldn't be pure. I must've been kidding myself.

"Did you even get to eat?" I asked.

"We'd only had drinks. He had an appetizer, but I can't eat that crap anyway. We were supposed to order the main meal right when you crashed."

"Let me buy you dinner. It's the least I can do for *crashing* your date." I held my palms up. "I promise. No funny business. Just a friendly dinner between friends." I winked. "*Friends.* That has a nice ring to it, doesn't it?"

To my surprise, she agreed. "Yeah. Okay. But you're not paying for me."

"We'll talk about it," I said, knowing damn well I wouldn't let her pay. "You wanna eat at that place or somewhere else?"

"Actually, there's a Japanese restaurant around the corner I've been wanting to try."

"Cool. Let's go there, then."

Since it was so close, Aspyn chose to meet me there while I found parking in the same area where she told me she'd parked her car.

Once I found a space, it was only a three-minute walk to Yamaguri House of Sushi. You had to go down a set of stairs to enter the restaurant in the basement. It was a cool little place with bright red wallpaper, relaxing lighting, and a large tank filled with tropical fish in the center of the room. We got a table in the corner. A small candle flickered between us as we opened our menus.

She sighed. "This is so much better."

"Sitting across from me instead of Brian, you mean?" I smirked.

"Well, I was referring to the place, the food, the ambience... But I guess the company is a step up, too."

"Unfortunately, considering who you were with, that's not saying much."

"True." She giggled.

Okay. That fucking giggle? I could get high off it.

One step closer to making her scream.

Jesus.

Where did that come from?

My horny subconscious mind must have thought it could crash this party, too.

Ignoring the fact that my dick was having a field day, I casually asked, "You said you've never been here before?"

"It's my first time. I love sushi. It's one of the only restaurant foods I can eat without having to be a pain in the ass to the waiter, asking to modify everything."

"If you don't mind my asking, what's up with all of your dietary restrictions?"

"You probably just assumed I chose to be miserable, right? You know, bitter coffee girl and all?"

"I didn't say that…" *This time.*

She took a sip of her water. "Let's order first. The answer to your question is not a quick one."

That had me curious. "Okay," I said, perusing the menu.

I wasn't typically a sushi guy. I liked my fish cooked. So, I opted for a chicken teriyaki dish. Aspyn asked for two orders of raw salmon and tuna wrapped in cucumber and a side of edamame.

After the waitress left with our menus, I crossed my arms. "Okay, so now tell me about your diet."

"It's not a diet," she corrected. "It's a way of life. And it has nothing to do with a need to be boring."

"Tell me more."

She exhaled, playing with the wrapper from her chopsticks. The skin on her neck reddened a bit. "A couple of years back, I started having all of these weird symptoms.

At the time, I didn't know if it was stress-related or if there was something more to it."

My eyes narrowed. "What kind of symptoms?"

"Weakness, tingling, fatigue, some weird rashes that would come and go."

"Okay..."

"The doctors ran a bunch of tests for things like MS, lupus, thyroid issues. Nothing came back definitive. They basically ruled those specific things out, but some autoimmune markers in my bloodwork were mildly elevated. So, they came to the conclusion that I have some form of autoimmune disease, not otherwise specified."

"I'm sorry... I don't know much about autoimmune diseases. How bad is that?"

My question probably sounded ignorant. But I genuinely knew nothing.

"Well, it *can* be bad if you can't control the symptoms. I did a ton of research and found that there are autoimmune dietary protocols a lot of people swear by. But the only way they work is if you're super strict in cutting out inflammatory foods."

"So, like what types of things do you eliminate? I know sugar is one..."

"Gluten—so all bread and pasta, that kind of thing. Plus, all dairy and sugar."

Damn.

"Is there anything left to eat?"

She laughed. "All fruits and vegetables, all meats and fish. And some non-gluten starches, like potato and rice." She sighed. "It's really not that bad once you get used to it. It's mainly annoying when you go out to restaurants."

"Or when assholes like me accuse you of being a bitter person because you don't put sugar in your coffee."

"Exactly."

"If you don't mind my asking, eating like that—how do you not shrivel up into nothing? Your body is healthy, and I mean that in the best of ways."

"Nuts keep junk in the trunk." She chuckled. "I eat lots of them. They're healthy fats, along with things like avocado and full-fat coconut milk."

"Got it." I smiled. "So, how do you feel nowadays?"

"Honestly? I feel amazing. Better than I've ever felt, even before all of those symptoms started. Which is why I'm not willing to go back to the way I ate before. I tried reintroducing some of the old foods once just to experiment, and many of the symptoms came back."

"That's cool that you were able to figure this out on your own."

"I feel lucky."

"Thank you for explaining it to me. It makes total sense." I lifted the green tea at the center of the table. "Can you have tea?"

"Yes." She smiled. "I drink it all the time, actually."

I poured her a cup before doing the same for myself.

"Speaking of my eliminating bread and sugar..." she said. "I would imagine that's particularly hard for you to fathom since your grandparents owned an Italian bakery growing up."

"You knew about that, huh?"

"Yeah." She smiled.

"Nonno and Nonna were legendary in Meadowbrook. He'd get up at 3 AM every day to head in to work and bake stuff. She'd follow him soon after. And they kept the place open till seven to catch the after-work crowd. So it was a long-ass day. They'd get home late every night. And I'd have a late dinner with them. Usually some kind of pasta."

"Italians having pasta! You don't say..." She teased.

"Imagine that?"

"Wait..." she said. "Did you live with them or your dad?"

"Both. We lived in a two-family house growing up. My father and I lived on the second floor, and my grandparents were downstairs. My dad worked a lot of night shifts at the fire department. There were times I was home alone and times when I was with my grandparents, but most nights ended with a late dinner and whatever bread needed to be taken home because it was too stale to sell at the bakery."

"I visited that bakery a few times, but never knew who the owners were or that they were your grandparents."

"If you had known in high school, you definitely would've stayed away, right?"

"Not if the cannoli was good." She laughed.

"Oh, it was. Believe me."

She sighed. "Anyway, from everything you describe, it sounds like an idyllic life. Delicious Italian meals every night, all the bread you could eat, getting to grow up with grandparents around who lived in the same house." She paused and looked deeply into my eyes. "But I'm sure it wasn't easy growing up without a mom."

A tension built in my chest. If anyone knew what that might have been like, it was Aspyn. Because she was raising a kid in that exact situation.

"It wasn't easy," I agreed, choosing not to get into it more right now. I didn't want to ruin the mood of this evening. Instead, I shifted the topic. "I know you can understand that because of Kiki."

"Yup. No matter how much love I give her, I can never replace her mom. That's just the way it is."

I wanted to ask what had happened to her sister, but again, I felt like it wasn't the right time. That would make me feel obligated to talk about my mother. And I wasn't ready to go there. But for some reason, tonight made me feel like I *could* go there. Aspyn would understand, and she was a good listener. I could've stayed here all night talking to her—just not about my mother.

"Does your dad still live in the house you grew up in?" she asked.

"When Nonno went into assisted living, my dad and he sold the house. I was living in Seattle by that time. My father bought his own place, which is where I'm staying now."

"I see." She sipped her tea.

"Do you own your house or rent?" I asked.

"I own it. Barely cover my mortgage every month, but I'm somehow making it work."

"Good for you. It's smart to own. And it's a nice little place. Very homey. Even if the last memory I have of it is getting attacked there."

"Sorry again about the water gun."

"Maybe one of these days you'll invite me over for black coffee and air, and I can show Kiki I'm not really the bogeyman."

She nodded, clearly not committing to anything.

Over dinner, we fell into more easy conversation. She asked me about my college experience at the University of

Florida and why I went into finance. I told her a little about my life in Seattle. She talked some more about what it was like helping to raise her niece. If I didn't know better, I would've said this night felt an awful lot like a damn good *date*. But I wasn't going to ruin it by insinuating anything. Despite getting along for at least one night—and despite the fact that I couldn't help noticing how the lights in here caught her green eyes—I knew Aspyn and I likely couldn't ever be anything more than friends. Her accepting me as a friend *was* the best-case scenario. And that sucked because tonight had made me realize how much I liked her.

Fuck.

I really like her.

Chapter Five

Aspyn

On Monday at work, one of the nurses, Shala, asked about my date this past weekend. As we ate lunch in the dining room, I filled her in on what had happened and how I ended up actually having dinner with Troy Serrano. My failed date had essentially turned into a date with Troy, and I still didn't understand how I truly felt about that. I'd had a good time with him, though. That was undeniable.

Shala was all too amused by my story.

"Honestly, what are the chances?" she said. "It's like you can't get away from the guy. I love it, though."

"I know. And it turned out to be a pretty nice dinner."

It was the first time I'd been able to spend time with Troy without dwelling on the past. I'd gotten lost in conversation—and a little lost in his gorgeous eyes at times.

"Sounds like you dodged a bullet with that Brian, too."

I nodded. "Without a doubt. It's always nice when someone shows their true colors off the bat. Saves you time wasted. Although, I wasn't attracted to him in person, so it likely wouldn't have gone anywhere even if he'd turned out to be a stand-up guy."

"Physical attraction is important." She took a bite of her sandwich and chewed. "Speaking of attractive, what about Troy? What are *his* true colors? Do you think he's still that jerk he was in high school?"

I shook my head. I hadn't figured grown-up Troy out yet. "I've always been taught to believe that people don't change. I can't say there are never exceptions, though. But I don't have enough current-day experience to deem him trustworthy."

She shoveled some chips into her mouth. "That's too bad, because he's so damn good-looking."

"If Troy were as trustworthy as he is hot, we certainly wouldn't have a problem, now would we?" I chuckled.

We continued chatting as the subject changed from Troy to Kiki. Shala had three kids, one of whom was eight like my niece, so I often looked to her for advice.

Our conversation was interrupted when she looked over my shoulder. "Oh my. Look who's here."

I turned to find a smiling Troy walking toward our table.

I wiped the side of my mouth with my napkin. "What are you doing here?"

"What do you think I'm doing here? I'm visiting my grandfather."

"I know...but your days are usually Tuesdays and Thursdays."

He pulled up a seat next to me. "It's not an exact science, Dumont. Those aren't the only days I ever come see him, just the days we go out. Sometimes I pop in at random times—bring him a donut or say hello during my lunch break." He looked down at my empty plate. "What are you up to...eating?"

"Yeah." I tucked a piece of my hair behind my ear. "Just finishing up." The hair on my arms stiffened; the way my body reacted when he was close definitely unnerved me.

"What's going on the rest of the day here?" he asked.

"We're doing a singalong later."

"Nice. How does that work?" he asked.

"I play the piano and sing and everyone else..." I stopped, momentarily distracted by his...*face*.

"Sings along." He grinned, finishing my sentence.

"Yeah."

"What tunes?"

"We usually pick one band or artist and go through a number of songs from their catalog. Today it's The Carpenters."

He scratched his chin. "Oh yeah...the brother and sister from the seventies. Tragic how she died. What made you pick them?"

"Their songs are pretty easy to play, and they're a fan favorite."

Just then the facility director, Nancy, popped her head into the dining area. She asked it she could pick Troy's brain about some financial questions. He agreed, and after he excused himself, I didn't see him for the rest of the afternoon.

The singalongs, which we did a couple of times a week, were usually held at 3 PM. I liked that they made the last hour of my shift go by pretty fast.

Knowing how to play the piano had never come in handy until I got this job. I used to think my years of lessons as a kid had been a total waste, but being able to play for the people here was one of my greatest joys. I chose songs they might remember from their younger years and passed around sheets with the lyrics.

Today's singalong started routinely enough, as everyone got situated in their spots. After I'd passed out the lyric sheets, I spotted Troy wheeling his grandfather into the room. *He's still here?* Not only that, he had a guitar over his shoulder.

What the...?

He parked Mr. Serrano at a spot in the front, close to my piano.

"What are you doing?" I asked.

Troy put the guitar down. "I hope you don't mind. I figured the more, the merrier."

"You play the guitar?"

"Yeah. I used to teach myself in my spare time."

"Oh. That's right. Your *obituary* mentioned that."

"I ran home and downloaded The Carpenters' sheet music and printed it out. Figured I could play along—unless you'd prefer I didn't?"

What am I supposed to say...no? "Uh, sure. That's fine."

"You sure?"

I nodded, although the prospect of him playing alongside me put me on edge. I'd never had to stay in sync with anyone else before. This was supposed to be an informal singalong in a nursing home, not some bizarro-world duet performance.

"Which song are we starting with?" he asked.

"'Close To You'." I felt my face heat up.

He nodded and began to sift through his music sheets.

Rather than let my nerves consume me, I forced myself to sit down at the piano and just start. I wasn't the best singer, but I typically didn't worry about how I sounded, because as soon as I belted the first notes, my voice was drowned out by every other out-of-tune voice in the room. Except today, all I could hear was Troy—because he was right next to me. And you know what? He had a really nice voice. He also managed to keep up with me. Or maybe it was me managing to keep up with him. Either way, the guitar really complemented the piano, despite my earlier doubts. We were an unlikely musical pairing, but it worked.

I think everyone appreciated the change of pace Troy and his guitar brought to the occasion. All of the elderly women were understandably charmed. We played five Carpenters songs, with plenty of pauses for reminiscing in between, ending on an encore of "We've Only Just Begun." The hour flew by even faster than usual.

After our time was up, I wheeled the piano back to the corner of the room and walked over to Troy.

He put the guitar strap over his shoulder. "It's four o'clock. You're off now, right?"

"Yup. Pretty much—after I pick up all these music sheets."

"Cool. I'll help clean up and walk you out."

As I went around the room, I got goosebumps. It felt like something had shifted between Troy and me since the other night.

After the room was clean, Troy waited as I grabbed my personal items from my cubby. Then we walked together slowly out to the parking lot. He gave off a vibe that there was a reason he'd wanted to wait for me.

When we stopped in front of my red Honda Civic, Troy said, "The feeling is mutual, Aspyn."

The feeling is mutual? "What are you talking about?"

"What you said about me to that chick you were eating lunch with."

What? My brain raced to backtrack. "You were listening in on our conversation?"

"I was in the hallway outside the dining area—right around the corner at the desk signing in. I couldn't help overhearing."

I cleared my throat, fearing the worst. "I don't remember what I said."

"Technically, it was half-insult, half-compliment, but I'm choosing to look at it positively."

I licked my lips. "What did I say?"

"You said you wished I was as trustworthy as I am hot."

Fuck.

Fuck.

Fuck.

There was no way to deny what he'd heard. I just had to come clean.

"I obviously didn't mean for you to hear that."

"Clearly. But it's okay. I already know you don't trust me, nor should you—yet. But I have to say, I was pleasantly surprised to receive that compliment."

My cheeks burned. "You know you're a good-looking guy. Why is that news?"

"It is *absolutely* news to me that I don't physically repulse you. You've referred to me in the past as 'annoyingly handsome' but never hot. It surprises me that you find me attractive, because sometimes if you can't stand someone, you can't see past your dislike for them, no matter what they look like."

Swallowing, I did my best at damage control. "Well, it doesn't mean anything. It's just an observation. I think Ted Bundy was kind of good-looking too—in his own way. That doesn't mean I would have let him into my house." *Shit. What the hell did I just say?* My nerves had me spouting out nonsense.

He narrowed his eyes. "You did *not* just compare me to a serial killer."

"I was trying to make a point."

"You made it, alright," he scoffed.

Shaking my head, I looked down at my shoes. "I'm sorry. That did sound terrible. I'm a bit embarrassed, to be honest. I guess I'm not handling it well."

"That's because I intentionally embarrassed you when I called you out. See? I'm already proving your point. I can't be trusted." He sighed. "I'll cut the shit now."

"Thank you."

"On one condition…" His mouth curved into a smile.

"You're evil." I chuckled.

"Not as evil as a serial killer."

I crossed my arms. "What's your condition?"

"My condition is that you give me a chance to transform your opinion of me before I have to go back to Seattle. I want you to deem me as trustworthy as I am…" He paused. "Well, you know…"

"I get your point." I rolled my eyes. "I don't understand why it's so important to prove yourself to me."

The sun reflected in his gorgeous eyes as he looked at me. "I can't explain it either, Aspyn. All I can tell you is the second I landed back here, after so much time away, it hit me that these past ten-plus years have gone by in a blur. The way you looked at me and acted toward me when we first reconnected—I didn't like it. Being home alone in my dad's house has caused me to reflect on a lot. Even though I'm successful financially, there are areas of my life that still need work. Despite my glowing fake obituary, I haven't done anything truly positive with my time on this Earth. If it all ended suddenly, I don't want to be remembered as that asshole from Meadowbrook High."

"I don't understand what you becoming a better person has to do with me. Like I've said before, I don't want to be your charity case or test subject."

Troy sighed. "Look, you're someone I indirectly hurt in the past. Even though you say you forgive me, I don't believe you. And you *clearly* don't trust me. You said it yourself." He flashed an impish grin. "But also...you're a *fun* test subject. We're getting along better, and when we're not, I like our arguments, too. So, win-win."

"I did have a good time when we went for Japanese food the other night," I admitted.

"Except you never actually intended to hang out with me. We got there by default because loose-suit Brian was a loser."

"That's true."

"What are you doing this weekend?"

"I can't do anything this weekend. I have Kiki because my parents are going to a wedding in upstate New York."

"I could bring by a pizza or something?" He quickly shut his eyes. "Shit...you can't have pizza." He snapped his fingers. "I'll pick up some of that sushi you like. Does Kiki like pizza?"

"Yeah, she loves it, actually."

"Then I'll get pizza for her and me. And sushi for you. Text me exactly what you ordered, though, so I don't get the wrong thing. Do you prefer Friday or Saturday?" he asked, rushing out the words as if to prevent me from having a chance to say no.

"I haven't agreed to this yet," I said, though I knew this time I was going to.

"Sorry. Am I jumping the gun on Operation Trust?"

I sighed. "Saturday."

"Cool."

Choosing Saturday would be far less stressful than having to make my house presentable on a work night. *I guess this is happening.*

"What does Kiki like to drink?"

"Beer."

His eyes widened.

"Obviously kidding. You don't need to bring anything for her to drink. We have plenty of stuff at home that she likes. I buy in bulk."

He tossed his keys in the air and began walking backwards toward his car. "Just text me her favorite toppings when you send me the sushi order." He called out, "Make sure you tell her not to attack me, though. I'm determined to make her like me, too."

I laughed. "If you think *I'm* hard to please, you ain't seen nothing yet."

• • •

Saturday evening, Kiki followed me around the house as I went from room to room to make sure everything looked presentable.

"So why is he coming over again?"

Fluffing throw pillows for no reason, I answered, "He's a friend."

Troy would be here any minute, and my nerves were getting the best of me. Whenever I got tense like this, I'd rush around the house and tidy up, even if things didn't need fixing.

"A boyfriend?"

"No, definitely not."

"Boy toy?"

I whipped my head in her direction. "Where did you hear that term?"

"I don't remember." She giggled. "Wait! Not boy toy. Boy *Troy*."

"Very funny." Chuckling, I shook my head. "He's just a friend, Kiki."

The doorbell rang, saving me from further inquisition.

I took a deep breath in. "That's him. Be nice, okay?"

She nodded.

I swiped my hand through my hair and headed to the door, opening it to find Troy juggling a bunch of items.

"Hey!" he said, a huge grin on his face.

I could barely see him behind all the stuff he was carrying.

"Wow, you really went all out." I moved aside to let him in.

He carried two pizza boxes with a large paper bag on top. Under his right arm, he clutched a Tupperware of some kind.

Did he bake something?

"It's not much." He looked around. "Should I just put all this on the kitchen counter?"

"Actually, you can take it to the dining room. We'll eat in there."

Troy followed me and laid everything out on the table.

When we returned to the living room, he looked over at Kiki. "No gun today?"

"Auntie Aspyn told me I had to behave."

"Well, that's no fun. But I appreciate the mercy. Maybe I'll let you get me on purpose sometime. I just need to come prepared—wear some waterproof pants." Troy rubbed his palms together. "Your aunt told me you like black olives on your pizza but nothing else. I made sure they got it right."

"Thanks." Kiki offered a hesitant smile.

She definitely wasn't an easy sell. She didn't trust very easily, but when she did, she gave her whole heart. I guess she was a lot like me that way.

The three of us moved back into the dining room and sat down at the table.

I'd made some fresh lemonade and brought the pitcher out. I'd bought some beer in case Troy wanted one, but when I offered it, he opted for lemonade instead.

Kiki served herself a slice of pizza and blew on it while she waited for it to cool. She watched Troy intently as he poured hot red pepper flakes onto his own slice. I opened my sushi, which looked so fresh and vibrant, an array of bright pink and coral colors.

"That stuff makes my tongue want to fall out," my niece announced as she stared over at Troy's pizza. "I accidentally ate some once."

"They're not for everyone." He winked. "But I can take the heat."

Pouring Tamari sauce into a small, glass dish, I said, "Thank you for making an extra trip to get the sushi. That was really thoughtful."

Troy smiled. "It was no problem at all."

We dug into our food.

"So, what do you like to do for fun, Kiki...besides water gun attacks?"

She momentarily stopped chewing. "Play video games, I guess."

He wiped his mouth. "What do you play?"

"Super Mario."

"I used to play that when I was a kid, too."

"Mario was around back then?" she said.

Troy looked over at me and laughed. "Yeah, in the Stone Ages when I was a kid, they had that game. It's a classic."

"You went to school with my aunt in the Stone Ages?"

"Yup. Hopefully, she didn't tell you too much about those days, though."

"I didn't say a word," I assured him.

"Phew." He pretended to wipe sweat off his forehead.

"Did you know my mom?" Kiki asked.

Troy paused. "No." He looked over at me for guidance.

"Your mom was a few years older than us," I told her. "And she went to a different high school."

"Oh," she said.

"I didn't know her, but I wish I did," Troy added.

"I never knew her, either." Kiki frowned. "At least I don't remember her. I was only six months old when she died."

The mood suddenly turned somber.

"I'm sorry," he said, setting his slice of pizza down. He was silent for a while. "I know how it feels not to have a mom around growing up."

"You do?" Kiki asked with a mouth full of pizza.

"Yeah…" he whispered. "I do."

My heart clenched.

"Your mom died when you were little?" she asked.

He was quiet for the longest time before he finally answered, "No…"

My eyes widened. Jasmine had told me Troy's mother passed away when he was a baby.

"What happened?" my niece asked.

Troy wiped the corner of his mouth. "There are different ways to lose parents. The worst way, of course, is if your parent dies. Nothing is worse than that. But my mom…she left when I was a baby because she didn't want to be a mother."

What?

Kiki tilted her head. "You never saw her when you were a kid?"

"She left when I was too young to remember. But… she's since passed away."

"Wow," I said. "I'm so sorry."

"It's okay." He nodded. "Thank you." He looked back over at Kiki. "Anyway, I'm telling you this because I know how it is to feel like you're different from all the other kids because they have a mom and you don't. I totally get it, Kiki. But you know, your mom never wanted to leave you. She'd be here with you if she could. And I'm sure she's with you in spirit every day."

My niece nodded. "Yeah. My dad, too. They died together. They watch over me and Auntie Aspyn. And Grandma and Grandpa."

"Yup." He smiled.

I had never spoken to Troy about the accident. I'd have some explaining to do later. My heart felt heavy as we continued to eat in silence for a few minutes. Everything I thought I knew about Troy's situation had gone out the window.

Kiki suddenly got up from the table. "I have to go to the bathroom."

"Okay," I said as she ran down the hall.

I hoped she was alright. I couldn't tell if she actually had to go or was just feeling emotional.

After she was out of earshot, Troy turned to me and whispered, "Well, that was a heavier conversation than I was expecting to have over pizza."

"Things escalate fast in this house sometimes." I cleared my throat. "I didn't know that about your mother. Jasmine told me she died when you were little. Did you never tell her what actually happened?"

He shook his head. "Back then, I was really bitter. Whenever anyone asked me where my mother was, I told them she died when I was a baby. Because she was dead to me, you know? In retrospect, that was dumb. I should've never lied about something like that. But I didn't give a fuck back then. Didn't know better. I didn't realize the extent of that mistake until she *actually* died, and I knew I'd never have a relationship with her."

This story added a new layer to Troy, and it explained a lot about some of his behaviors in high school, why he'd acted out.

"What happened, if you don't mind my asking? You don't have to talk about it if you don't want to, though."

"How she died or why she left?"

Pushing my plate away, I said, "Both, I guess?"

Before Troy could answer, my niece ran out of the bathroom.

"I'm bleeding!" she announced from the hallway.

"What?" I jumped out of my seat and ran over to her.

My first instinct was to look at her nose, but when that appeared clear, I looked down and spotted the red spot on her pants.

It can't be. "Oh no." I rushed her back into the bathroom.

"What's happening?" she cried.

I lowered my voice. "You're not hurt. I think you just got your period."

"My what?"

"Remember that time you found my tampons, and I explained what happens to older girls each month?"

"Yeah?"

"That's what this is. It's just earlier than I thought you'd get it. *A lot* earlier."

I knew it was possible for girls to get it as young as eight, but I assumed that was rare. I'd been eleven myself, which I'd thought was on the young side. So, I was less than prepared for this. Not to mention, I didn't have a single maxi pad in the house, since I only used tampons.

Patting her on the shoulder, I said, "Stay here."

I ran into the kitchen for a bunch of paper towels and returned to the bathroom. I instructed her to place them in her underwear.

"Is everything okay?" Troy hollered from outside the door. "Do you need anything?"

"Everything's fine. Be right out!"

Of course, this has to happen the one night he's here.

I opened the door. "Kiki, go to your room for a bit and watch some TV, okay? I'll be right in."

"Can I have ice cream?"

"Sure. Are you done with your pizza?"

She nodded.

"I'll bring some in to you," I said, giving her a hug before she disappeared into her room.

I caught up with Troy back in the dining room.

"Hey," I said, a bit out of breath.

He looked up from cleaning some of the mess we'd made. "What's going on?"

"So, unfortunately, it seems she got her period," I whispered.

His eyes went wide. "What the heck? Really? She's practically a baby."

"I know. But it *is* possible to get it as young as eight. She's eight and a half."

"Okay..." He blew out a long breath and stared off. "Well, shit."

Pulling on the top of my hair, I sighed. "I wasn't prepared."

"Yeah, I can understand."

"I mean, I'm *literally* not prepared. I don't have any pads, and she's too young for tampons. I need to go to the store."

"I'll go," he immediately offered, officially making tonight even more bizarre.

Normally, I would've called my mother and asked her to run to the store, but my parents were away. I didn't want to send Troy, but taking advantage of his offer made the most sense.

"I hate to do that to you, but it would be great. I just need maxi pads. Nothing fancy. Any kind."

"There's more than one kind?" Confusion crossed his face.

I suppressed a smile. "There are lots. But just get any kind that's medium absorbency." I shook my head. "I can't believe I'm having this conversation with you."

"Well, there's a first time for everything, right?" He lifted his keys from his pocket and tossed them into the air. "This is my first official maxi pad trip. Do you need anything else while I'm out?"

"No, thank you."

He flew out the door as if there was only one box of maxi pads left in the world, and he needed to rush to seize it. I watched from the window as he drove off.

Then I went to the kitchen to make Kiki's bowl of ice cream. A few minutes later, I entered her room and placed the bowl on the table next to her as I sat at the edge of the bed. "Are you okay?"

"Yeah." She sat up against the headboard, pulling her floral comforter in closer.

"I sent Troy to the store."

"Did you tell him what happened?"

"I had to. He was worried, thinking you were hurt. It's okay. He knows what it's all about, even though he's a guy. It's nothing to be embarrassed about. It happens to every girl."

I spent the next twenty minutes answering Kiki's questions about the monthly cycle.

"You might not be regular in the beginning. But it usually comes every twenty-eight days or so."

"How do you know exactly when it's going to come?"

"You don't." I frowned. "It's sort of like a surprise you don't really want."

A look of worry flashed across her face. "Like I'll be in school, and I'll just start bleeding?"

"Yes. But you can wear something a couple of days ahead of time just to be on the safe side."

"I wish I could go back to yesterday when my life was simple," she cried.

I leaned in and kissed her forehead. "You and me both, kiddo. That feeling only gets worse the older you get."

I sat with her for a little while, watching the cartoon she'd chosen on TV. When the doorbell rang, I placed my hand on her knee. "That's him. Be right back."

I went to answer the door and found Troy holding a large bag. "Did you buy out the whole store?"

Looking like he'd just returned from war, he stepped inside and placed the bag on the counter. "Honestly, I didn't know what kind to choose, even though you told me medium. There were too many choices—long, super long, nighttime, wings, no wings. What, do you women fly away or some shit? Anyway, I got like five different kinds."

"Five? We might be set till she's a teenager." I laughed as I sifted through the bag. I lifted one of the packages. "These are for bladder incontinence."

He shut his eyes. "Shit."

"I can return them," I said.

"Or we can donate them to Horizons," he suggested. "I'm sure they can use them for someone."

"Good point."

The next item in the bag was a stuffed, pink unicorn. "What the heck?" I laughed.

"I didn't want the cashier to think I had a maxi pad fetish. So, to distract from my collection, I threw that into the mix."

"I feel like that many maxi pads *and* a unicorn might have made you come off as even weirder."

"Solid point. But, hey, it's cute. It's for Kiki... obviously."

"That was very sweet of you."

I peeked inside and noticed the last item was a bottle of cabernet.

"That's for you," he said. "I figured you could use it tonight."

"Damn right. Thank you."

"I didn't think to ask you if you drink wine—with all of your food issues. But you mentioned drinking the night you were out with that Brian tool."

"I do drink wine, just in moderation. But I will *definitely* be partaking in this tonight."

"Would you prefer that I leave and let you relax?"

I paused. Telling him to leave after he'd gone to the store for me didn't seem right. But more than that, did I *want* him to leave? I'd been enjoying his company tonight, despite everything.

"Just give me a few minutes while I go tend to her. Make yourself comfortable in the living room."

"Cool." He smiled.

I took the supplies Troy had bought to Kiki's room and had her go to the bathroom and change. After she returned, I gave her the pink, stuffed unicorn.

"What's this?" she asked.

"Troy picked it up from the market."

"It's for me?"

"It is."

Kiki stared down at it before hugging it to her chest. "Tell him I said thank you."

"You don't want to tell him yourself?"

She shook her head. "I just wanna go to bed."

I couldn't blame her. "Okay." I kissed her on the head. "I understand. Holler if you need anything, okay?"

"I will."

Troy was watching TV when I returned to the living room.

He lowered the volume. "Everything okay?"

"Yes. She wants to go to sleep early." I sat across from him. "Thank you again for going to the store. You saved the day. I really appreciate it."

"Anytime." He grinned. "What do you say we crack open the wine?"

"Yeah." I stood up. "That would be great. We can sit right out back. It's a nice night."

"I'll bring out the special dessert I brought you. It's something you can eat. At least I hope I got it right."

"I totally forgot about that Tupperware you walked in with. I have to say, you have me curious."

"Go make yourself comfortable. I'll take care of everything."

Well, I wasn't going to argue with that—certainly not tonight. "The wine glasses are up there," I said, pointing to the cupboard. "There's an opener in the second drawer from the left."

I couldn't remember the last time a man had told me to make myself comfortable while he prepared a glass of wine for me. Troy might have had his faults, but he seemed to know how to take care of a woman when she needed it.

My imagination, of course, took the opportunity to run wild with all of the various ways Troy might *take care* of me.

Chapter Six

Troy

I carried the bottle of wine and two glasses outside with the Tupperware container tucked under my arm. Crickets chirped, and the weather was cool and comfortable on this dry, summer night. To say this evening had turned out nothing like I'd imagined it, though, would be putting it lightly.

I poured us each a glass of the cabernet before reaching for the Tupperware.

Rubbing over the top of the container, I said, "Okay, I wanna preface this by saying these probably taste like dirt. So, go easy on me. It was my first time baking anything like this."

"You baked something?"

"I did. I like to bake, actually. I'm not much of a cook, but cookies? I'm the cookie master. I know you can't have sugar—or gluten or dairy. So, I Googled around for paleo desserts. I found this recipe for banana cookies. They're sweetened with ripe banana and dates and made with almond flour." I panicked for a second. "Shit, you can have eggs, right?"

"Yes, in moderation."

"Phew. Okay."

She looked down at the Tupperware and smiled. "This was amazingly thoughtful of you."

"I tried one earlier just to make sure they didn't taste like shit."

Her brow lifted. "And?"

"I don't know. I can't tell. They're not horrible, but…"

"Well, I'll definitely try one since you went through the effort of making them."

When she reached for the container, I felt my pulse race a little. That was a new feeling for me—getting nervous about someone trying a recipe I'd made. What was my life coming to?

Aspyn took a bite and closed her eyes to concentrate on the taste. She chewed for a while before she finally said, "They're not bad!"

"Really? Be honest."

"They taste like…bananas…and dates…and a hint of plaster."

"Ouch." I laughed.

"Seriously, it's so hard to bake without dairy, flour, and sugar. It's like a science experiment. I give you a lot of credit for even trying."

"I shouldn't give up my day job, right?"

"Probably not." She took another bite. "But I swear, they're not bad. In fact, these will be even better warmed in the microwave with coffee in the morning."

"Or you could toss them in the trash after I leave. I won't be offended."

"I won't." She smiled.

Taking a long sip of my wine, I leaned back and relaxed into the chair. "This night was certainly unexpected."

She stared up at the sky. "You're telling me."

"It really showed me how different your life is. How much responsibility you have. I mean, I go home, and all I have to do is feed Patrick."

Aspyn squinted. "Patrick?"

"My dad's cat. He's certainly not gonna get his period."

"Let's hope not." She cackled for a long minute, and then wiped her eyes. "God, I needed that laugh. Thank you."

"It's good to see you laugh, Aspyn."

"Sometimes I have to laugh so I don't cry." She took another sip of her wine. "Tell me more about Patrick."

I crossed my legs. "Well... Patrick is a tabby cat with a fat head and no neck. He likes his belly massaged and to rub his asshole on my feet occasionally. He's pretty good about using the litterbox, but conveniently misses when he's been neglected. He's also got agoraphobia."

She chuckled. "How do you know he's agoraphobic? Did he tell you?"

"It's obvious. He doesn't like to go out. He went ballistic on me when I tried to get him into the crate to take him to the vet the other day."

"Well, he's an indoor cat, I assume?"

"Yeah."

She gestured with her glass. "So, what do you expect? You train him to be inside when it's convenient for you and then force him out into the world randomly."

"I guess that's true."

She took a bite of her cookie. "How did you finally get him out?"

"I was never able to get him into the crate, because of the negative association he has with it. I have no clue how my father does it. So, I had to go out and buy one of those slings—you know, a baby carrier."

She cracked up. "He let you put him in that no problem?"

"Yup. He was still shaking and nervous and all that, but he trusted it more than being put in a crate. I think he figured if he was going down, I was going down with him."

She nodded. "I don't blame him. Also, I'd pay money to see you carrying him around in that sling. That's sort of adorable."

"I'll send you a photo next time, if it earns me trust points." I winked.

Aspyn chewed. "Trust points, huh?"

"Yeah. You didn't know I'm trying to earn those?"

"Well, I'll give you at least one after what I put you through tonight."

I fist pumped and mouthed *yes*.

She sighed. "Anyway, your cat sounds like he has a lot of character. I've wanted a cat, but I can't take on any additional responsibility."

I wriggled my brows. "You can come over and play with mine."

She seemed to blush as she finished off the last of the cookie.

When she finally looked over at me again, my eyes lingered on hers. "You know, Kiki is really lucky to have you. If I'd had someone like you growing up, I might not have turned into such a dickhead in high school."

"You had your dad, though, right?"

"Of course, yeah...and my grandparents. But I wasn't ever really—I don't know—nurtured? I was fortunate to have them. I know that. People have it a lot worse than I did. But something was missing." I shook my head. "I sound like a pussy."

"Not at all," she said. "Tell me more about your childhood."

I took a deep breath in and let it out. "As I've alluded to before, my grandparents and father were always working. Dad tried his best, but he was in over his head—not that I needed to be drowned in attention, but there was a lack of affection for sure. Not of love—just affection. It wasn't their fault...just their nature."

"That's so funny, because your grandfather is the sweetest man."

"He's softened over the years. He was a lot more serious when he was younger. In many ways, he's like a totally different person now—even softer since my grandmother died."

Aspyn's eyes wandered over to the trees blowing in the breeze before she looked back at me. "You started to tell me what happened with your mother earlier before Kiki came out bleeding."

I nodded. "To make a very long story short, my dad barely knew my mother when he got her pregnant. My grandparents had a cottage down at the shore. They rented it out the majority of the time, but occasionally they'd close the bakery and head down there. They let my dad stay there alone when it wasn't rented out. He met my mother there one summer. She was vacationing by the beach with her family. Dad was twenty-two, and she was eighteen." I exhaled. "One thing led to another, and she got pregnant. She went back home to Boston and then contacted him to tell him she was pregnant and probably getting an abortion. Her parents also wanted that. And even though my dad told her he'd support any decision she made, he begged her not to terminate me. He told her he would raise me himself. Anyway, he traveled to Boston, and somehow he was able to convince her to have me. Her parents weren't happy. After I was born, she signed her rights over to my father."

"Did you ever meet her?"

"Once...when I was fifteen. My dad had sent her photos over the years, although she'd never contacted me. I didn't know he'd kept in touch with her until my teens. I finally decided to reach out to her myself my sophomore year in high school. She agreed to come to New Jersey to meet me, but I was still so filled with anger toward her for abandoning me that I didn't open up much when we met. I just wanted to meet her out of curiosity. She was nice enough, but I didn't feel a strong connection. I think I was also blocking the possibility of that as a protective mechanism."

Aspyn nodded. "What had become of her life?"

"She was some sort of executive—traveled a lot for work. She'd always put her education and career first. She never had any other kids." I paused, feeling an unwanted tension bubbling in my chest. "When I was in grad school, I got an email from her saying she was sick. She asked me to come visit her, said she wanted to talk to me about some stuff. I'd planned to go the week after my finals. But she passed away before I had the chance." I took a slow breath.

"I often wonder what she wanted to say to me. She left me a good amount of money, but I'd give it all back for a chance to talk to her."

Aspyn surprised me by reaching across the table to squeeze my arm. "I'm so sorry."

"Thank you."

"What kind of illness did she have?"

"It was an aggressive form of breast cancer. I did go to her funeral." I shook my head. "It was surreal."

"You met her family there?"

"I did. Her parents and brother. But like when I met my mother, the connection just wasn't there. I think knowing her parents hadn't wanted me in this world made me incapable of bonding with them in any way. But my mother went against them to have me. So, I could forgive her, but it was hard to want to form any connection with her parents."

"I get it," she whispered.

"What happened to your sister...and to Kiki's father?" I asked after a moment.

Aspyn swallowed. "They had a car accident on a rainy night. Ashlyn and her boyfriend, Toby, both died on impact."

"God, I'm so sorry."

"As Kiki alluded to earlier, she was only six months old at the time, so she doesn't remember them. I'm just so grateful she wasn't with them that night."

"I can imagine." I paused. "Look, I want to apologize again for what I said that first day—about you being stuck in a time warp. That still eats away at me. Obviously, I didn't know shit about your life, and I still don't know shit about what it's like to walk in your shoes."

Aspyn smiled. "I didn't blame you for your ignorance then. And it's true that it would have benefitted me to experience life away from Meadowbrook. There's no denying that."

"Despite what I said, the grass isn't always greener. The more I spend time here, the more I'm starting to think there really is no place like home—as corny as that sounds." I laughed. "I think I'd been so focused on getting the hell out of here before college, I never stopped to appreciate what a great place this was to grow up. It's like I can see it through a different lens now."

She swallowed some wine and set her glass down. "But yet you'd never choose to live here again…"

"It probably wouldn't be my first choice, no," I admitted. As much as this place was growing on me, it was a reminder of the emptiness I'd felt as a kid.

She reached for another cookie.

"Wow. I guess they can't taste *that* bad if you'd willingly consume another one?"

She winked. "Wine makes me hungry. I'd eat a brick right now."

"You pretty much are."

Aspyn laughed. "Tonight will forever be remembered as the bizarre night that Kiki got her period and Troy Serrano baked me paleo cookies."

"What is this fuckery, right?" Feeling hungry myself, I reached for one of the smaller cookies and took a bite. They didn't taste half as bad as I remembered. "So…" I asked. "Have you told Jasmine you've had to spend time with me?"

Aspyn nodded. "She thought the whole thing was as weird as I did."

"Does she still hate me? I mean, I know she friended me on Facebook, but that doesn't mean she doesn't still hate me on some level."

"Actually, no. She doesn't. She's moved on."

I winked. "Unlike some people."

"I thought we were supposed to be getting along tonight."

"We are. I'm teasing."

She smiled from behind her wine glass. Whatever I was doing, it was working. I felt Aspyn slowly warming to me. So, I took further advantage.

"Confession time…" I announced.

She narrowed her eyes. "Depends."

"Depends…isn't that what I bought earlier tonight instead of maxi pads?"

Aspyn snorted. "Close." She wiped her eyes. "Okay, what's your confession?"

"It's actually a question for both of us." I paused. "What was the worst name you ever called me behind my back in high school?"

She sighed. "God, there were so many. I'd have to think about it. Why don't you go first. What was the worst thing you ever called me?"

"CPB."

"CPB? What does that stand for?"

"Crazy psycho bitch."

She chuckled. "I knew about Psycho but hadn't heard that particular take on it."

"That was your main nickname."

Aspyn rolled her eyes. "Lovely."

I took another bite of my cookie. "Your names for me are so bad you can't even decide which one is worst.

Either that, or you don't want to say them because they're so wrong…"

"I don't remember them all, really…"

I popped the last piece of cookie into my mouth. "Because you called me every name in the book."

"I do remember one."

My brow lifted. "And?"

"Whoreannosaurus."

I spit out my wine. "Oh my God, like Tyrannosaurus, but a whore."

"I'm sorry. You asked."

"No. It's all good. It was fitting for me, I suppose. I deserved it."

Her tone softened. "Knowing what I know now about your mom…it explains a lot."

I took another sip of wine and nodded. "There's no doubt I acted out because of my anger toward her. That's no excuse, though. Things only got worse after I actually met her. In some ways, it was easier when she basically didn't exist."

"You have every right to feel hurt about what she did."

"Maybe, but sometimes I feel like I should just let it go. She's dead, for Christ's sake."

"We don't always get to choose what we hang on to."

I pinned her with a look. "Like your hatred for me."

"That wasn't what I was referring to."

"I know. I understand what you're saying." I exhaled. "Not having a mother shaped my entire life. It shaped my perception of myself…my perception of women."

Aspyn tilted her head. "In what ways?"

"Well, I guess her not wanting me made me feel… unlovable. At the same time, it's why I don't look at relationships with women as permanent. Like, 'don't you dare get attached to someone who will leave like your mother did, Troy.' It's messed-up shit."

She stared at me for a few seconds. "But you must know on some level that not all women leave."

"Yeah, but it's hard to trust that, I guess." I shook my head. "I'm sorry, I must sound like such a pussy." I sighed. "First the cookies, now this."

"No. You don't. I'm liking this conversation. It's honest and showing me a side of you I never knew existed."

"Don't encourage me. I might keep you up all night unloading my screwed-up shit. Or start crying or something." I raised my forehead. "Wait—would that earn me a trust point?"

"Don't push your luck." She smiled. "Seriously, though, I don't mind listening. It's good to talk it out."

I looked up at the sky. "I don't know, Aspyn. I also worry that maybe I'm more like my mother than I want. Part of why it's so important to get you to trust me is to confirm whether it's safe to trust *myself*. I don't want to be the type of person who flies through life hurting people."

She nodded. "It's amazing how much our parents shape us, whether they're around or not."

"Your upbringing was pretty normal though, right? You mentioned your parents are still together and everything."

She downed the last of her drink. "My dad…"

"What about him?"

"My parents *are* still together, but my father hasn't been faithful to my mother. He's strayed more than once."

"Your mom continues to stay with him, even though he's cheated?"

"Yeah." She frowned. "I think after Ashlyn died, she couldn't bear to break the family apart any more. So she's put up with a lot. But the issues with my father started years before that."

A lightbulb went on. "Might that have anything to do with why you went ballistic on me after I cheated on Jasmine?"

Aspyn rested the tip of her finger at the corner of her mouth and pondered my question. "I never really thought about that... But yeah, that very well could have had something to do with why I reacted so intensely."

"It's interesting that we can look back now on our behavior as kids and see the deeper meaning behind certain things." I lifted the bottle. "You want some more?"

Aspyn held up her palm. "I'd better not."

"You're so disciplined."

"I'm picky about what I put in my body, yeah."

"I'm not gonna touch that one." Of course, my dirty mind had to go there.

She blushed.

"Speaking of which...find anything good on the dating app lately?" I asked.

Aspyn rolled her eyes. "Nice segue."

"I thought so."

"No, actually. I'm taking a break from it after Brian."

"Brian would be enough to scare me off it for a while, too."

"What about you? Any good ass for you on there lately?"

Sadly, the only ass I'd been thinking about was Aspyn's, but I wouldn't confess that tonight.

"I haven't actually matched with anyone since you picked me."

"Oh, yeah...I *picked* you."

"Accidentally or intentionally, it happened. Still not quite sure how someone drops a phone and swipes right at the same time. But whatever." I winked. "I guess you have mad skills."

Her face turned red again.

"You okay?" I asked. "You seem flustered."

"I'm fine." She attempted to take another sip of her wine, forgetting that her glass was empty.

I held up the bottle again. "Will you please let me pour you the last of this?"

She conceded, sliding her glass over to me.

I watched her sip as she gazed up at the dark night sky. We finally seemed to be getting comfortable, but I didn't want to overstay my welcome. Especially since tonight had been *a lot.*

Turning to her, I forced the words out. "I probably should go..."

Aspyn set her glass down. "Okay..."

Alrighty then. I was hoping she'd try to convince me to stay, but once again, she apparently couldn't wait to get rid of me. But I sensed it was a little different this time. Maybe she thought she'd opened up too much. I couldn't figure it out. She'd seemed to be enjoying my company. All I knew was that I could have stayed here all night talking to her.

I stood from my seat. "Well, it was a pleasure..."

She got up. "A pleasure? After what happened tonight? Liar."

"I had a really good time, Aspyn." I made sure to look her straight in the eyes so she could see I was being sincere. "It's not often I open up like this. It felt good. Thank you for listening."

She broke the eye contact, looking down at her feet. "Thank you again for making me the cookies. The fact that the first person besides my mother to bake anything for me is *you* is pretty funny."

"You want me to make them again?"

"No! Not necessary." She laughed.

I chuckled. "I'm gonna try to make them *better* next time. They're a work in progress."

She walked me back inside and to the front door before we faced each other one last time.

"Well...goodnight, Aspyn."

She smiled. "'Night, Troy."

I walked out, and rather than hearing the door slam behind me, this time Aspyn stood waiting as I got into my car.

After I started the engine, I lifted my hand in a wave, and she waved back. Something in my chest moved. A muscle? My heart? I didn't know what it was, nor was I willing to acknowledge that it had something to do with the woman who seemed to be infiltrating my mind twenty-four-seven lately.

I got back to my dad's house, and it seemed emptier than usual. As I lay in bed with Patrick curled into the spot next to me, I talked to him as if he were going to respond.

"I don't know, Pat. Clearly, she's not as comfortable around me as I am around her. She keeps trying to get rid of me. Maybe I shouldn't even try. I've never been the type to throw myself at anyone." I rubbed my fingers into the top of his head as he closed his eyes. "But she did wait at the door when I left. That means something, right? It means she probably doesn't hate me? Or maybe she's starting not to?" Unable to relax, I sat up in bed. "Why don't you ever answer me? This is not helpful, you know."

Leaning my head against the headboard, I looked up at the ceiling. "Anyway... You want to know something messed up—as if this night wasn't messed up enough?" I looked over at the cat. "Okay, I'll tell you." I paused. "I'm not even sure of my motives anymore. I tried to convince myself I was just trying to get her to trust me. But I think this is more about me liking her now. Which is dangerous. Where's that gonna get me if she doesn't like me back? Or if she likes me but doesn't trust me? You see how complicated this situation is? You have no idea how lucky you are, Patrick, not having to worry about this kind of shit. As long as you have your food and your water and some foot to rub your asshole against, you're good. You don't need validation or affection or sex. You're better off."

I heard a rumbly purr—a snore, actually. Patrick had fallen asleep. I couldn't blame him for shutting my rambling out.

As I tried to fall asleep myself, I kept picturing Aspyn's face, at the same time trying to convince myself to stop thinking about her that way. But like usual, the more I willed the thought away, the more it stayed.

Chapter Seven

Aspyn

Tuesday morning, my mother came to pick up Kiki and take her to school. Even though I normally drove her, Mom wanted to have breakfast with us to tell me all about the wedding she and my father had attended over the weekend. They'd just gotten back late last night. Mom had really missed her granddaughter and felt bad that she wasn't here when Kiki got her period for the first time.

My niece lifted the stuffed animal Troy had bought her at the supermarket. "Grandma, look at my new unicorn."

"Very cute! What's her name?"

"Menses."

I jerked to look at Kiki as I stirred my coffee.

"Strange choice, but I suppose given the circumstances, I can understand," my mother said.

"I looked up another name for period and saw that," Kiki explained. "This toy reminds me of my period. Aspyn's friend Troy bought it for me."

My mother looked over at me. "I see. Well, *Menses* is very pretty."

I rolled my eyes at the ridiculousness of the name choice. I'd filled my mother in on everything that happened the other night, including my recent interactions with Troy, before Kiki woke up.

After Kiki left the breakfast table to get dressed, my mother turned to me as she finished the last of her coffee.

"So...this Troy. You think you'll invite him over again?"

I hesitated. "I'm not really comfortable with that."

"Why are you uncomfortable? Because you like him despite your history?"

"Who said I like him?"

She gave me a look that said, *stop lying to yourself.*

"I don't *want* to like him." I sighed. "I'm extremely attracted to him, though I don't like admitting that. And I think that's why I'm so focused on him lately. It's like I can't think straight around him because I have these blinders on."

Her brow lifted. "There's nothing more to it than physical attraction?"

I'd tried to blow off all of the other things brewing inside me since the other night. He'd been so sweet to step in when I needed help with Kiki. He'd opened up to me. I actually hadn't wanted to flee when we were talking out on my deck.

But I shook my head. "There can never be anything more between us than this friendship of sorts. Number one, he doesn't want a relationship. Number two, I don't think I could ever trust him fully after what he did to Jasmine in high school. Number three, he doesn't even live here full time." I pointed my index finger toward her. "You know what? Thank you for helping me see the light."

"I didn't even say anything, Aspyn."

I turned to pack my lunch into a container. "Well, talking it out still helped me realize I need to get these weird feelings in check."

I took one of Troy's cookies from the container and bit into it before placing the rest in some plastic wrap so I could take them to work. They somehow tasted better after a few days.

Damn Troy, and damn his cookies, too.

• • •

It was an ordinary Tuesday at Horizons until I walked into Mr. Serrano's room at two. I'd assumed I'd be accompanying Troy and him on the usual excursion, and I'd been looking forward to it all day—despite everything I'd fed my mother this morning.

But when I got there, Nancy was already sitting with Mr. Serrano.

"Hey, Nancy. What's up?"

"So, change of plans, Aspyn. You're no longer needed to accompany Mr. Serrano."

A deep voice from behind me said, "What?"

I turned around to find Troy in the doorway, looking just as taken aback as I was.

"Today or moving forward?" I asked her.

"Moving forward."

Troy's eyes widened.

She looked over at him. "I think Troy here gets the picture about how serious we are about sticking to the rules. There's no need to waste you as a resource any longer. We're going to start adding more afternoon outings for some of the other residents soon, and we'll need you for those. Today we're doing games in the dining room, though. So that's what you'll be overseeing instead of going out."

I didn't know how to respond. "Wow, uh, okay. Thank you for letting me know."

She nodded at Troy as she headed toward the door. "Good to see you." Her heels clicked as she made her way down the hall.

Troy and I just looked at each other.

Mr. Serrano interrupted the silence. "Well, I'm certainly gonna miss your company."

"This fucking blows," Troy finally said.

"Watch your language," his grandfather warned.

"Sorry, Nonno."

"Yeah, it does suck," I admitted. "I was sort of getting used to these little trips."

"You're wearing your Goofy scrubs, too. What a waste." He frowned.

To add insult to injury, I *had* decided to wear Troy's favorite scrubs today. I'd figured it was the least I could do after how good he was to us the other night. And now look where that decision had gotten me—straight into some crappy luck.

God, why does he look so adorable frowning now? I forced myself to move toward the door. "Well, I'd better get going. You two have fun, okay?"

They both had the exact same pout on their faces.

"Bye," Troy groaned.

Almost out the door, I turned back around, paranoid

that Troy had been watching my ass jiggle—AKA Goofy laughing. He flashed a guilty smile. I rolled my eyes and made my way down the hall.

Twenty minutes later, I was setting up a game in the dining room when my phone chimed. It was a photo from Troy. It looked like they were at the park. His grandfather was eating his McDonald's ice cream cone on a bench, and Troy lifted a coffee.

Troy: Drinking a black coffee in honor of you.

Grinning like a fool, I typed.

Aspyn: Does it taste as bitter as my personality?

Troy: Okay, confession. I might have snuck a little sugar in.

Aspyn: Wuss. Go pay attention to your grandfather and stop texting me before you lose him.

Troy: I only lose him when you're with me. Anyway, he's right here, chatting up this lady sitting across from us. I feel like a third wheel. I'm missing the fourth wheel a lot right now.

The fourth wheel? *Me.* Why was he turning so... mushy? He needed to stop because I was starting to fall for his shit. I slapped my own cheek. *You need to remember who you're dealing with, Aspyn. This is the same guy who cheated on your friend. The same guy who called you names behind your back, causing a rumor that you were actually crazy.* (Which might have been a little correct at the time.)

My phone chimed again, snapping me out of my thoughts.

> **Troy:** Seriously, I'm bummed that they took you off my case.

> **Aspyn:** What are you, a criminal? You shouldn't have a "case." Behave so you don't lose your privileges.

> **Troy:** You just gave me an idea.

> **Aspyn:** Uh-oh.

> **Troy:** If I'm late bringing him back, will they send you out with us next time?

> **Aspyn:** Pretty sure next time it's gonna be Nancy accompanying you.

> **Troy:** I'd better not risk it then. She seems mean. Like black-coffee-drinker mean.

> **Aspyn:** Actually, from what I hear, she's quite fond of you.

> **Troy:** In what way?

> **Aspyn:** In "that" way…

Troy: Really? That's a little icky. She's old enough to be my mother.

Aspyn: You didn't hear that from me.

Troy: What made you wear the Goofy scrubs today?

I lied.

Aspyn: Everything else was dirty.

Troy: Like my mind...

Aspyn: Yes.

After about a minute, he wrote back again.

Troy: I really enjoyed talking to you the other night.

Heat washed through my body. I felt like I knew where this was leading, and if I agreed, it would only encourage things. So, I didn't agree that I, too, had enjoyed our conversation.

Aspyn: Thanks again for going to the store for me.

Troy: How's Kiki doing with everything?

Aspyn: She's hanging in there. Getting used to her new normal.

Troy: I'm glad she's okay.

Aspyn: How's Patrick?

Troy: Still rubbing his asshole on my feet.

Aspyn: LOL

Troy: I'd better let you tend to your games.

Aspyn: Yeah. Good idea.

Troy: Don't leave until I get to say goodbye later. I'll meet you out in the parking lot after your shift.

My heart fluttered. *Shit*.

Despite organizing several card games that afternoon, my mind wandered as I wondered what Troy and his grandfather were up to. I hadn't realized until today just how much I'd looked forward to hanging out with them.

When 4 PM rolled around, I wasn't surprised to find Troy waiting for me out in the parking lot, as promised. What did surprise me? He was holding a bouquet of flowers. Upon closer look, they were roses. *Black* roses.

"What's this?"

He held them out to me. "These are for you."

I smelled them. "Did your grandfather buy them?"

"No. This time it was all me. They're to thank you for putting up with my ass these past few weeks and chaperoning me. Black is more fitting for you, don't you think? You're no boring yellow rose. You're the black rose. Deep, mysterious, complex...and beautiful."

My heart was practically pounding out of my chest.

Stop.

I cleared my throat and sniffed them again. "Well, thank you. They're really nice."

"Can we talk about how much it sucks that I no longer have an excuse to see you twice a week? I feel like it's the end of a small era."

I wanted to stomp on my heart right now. I couldn't allow myself to continue to react to this man. Butterflies had been swarming in my damn belly all afternoon—from the moment I'd caught him looking so down when he found out I wasn't joining them today. As much as I hated to admit it, I had a massive crush on him that had apparently started to suck the rationality out of me. Case in point, my intentionally wearing the Goofy scrubs I knew he loved. I was setting myself up for failure.

"What are the chances you'd let me take you out this weekend?" he asked, interrupting my thoughts.

A wave of panic swept over me as my heart wrangled with my better judgment.

"I can't do this anymore, Troy..." I blurted.

"Oh...kay?" The color drained from his face.

I understood why he might've been confused by my response. Things had been going well between us. I had every reason to say yes. But the underlying fear that I was somehow being punked by this man just wouldn't let up.

"I'm sorry for reacting so abruptly." Staring down into the roses, I said, "I just don't see this ending well."

A muscle in his jaw twitched. "In what way?"

"I don't think it's a good idea to get closer to you."

"Because you don't trust that I only want to be your friend..."

"It's not just that. I don't trust *myself*."

He took a few steps closer. "Elaborate."

"I'm only human. And...I can see this going in the wrong direction if we keep spending so much time together under the façade of friendship."

I could feel the heat of his body. "The wrong direction... What does that mean?"

"I think you *know* what it means."

"You think I want to sleep with you..." He paused for several seconds. "You're right."

My eyes widened. "I am?"

"I'm very attracted to you, yes. I want to sleep with you very badly. And when we argue..." His eyes rolled back a little. "I want to fuck you even more."

That eye roll and what he'd just said made the muscles between my legs contract, just another indication of my lack of control. My body buzzed as my breathing sped up. But I said nothing—I was speechless.

He exhaled. "Look... Part of getting you to trust me is being honest with you. So I'm not going to stand here and deny that I have *those thoughts* about you...all the time." His eyes wandered over me. "Especially when you're in those damn Goofy scrubs." He inched closer, putting my body on full alert. "Do I think I'm right for you? No. That's me being honest, too." He swallowed, his Adam's apple moving up and down. "I'm confused. That's the truth. All I know is that I haven't been able to stop thinking about you."

"I've been thinking a lot about you, too," I admitted. "That's the problem."

He looked down at me, the sun shining in his eyes as his hair blew slightly in the wind. "What do you want, Aspyn? You want me to back off? Stop trying to get closer to you? Because if that's what you *really* want, I promise you, I will. I come on strong when I'm determined. But I know how to walk away just as fiercely. I *do* have pride—a fuck ton of it, which is why my mother never saw me knocking on her door."

That broke my heart. I hated that this situation had somehow reminded him of that.

"All you have to do is say the word," he said. "And you won't see or hear from me anymore."

An undetermined amount of time passed as we stood facing each other in silence. Shala walked by as she headed to her car. She gave me a look that said, *you'd better fill me in later.*

I had two choices—either admit that I was scared of my budding feelings for him, or agree that not seeing each other was best. I chose the latter.

"Yeah. I do think it's best if we not see each other anymore."

Those words left a bitter taste in my mouth. I guess that's the way it tastes when you let fear win. Emotions twisted inside of me. I'd just said the opposite of what I wanted. But it felt like the safest choice, the one that would ensure I didn't get hurt in the end.

The disappointed look on his face told me that it wasn't the answer he was hoping for. I'd been giving him mixed messages, and he didn't deserve that—another reason this couldn't continue. I wouldn't blame him if he never spoke to me again, though.

A vein popped out in his neck as he finally nodded. "You got it."

That was the last thing he said before he got into his car and took off.

Chapter Eight

Aspyn

A week passed, and it felt like forever since I'd seen Troy Serrano. After being a constant presence for almost a month, he'd disappeared from my life. He somehow managed to avoid me altogether when he came to take his grandfather out and made no effort to contact me. This was exactly what I'd asked for, but the more he stayed away, the more I thought about him. Funny how that works.

One night over dinner, my niece caught me staring down into my plate.

"Are you okay, Auntie Aspyn?"

I looked up suddenly. "Yeah, hon. I'm fine. Just thinking about some stuff."

She cocked her head. "What stuff?"

"Adult stuff."

Kiki rested her chin in her hand. "Is it about Troy?"

Her perception surprised me, since I hadn't mentioned him. But maybe the fact that I'd not uttered a word about him at all clued her in.

"Yeah," I admitted.

"Did he do something bad?"

"No." I stared down into my salad. "Not at all. He actually did something...good."

"Then why are you sad?"

"Because I miss him," I whispered.

The fact that I'd admitted aloud what I'd been thinking for days shocked me. And to Kiki, of all people. I missed Troy? Damn, I did. I missed his humor, his presence, his smell. I missed it all.

"Then why don't you call him?"

Her question made total sense, but the answer didn't seem simple.

"Because sometimes you have to choose to walk away from something because you know that ultimately, it's not right for you."

"Like candy?"

I laughed. "Exactly like candy."

Troy *was* like candy, except I hadn't even gotten a taste. I'd stopped it before it could happen because I sensed that *tasting* was exactly where things were headed. I could feel it in every fiber of my being. And I knew that taste would be as addicting as it was dangerous. Ironically, sex fantasies of Troy seemed to be all I thought about whenever I lay in bed at night. Would *one time* have really killed me? I shook my head.

"Why is Troy not good for you?" she asked.

My niece was really testing me tonight. But that was a fair question.

"There's not a simple answer to that. But for one, we have a lot of negative history from our high school days."

She leaned her elbows against the table. "Like what do you mean?"

"We were mean to each other, and he did some things that make me not trust him fully."

"Troy scared me at first," she said. "I thought he was trying to steal from us. But now I like him. He seems nice. And he bought me Menses."

"I know he's nice. That's not up for debate. But I worry that a part of him is still the boy I used to know. Maybe that's all in my head, but it interferes with our relationship. More than that, he's not even here in Meadowbrook permanently. I don't think he likes it here. And I don't want to get attached to him if he's only going to leave. So, like I said, there are lots of reasons why he's not good for me."

"Why can't you just be friends until he leaves? My friend Ben from school moved away. I don't talk to him anymore. But I'm glad I was friends with him while he was here."

I smiled. "Things are a little different when you're older. Friendships between men and women can be complicated. They sometimes lead down paths where you didn't intend to go. And then someone gets hurt."

Her forehead crinkled. "I don't understand."

I chuckled and sighed. "Someday you will."

I'd thought the conversation was over until she shocked the hell out of me with her next question.

"Does he want to stick his penis in your vagina? Is that why things are weird?"

My mouth fell open. "What do you know about that?"

"I was reading about periods, and I found out about sex."

"Please tell me you didn't see anything online you weren't supposed to?"

"No. It was in a book Grandma got me. It talks about periods and how babies are made. Then I started asking her questions, and she told me sometimes people have sex even if they're not trying to make babies."

Thanks a lot, Mom, for giving me a heads up about this.

"Well, that is true. Adults might choose to do it when they are not trying to have a child. Sex is definitely something that makes relationships between grown men and women complicated...if there's an attraction."

"Did Holden stick his penis in your vagina?"

She'd almost never brought up my ex since he moved out. And this context was definitely awkward.

Why did I not have wine with this dinner?

I kept my answer generic. "I've had sex, yes. Because I'm an adult. And when you're an adult, you can decide whether that's a decision that's right for you."

She crinkled her nose. "Why did you do it?"

"Because...it can be pleasurable with the right person."

"It sounds horrible to me—like it hurts." Kiki cringed. "I'm never gonna do it."

"You don't need to think about it for a very long time."

I could only hope that when Kiki was my age, she handled such matters better than I had.

• • •

The following Saturday, Shala's husband offered to take care of the kids so she could get out for a night. She'd asked if I wanted to meet her at one of the bars in Meadowbrook Center. I'd spent enough time lamenting the self-inflicted end to my "friendship" with Troy, so I figured a night out would do me some good. A distraction was much needed.

As expected, the Kaleidoscope Lounge was packed when I stepped inside. There weren't a ton of options in Meadowbrook, but the few bars we had were all modern and popular.

Shala had her purse on a stool next to her to hold the seat for me until I arrived. A band was setting up in the corner as the singer tested the mic.

She lifted her glass. "I'm already on my second drink. Is that bad?"

"No. That's why we both got Ubers, right? And you totally deserve to get drunk tonight, mama."

I ordered a glass of red wine, pretty much the only alcohol I allowed myself since I could justify the resveratrol as a health benefit.

"How's Kiki doing with the whole period thing?" she asked.

"She's handling it okay."

"I'm so glad. I suppose I'm fortunate to have boys in that respect."

"See? I couldn't imagine dealing with a boy. I think we're comfortable with what we know."

"You're amazing for doing what you do for her."

I shrugged. "It's not that commendable. Anyone would have done it for their sister."

"I beg to differ. Some people would've taken off and let their parents handle it all. I know that's what my selfish siblings would have done. You didn't have to do what you did."

I'd never looked at it that way, especially since I took some of the blame for my sister's death. But even if things were different, I couldn't imagine leaving Meadowbrook and Kiki behind.

After a few minutes, the wine started to hit me, and I felt relaxed for the first time in a while.

Three glasses and nearly two hours later, the feeling of euphoria was even better. That, unfortunately, came to an abrupt end the moment I spotted him. My stomach dipped.

Troy Serrano.

He was at a table across the bar, sipping on a bottle of beer and laughing as if he didn't have a care in the world.

My heart began to race. *Why?* He looked so damn good. His hair was damp and slicked back off his face. And the white sweater he wore accentuated his tanned skin and clung to his pecs perfectly. There was no denying how beautiful he was. I just wished I didn't have to bear witness to it tonight when I was trying to forget about him. Why he'd chosen not to venture to Trenton or Philly instead of staying in Meadowbrook, I didn't understand. Shala and I only came here so she'd be close to home. She wanted the option to head back quickly if she needed to.

Damn it.

Troy hadn't noticed me yet. He seemed surrounded by both men and women. I couldn't tell who he was here with or who he'd just happened to meet. The inability to distinguish drove me crazy.

I wondered if I should make up an excuse and leave so I didn't have to deal with this.

"Are you okay?" Shala asked.

It was no wonder she'd figured something out, considering how long I'd been staring over in Troy's direction.

"Yeah. I just noticed that Troy is here."

She turned around to get a look at him. "Oh wow. Yeah. Is that a bad thing?"

"Can we switch seats so I'm not facing him?" I asked.

That was cowardly. But the only way I could continue to relax tonight was if he didn't notice me.

Shala narrowed her eyes in confusion but complied. "Sure."

Once my back was to him, I felt a little better, albeit still preoccupied with the fact that he was just across the room. Of all places, why did he have to be *here* tonight?

"Everything okay with you and him?" Shala asked.

"We don't really interact anymore after I stopped chaperoning the outings."

"I never asked you about the day I saw you in the parking lot. Things seemed tense. Something tells me there's more to the story here."

I took a long sip of my wine and set the glass down. "There is. But I'd prefer not to get into it right now."

The conversation temporarily moved off of Troy until I noticed him at a new table, diagonally across from me. *He'd moved!* And now I was facing him. So much for switching seats. I wasn't about to play musical chairs, either. Poor Shala would think I was nuts.

This time, Troy was alone with a woman, and the other people were nowhere in sight. They were chatting away, and unfortunately I now had a front-row seat to it all. It was still unclear to me whether this was someone he'd just met or whether he'd planned to meet her here.

"What's wrong?" Shala asked.

I shook my head. "I'm sorry. Troy just moved seats, so he's facing me again. He's sitting over there with some girl. And I'm a little distracted." Downing the last of my wine, I slammed the glass on the table. "I'm the worst person to be out with tonight."

"No worries. I'm actually finding it amusing." She turned around to look at Troy and the girl, and when she faced me again, she examined my face. "You're turning red as a beet, Aspyn." She chuckled. "You have it bad, don't you?"

Her words were humiliating. Mostly because they were true.

I wiped my forehead with a napkin. "I'm sorry. I think I'm losing my mind." I cleared my throat. "There's no doubt he has an effect on me, but I wish that weren't the case."

"Please don't apologize. You're human. He's a very attractive man, and clearly you two were getting on pretty well for a while there."

"Nothing happened between us." I felt the need to clarify. "But it felt like things were starting to cross a line, and I told him I thought it was best if we didn't hang out anymore. That's not what he wanted. It's not really what I wanted either, if I'm being honest. But I thought it was the right thing to do. Seeing him here tonight is getting under my skin a little."

She nodded. "You like him."

"I don't *want* to like him, Shala. He was such a dick in high school. It hasn't been easy for me to accept that he's changed. But I *do* think he has. Even so, he's *still* not right for me. What I'm feeling is just an intense, mostly physical attraction to someone who's all wrong. He's my friend's ex, on top of everything. He doesn't even live here. And he doesn't want to settle in Meadowbrook. There are so many reasons to stay far away."

She smiled knowingly. "But you haven't been able to stop thinking about him. Sounds like you're using every excuse in the book to justify your decision. But feelings don't lie, Aspyn. You tried to write him off, but he's still in your head."

"Much to my dismay, yeah. Tonight was supposed to help me focus on something else." I glanced over in Troy's direction. "And now he's here. Just my luck."

Somehow, after all this time, Troy still hadn't seemed to notice me. When Shala got up to use the restroom, I opted to stay in my seat so as not to draw attention to myself.

About a minute later, from the corner of my eye, I noticed Troy's date leave their table and head toward the bathroom.

A few seconds later, my phone chimed.

Troy: Is this an eye for an eye?

I looked over at him.

Aspyn: What are you talking about?

Troy: You thought I was spying on your date that one time, so now you're spying on mine?

My fingers hit the keypad harder.

Aspyn: You're kidding me, right?

Troy: Yeah, actually, I am. But did you think moving earlier was going to keep me from noticing you? Even if you hadn't moved, I'd know it was you from the back of your head. I know your entire backside pretty damn well.

Aspyn: Well, aren't you talented.

Troy: You're like a laxative-filled Boston cream donut. You stand out in the bunch.

Aspyn: Thanks?

Troy: You look nice. I hope you're having fun. You deserve to let loose. Glad to see you out and about.

He thinks I'm a hermit.

His date returned to the table, and Troy put his phone down. I tried to ignore the burn of jealousy I felt at having his attention taken away from me so abruptly.

Shala returned to the table. "Did you survive without me?"

"Yeah." I breathed out.

I could see from the corner of my eye that Troy had now gotten up from the table.

A moment later, my phone lit up again with a text.

Troy: Meet me in the stairwell through the door in the far-left corner of the bar.

I kept staring down at my phone.

"What's going on?" Shala asked.

"Nothing." I looked up, my heart racing. "Actually, I have to...use the bathroom, too. Be right back."

The room swayed a little as I got up from my seat and headed to the back of the bar. *Am I seriously doing this right now?* How pathetic did I have to be to come when called like that? I needed my head checked, but I was too damn curious to stop myself.

Troy was standing in the stairwell with his arms crossed. His scent was dizzying. My nipples hardened, my body becoming aware of just how much it had missed being around him. And gosh, was he always this tall?

I took in a deep whiff of him and exhaled. "What was it you needed to see me about?"

"I have to admit, I'm a little insulted."

"Why is that?"

"You've been looking over at me all night, yet you never bothered to say hello."

"Why would I come say hello when you're on a date? It would be rude for me to interrupt."

"It's not a date."

"Sure looks like it."

He inched closer. "I just met her tonight. I was hanging out with my buddy, Eric, but he had to leave. Casey was with some work friends, and she started a conversation with me." His gaze traveled over my body, causing a chill to run down my spine. I could feel his breath on my face when he said, "You look beautiful tonight. That liner you're wearing really brings out your eyes, but at the same time, you don't need it." His eyes trailed down my neck. "I hope you don't mind me being blunt...but your tits look amazing in that shirt, too." He looked back up at me. "*You* look amazing."

I could hardly breathe, let alone form a response to that.

"All I've wanted to do was look at you. But I knew if I looked your way, you'd stop looking at *me*. I could feel you staring, and I loved knowing that your eyes were on me. I fucking loved every second of it."

I swallowed. "Well, I'm surprised you noticed me looking over at you at all. You seemed to be getting along so well with her."

"Not everything is what it seems. Because while I looked like I was getting along with her, I kept wishing she were you."

I'd been looking down at my feet, but he placed his hand on my chin and lifted it to meet his incendiary stare.

"Goddammit, please tell me I'm not alone. Are you feeling this, too, Aspyn?"

He was far from alone. Feelings of intense attraction and jealousy had consumed me tonight. I just couldn't get myself to admit it.

What he said next shook me.

"Casey *did* ask me to go back to her place for a nightcap. Any reason I shouldn't?"

I was burning up. I wanted to urge him not to go home with her, but then what? I'd have to admit my jealousy. And there would be no going back once I fell into that web.

"You should do what you want," I coughed out.

He leaned in, close enough that I could practically taste him. "What do *you* want?"

My chest heaved. "This has nothing to do with me."

"You sure about that? Because you seemed pretty invested tonight with the way you couldn't take your eyes off me."

My voice shook. "Your ego is atrocious. What do you want me to say? There's no need for me to answer if you've already drawn your own conclusion."

"I want you to admit that you've missed me as much as I've missed you this past week." He inched even closer. "Look me in the eyes and tell me you haven't been thinking about me."

As much as I wanted to put on a façade and attempt to stare him in the face and tell him just that, I was never a good liar. My gaze, therefore, stayed firmly planted on my feet. Because the second I looked at him, he'd know.

"You can't, can you?" he said.

I felt his hand on my chin again as he brought my face up to meet his. And it was in that moment that I decided to let go. "You're right. I can't lie. I *have* been thinking about you. And I hate it."

Troy's hand snaked around the back of my neck. He threaded his fingers in my hair before pulling me into him. Our lips smashed together, and a tidal wave of pleasure hit. A moan escaped into his mouth, and all sense of reality seemed to dissipate.

"You're all I fucking think about lately," he groaned over my lips.

I opened wider, letting his tongue in. He tasted sweet, with a hint of alcohol. My hands raked through his hair as

I became lost in the most amazing, all-consuming kiss I'd ever experienced. The heat of his breath seemed to warm my entire body, his scent enveloping me.

Troy suddenly pushed back, leaving me cold and starving for more.

"How do I make it stop, Aspyn? You say you want nothing to do with me, but it sure as hell doesn't seem like it." He cupped my cheek, gently rubbing his thumb across my lips. "I need to get you out of my system."

Shutting my eyes, I panted. "I never said I didn't want you. I *wish* I didn't want you."

"Really? Maybe you need to get me out of your system, too, then?" He shook his head slowly. "Look, I get that this can't really go anywhere. I'm going back to Seattle. You won't ever genuinely trust me. We're bad for each other. I'm Jasmine's ex. Yada, yada." He looked into my eyes. "But don't you feel like you'll always wonder...what if? What if we let nature take its course, just once? For a long time now, I haven't been able to think of any woman but you. I feel like it's an itch only you can scratch. If we're both curious, if we're both adults, then why the fuck are we fighting it so hard?" A long moment of silence passed. "I'm gonna ask you one more time. Do you want me to go home with her...or with *you*?"

My phone vibrated, and for a split second I thought it was the sound of my heart shooting out of my chest.

I looked down at it.

Shala: Are you okay?

Shit.

How long had I been out here with him? I had no damn concept of time.

Feeling like I was about to overheat, I made a rash decision. "My friend is worried. I need to go back to my table. You should do the same. Goodnight."

With lightning speed, I ran off, nearly crashing into a wall as I turned the corner in a haze.

Back at the table, a look of concern crossed Shala's face. "Everything okay? I thought maybe you passed out or something."

"Yup." I grabbed a water and downed the entire thing in one long gulp. I wiped my mouth with the back of my hand. "Everything is fine."

She sighed, looking down at her phone. "I actually have to get going. It's later than I told Felix I'd be home."

Tucking a piece of hair behind my ear, I nodded. "Okay, yeah. Thank you for coming out tonight. This was so much fun." *Until I turned into a hot mess.*

She stood up from her chair. "I'll see you Monday. Be careful getting home, okay?"

"I will." I nodded. "You be careful, too."

When Shala left, I noticed Troy return to his table. Soon after, he and Casey both got up. With his hand at the small of her back, they walked toward the exit together before eventually disappearing out the door.

I felt nauseous. *Well, ain't that a bitch.* I guess he was serious when he threatened to go home with her.

Asshole. I didn't know if I was swearing at him or myself.

Damn it, this stung. He'd riled me up, and now he was going back to her place to take my rejection out on her.

Would he fuck that woman just to spite me after the best kiss of my life? *If that's the case, it's just more proof that he's nothing but bad news.*

I grabbed my phone and scrolled to the app for a ride home.

After I took a few minutes to cool down with another glass of water, I got up and walked outside to wait for my ride.

As soon as the cool night air hit my face, a voice startled me.

"Boo."

I looked to my left to find Troy leaning against the building.

He was alone.

I clutched my chest. "You scared me."

"You didn't think I was really gonna go home with her, did you?" He took a few steps toward me. "I know you like to call me Whoreannosaurus, but even *I* don't go home with women I've only known for a matter of minutes." He was inches away now. "Besides, how could I even think of anyone else after the kiss we had?"

My heart fluttered.

"Cancel the car, if you called one," he said. "I'm taking you home. And no, you don't have to let me *into* your house—unless you want to. It's just a ride home, Aspyn. No expectations, despite what I said when I was all worked up in there."

"Can you even drive?" I asked. "I saw you drinking."

"When I met Eric earlier, I wasn't expecting to stay as long as I did. I stopped at two beers because I brought my car. I nursed the last one. I promise I'm sober. I wouldn't put you in danger." He paused. "That goes for more than just driving."

"Well, you've already been in one car accident since I've known you."

"Yeah. But that was *your* fault."

"My fault?"

"I saw you with that guy and got distracted."

"That was why you crashed your car? Because you spotted me? I didn't know that."

"Yep. See? That wasn't easy to admit. But I've already thrown balls to the wall tonight with you, so what's one more thing?"

Taking out my phone, I scrolled down to cancel my ride as my body buzzed.

Troy and I walked together in silence to the area where he'd parked his car. He opened the passenger door for me, and I got into his Range Rover, which was, per usual, the epicenter of his intoxicating scent.

The tension was thick during the ride home. I didn't know if it was the pheromones in the air, the alcohol in me, or what, but I wanted nothing more than for Troy to kiss me again. My panties were still wet from our first one. My body had come alive in a way that felt like a faucet of arousal that couldn't be shut off.

As we drove over the small bridge leading to my neighborhood, my gut told me something was going to happen between us tonight. And I wasn't going to fight it, because I wanted it just as much as he did. Maybe more. I needed this. I needed him. I was going to let myself have it.

Troy turned on the radio, and "The Best is Yet to Come" by Frank Sinatra started playing. I wondered if he was trying to send me a subliminal message.

When we pulled up in front of my house, he shut the ignition off before turning to me. But he didn't say anything.

My palms were sweaty. "Are you...coming inside?" I finally asked, immediately realizing how suggestive my choice of words was.

Coming inside my house? Coming inside of me? Tomato-tomahto.

"Only if you ask me to," he said. "Just to be clear, I'm not making any assumptions. I won't do *anything* unless you *ask* me to do it, despite all that talk back at the bar." He wrapped his arm around the back of my seat, causing the hairs on my neck to stiffen. "Look, I feel like I can read people pretty well. If I didn't think you wanted me to come back here with you, I wouldn't have pulled what I did tonight. I know your head is telling you I'm a bad idea. But what you actually *want* is a different story. Am I right?"

I swallowed hard. "You're right."

He nodded as his eyes fell to my lips.

What my body wanted was never up for debate. The main thing stopping me was fear of where my *head* would take things *after*. I didn't want to get attached to a man I'd deemed dangerous for me. And I also didn't want to deal with everything else that came along with it, like having to admit what I'd done to Jasmine—even if she'd already encouraged me to go for him. Aside from all that, I couldn't deny that I wanted him more than I'd wanted anything in a very long time.

"If you decide you want me to come inside," he said. "We'll let things happen naturally—only what you're comfortable with and only what you ask me for. And I won't stay the night. There doesn't have to be any mention of it tomorrow, either, or the next day. It can be noncommittal. It doesn't have to mean anything if you don't want it to, Aspyn. No pressure...just *pleasure*."

"That sounds like an advertising slogan." I laughed nervously. "Anyway, you make it sound so simple."

"I can also go home. And we can pretend this conversation never happened. But that would be painful." He shook his head and groaned, "Because I want to fuck you so badly. I'm sorry for being blunt. But I've dreamed of fucking you almost every day since the night I crashed my car."

His words sent chills through my body. "I don't want you to go home tonight," I whispered.

"Good. Because I *really* don't want to."

A rush of adrenaline hit as I forced out an awkward but important question. "Do you...have any diseases or anything? Are you clean?"

He pushed back a bit in his seat to look at me. "I'm glad you asked. I saw my doctor for my yearly physical before I left Seattle, and I got a full STD panel just to be on the safe side, even though I always use protection. Totally clean, and I haven't been with anyone since I've been here. Despite what you might have assumed, I don't take that stuff lightly. You?"

"Same. Clean bill of health and no diseases. Haven't been with anyone in over a year, and I've always been safe."

"Two things I want to make clear," he said. "I'm serious about not discussing anything that happens tonight. I just want you to enjoy it and not worry about attaching meaning to it."

I swallowed. "What's the other thing?"

"As I've alluded to, I'm not doing anything to you unless you specifically ask me for it."

"Is that some kind of sadistic need to hear me beg?"

"Nope. I just prefer knowing *exactly* what you want and not making any assumptions."

I let out a shaky breath as he placed his hand on my leg.

He squeezed my thigh gently. "You're so nervous. Don't be. I won't do anything you don't want me to. Just tell me to fuck off at any time, and I'll leave."

What made me more nervous right now were all of the things I *did* want him to do to me. Even the touch of his hand on my thigh had sent shockwaves through my body, which was so damn sensitized. I was as excited and turned-on as I was nervous.

I finally opened the car door and got out. He did the same and followed. His body behind me was palpable as we walked together toward my house. Then I fumbled with my keys until I managed to open the door.

Once inside, he looped his fingers with mine and locked my hand in his. He slowly brought me toward him until our lips pressed together. I exhaled into his mouth as our frantic breaths collided. Troy's tongue went in search of mine, and I knew I was a goner. *Hell*. This man was the best kisser. Every inch of me felt ready to explode. It had been a long time since I'd had sex, sure. But the sexual attraction I had for Troy was next level. I'd never felt this intense need for another person's body before.

I scratched at his back as our kiss intensified. As he leaned into me, his hard-on became apparent. I couldn't help remembering the rumor about his size. I wasn't proud to be thinking about what Jasmine used to say about him right now, but that's where my mind went. I wondered if I'd be able to take him, since the two men I'd been with had both been average-sized.

"Aspyn, I'm so freaking happy right now."

I didn't respond to that, but my body certainly echoed the sentiment. And it turned out, I was the one with the least patience between us.

"We should go to my room," I muttered into his mouth.

He spoke over my lips. "Lead the way, beautiful."

We broke the kiss before I took him into my bedroom. I paused in front of my bed to reach my arms around his neck and kiss him again.

With our lips still pressed together, he placed my hand on his belt. "Undress me."

Wrapping my fingers around his belt buckle, I slowly opened it like I would the most ornately wrapped present. Loosening the belt, I slid it out from the loops on his pants and threw it to the ground. The buckle landed in a loud clank. I tugged at the opening of his jeans, noticing the warm skin of his hard stomach. I looked down to find a thin trail of hair lining his abs. Fuck, he was beautiful. My mouth watered.

"You like what you see?" he asked.

Biting my bottom lip, I nodded.

"Wait till you feel me inside you."

Jesus.

Rather than push his pants down, I slid my hands up his bare chest to feel the contours of his muscles.

"I love the way you're looking at me right now...so much, Aspyn."

"Get over yourself," I teased.

"I can't wait to have *you* over me—and under me. Can't fucking wait," he said huskily, looking down at my chest. "Can I touch you?"

I nodded fast. "Mm-hmm."

"Can I take off your shirt?" he asked.

I nodded again.

He slipped my shirt over my head and reached out to gently cup my breasts through my bra, massaging them slowly. Having his hands on me felt freaking amazing.

"You know what I love about your body?" he asked.

"What?" I could barely form words, so aroused by his touch.

"How natural it is. I love that you're not skin and bones. I love that your tits aren't fake. They're phenomenally real." He placed his hand on my stomach. "And I love this."

A twinge of discomfort coursed through me. "You love my jelly roll?"

"It's a tiny pooch—and yes, it turns me the fuck on." He reached his hand behind me. "But what makes me absolutely crazy is your ass, Aspyn. I've been obsessed with it from the moment I first saw it jiggle in those Goofy scrubs, and I can't wait to fuck you from behind."

Turned on to the max, I leaned in to taste his lips again.

"Now tell me what *you* want," he whispered over my mouth.

I was too far gone to be anything but completely honest at this point. "You seem to want me to tell you what I want. But I don't want that."

He pulled away and arched his brow. "Okay?"

I decided to unleash my deepest, darkest desire. "I prefer it if you call the shots. Tell me what to do."

His breathing was labored as he cupped my breast again and squeezed. "That's what you like, huh? Well, I'll be damned. You sure you want to give me all the control like that?"

I dragged my teeth along my bottom lip. "Yes."

"Well, then you *have* told me what you want." He placed another hard kiss on my lips. "Take off your bra and panties so I can look at you naked."

After I slipped off the rest of my clothes, he looked me up and down, his eyes glassy with desire. "You have no idea how turned on I am just looking at you." Troy returned his eyes to mine. "Now, finish undressing me."

Placing my hand on his zipper, I lowered it and pushed his jeans down. A spot of wetness on his gray boxer briefs met my eye. I rubbed my palm against the heat of his bulge. I could tell how huge he was. That excited and terrified me all at once.

"Can you see how fucking hard I am?"

"Yes," I whispered.

"Take my dick out," he demanded.

I slipped my hand into his underwear, wrapping my fingers around his thick shaft, moving my hand up and down over the silky skin.

"Do I meet your expectations?"

I looked up to find him smiling at me mischievously.

"Your reputation preceded you, but it's better."

"You want to taste it?" he muttered.

I managed to whisper, "Yes."

He shook his head slowly and grabbed my chin. "Not until I get to taste you."

Troy placed a hard kiss on my lips before he knelt and began rubbing his thumb over my clit. He slowly moved two of his fingers inside of me.

"Fuck—and I worried you wouldn't be ready for this tonight. You're so freaking wet."

I was incredibly aroused, so much so that I could hear my wetness as he moved his fingers in and out of me. My eyes rolled back, but they opened suddenly upon the feel of his hot mouth, his tongue lapping at my tender flesh. I threaded my fingers into his hair as his head moved in sync with the thrusts of his tongue. A groan escaped him, the sound vibrating inside of me. He seemed to be getting as much pleasure out of this as I was, and that turned me on even more. I bent my head back and moaned in pleasure as he sped up the movements of his tongue.

He suddenly stood, wrapping his hand around my cheek and bringing my mouth to his. I tasted myself on his lips as he pressed his chest against mine and led me to the bed. He toppled over me, then lowered his mouth to my neck before going down to my breasts. He placed my nipple between his teeth and tugged lightly before sucking hard on it.

"Spread your legs for me." He spoke over my skin. "Wide."

Moving my knees apart, I made way for him as he repositioned himself between my legs, this time devouring me with even more vigor. Troy used not only his mouth, but moved his entire face in a circular motion as he licked and sucked. The feel of his hot breath, the pressure of his tongue—it was almost too much to bear. I wanted to come against that tongue but needed to hold back. I tensed over and over, doing everything in my power to keep my release from happening too soon. I couldn't give him the satisfaction of knowing just *how* out of control I was.

"Still want to taste me?" he asked.

Licking my lips, I nodded.

"I want to fuck your mouth while I eat you." He got up. "Come here." Troy repositioned himself so his rock-hard cock was in my face and *his* face was between my legs in the sixty-nine position. The tip of his crown glistened as I took it into my mouth and sucked, swallowing every remnant of the precum that had been dripping off of it. He tasted so amazing, the perfect mix of salty and sweet. I arched my neck, taking him deeper into my mouth as his cock scraped the back of my throat. My head bobbed as I moved him in and out, nearly gagging. He groaned in pleasure, bucking his hips as he lapped at my clit with even more intensity the deeper I took him. I'd never done this before. But something told me it wouldn't have been as good with anyone else.

"You taste so fucking good, Aspyn." He lifted himself off of me. "Get on your knees for a minute. I want to watch you give me head before I fuck you."

My arousal dripped down my thigh as I moved to the floor and once again wrapped my mouth around his throbbing dick. I took him even deeper down my throat from this angle to the point where I did gag once.

He pulled out of my mouth with a pop. "As much as I love to make you gag, that's my cue to stop for now. Any more of that, and I'm gonna come way faster than I'd like." He gestured with his fingers. "Stand up. I want to look at you again."

As I got up and straightened my posture, my clit throbbed. "What's next?" I asked.

His mouth curved into a smile. "Next I bury myself inside of you, if you're still up for that."

"I am."

"Let me get something." He ran over to his pants and returned with a condom. "This is all I have. So we need to make it last."

I didn't have any condoms, which was unfortunate considering I already knew I'd want him more than once tonight.

He ripped the package open as he looked at me, his eyes brimming with hunger. He then rolled it onto his cock and squeezed the tip before slowly approaching me.

"Aspyn..." he whispered, lifting my chin to meet his stare.

"Yes?"

Troy's eyes filled with mirth. "That little bit of hate you still have left for me in there somewhere?"

"Yeah?" I panted.

"I'm about to fuck it out of you. *Hard.*"

Chapter Nine

Troy

oly shit. My body felt like it was on fire. I couldn't remember being this damn turned on in my life. I'd never understand what I'd done to deserve this. Aspyn Dumont succumbing to my every sexual command—and actually loving it—per her *own* request? *What is this life?* It felt like I was gonna wake up any second and find Patrick in bed with me instead of this beautiful woman.

I lowered myself over her and spread her legs apart, keeping my eyes glued to hers. I needed to see what she looked like the very second I entered her. I normally didn't care about such things. But it was important to me to know I was giving Aspyn just as much pleasure as she afforded me. I wanted to see the exact moment she lost control. I wanted to bear witness to every second of this.

I licked my lips, savoring the remnants of her delicious taste as I readied myself.

Placing the head of my cock at her opening, I slowly slipped inside her hot, wet pussy, watching her intently. Taken aback yet again at how ready she was, I momentarily broke my vow to keep my eyes open as I closed them against the onslaught of sheer pleasure. I quickly returned my gaze to her face. I'd thought maybe she'd roll her eyes back the moment I was balls deep, but instead her eyes widened as she gasped, her mouth dropping open. Her reaction was even better than I'd hoped.

I pumped in and out of her. "I'm inside of you, Aspyn. You can't take it back. You will always have fucked me."

She laughed through her heavy breaths.

"You're so wet, but at the same time, so damn tight. It feels incredible." I sped up my movements. "How hard do you want it?"

"I can take whatever you've got, Serrano," she said, her eyes glinting.

Damn.

Damn.

Damn.

I thrust harder with each second, pulling almost all the way out and slamming into her deeper each time. My hands spread her knees apart to make more room for me. I kept my gaze on hers, not willing to miss a single reaction. My balls slapped against her as I moved even faster, willing away the intense urge to come, since this was the only damn condom I had. If it were up to me, I'd be up all night fucking her every which way. As much as I wanted to flip her over and fuck her from behind right now, watching that beautiful ass jiggle as I pounded into her, I needed to pace myself.

But even though she'd loosened up a little, she was still so damn tight. The uncontrollable urge to release my load took hold of me and wouldn't let go. Before I could stop it, I felt my body shudder as I let go.

"Shit, Aspyn. Shit! Fuck…" I groaned as I came hard inside the condom, too caught up in the intensity to be that disappointed in myself for losing it like this.

Within a few seconds, she let out a shriek. And it was loud. She bucked her hips and trembled beneath me. As my orgasm came to an end, my eyes flew open, needing to see the look on her face as she climaxed. Her muscles tightened around my cock—between that sound she'd made and the pressure of her pussy convulsing, it was the most beautiful orgasm my dick had ever had the pleasure to take part in. Even in the dark, I could somehow see how flushed she was. I moved in and out of her until her muscles stopped pulsing.

My body was sated, but I wanted so much more. This felt like only the tip of the iceberg.

After I pulled out and discarded the condom, I felt like just lying in bed and holding her. This was so much more than I'd bargained for, despite the boundaries I'd set earlier tonight. And that was exactly why I needed to keep my promise and not linger here, not be as goddamn needy as I felt right now. Because not only did I want to fuck her again—even harder next time—I wanted to cuddle with her after. *And therein lies the problem.*

I kissed her softly…down her face to her neck and onto her stomach. My dick was already throbbing for more, but I forced myself to speak. "I'm gonna leave you alone to get some sleep."

She straightened up against the headboard, allowing me a perfect view of her beautiful tits as they bounced. "You don't have to go…"

I didn't want to go. But I'd promised to slip away with no words spoken of what we did tonight. "That was our deal, remember? Pleasure, no pressure."

She nodded, seeming disappointed. "Okay."

Her reaction made me feel conflicted. I'd thought this was what she wanted. Fuck, if she begged me to stay I would, even if it was against my best judgment.

Leaving is the right decision. Things had escalated very fast tonight, and I felt a responsibility to protect her from...well, *me*. If I couldn't guarantee I could be more to her than a sexual fling, I needed to act like the fuckboy I was and leave, not make any promises. Plus, with no more condoms, it would be painfully difficult not to try to fuck her again if I'd stayed. I needed to be better prepared next time. And God, I hoped there was a next time.

I reluctantly rolled off the bed and went in search of my pants. I spun around fast to see if she was checking me out. She was.

"What are you looking at, Dumont?"

Caught red-handed, she looked away suddenly.

Have I mentioned I really don't want to leave right now?

The cold floor at my feet was most unwelcome. Almost as unwelcome a feeling as this fucked-up desire to cuddle.

Stop being a pussy, Troy.

I walked back over to her and sat at the end of the bed, leaning in to kiss her forehead. I'd planned to leave her in bed, but she suddenly stood up, giving me a glorious view of her stark-naked body.

"You don't need to get up," I told her.

"Well, I need to lock the door behind you."

"Ah. Duh. Right."

Her boobs swung freely as she walked over to the closet and grabbed a short, silk robe, which she wrapped around her body.

We walked together to her door and with each step forward, I wanted to leave less and less.

As we faced each other, she stumbled over her words. "Well, thank you. That was…"

I finished her sentence. "It was fucking amazing." I wrapped my hand around her cheek. "Remember, we don't need to speak of this tomorrow—unless you want to. But, you know, either way, we should *really* do it again soon."

She smiled. "I'd like that."

Adrenaline pumped through me at that prospect.

"'Night, beautiful."

"'Night, Troy."

On the way out, I nearly walked into the shrubs outside her house. My head was still in a sex-induced haze. After getting into my car, I leaned back on the seat, feeling like I couldn't move, like the wind had been knocked out of me. Then I realized she was still waiting at the door, so I needed to move before she thought something was wrong with me, sitting here staring into space.

But there *was* something wrong, wasn't there? I was supposed to have fucked her and left, but it somehow felt like a piece of me was still inside that house. This was not how it normally felt for me after sex. In fact, this wasn't like anything I'd ever felt before, and I needed to get myself in check *fast*.

Once I got home, *getting myself in check* consisted of an intense jerk-off session in the shower as I pretended my hand was Aspyn's pussy and relived every taste, smell, and sensation from tonight. After I came, I leaned forward against the shower wall, letting the water rain down on me as I willed myself to get a grip.

I then got out and dried myself off, but the shower had done nothing to relax me.

As I lay in bed with Patrick at my feet, I was wired.

Deciding to just get up, I ventured into the kitchen. It was 3 AM—practically morning anyway. I poured myself some of the stale coffee from the previous morning and looked out the window at the trees in the darkness.

A few seconds later, Patrick wandered in to join me.

I lifted my mug to the cat. "You can't sleep either?"

He meowed, probably yelling at me for ruining the cozy situation he'd had in bed. Then he circled around my legs and purred. He was very forgiving.

I bent to scratch between his ears. "You know, you've got the right idea. Never leave the house. If I'd just stayed in this freaking house, tonight wouldn't have happened. I wouldn't be pussy-whipped—no offense—right now for a girl who wants nothing to do with me because she knows what's right for her. Well, there's *one* thing she wants to do with me—and believe me, I delivered."

I stood up. "I'm gonna tell you a secret, Pat. You know how you like to snuggle with me? That's what I wanted to do with Aspyn tonight. Isn't that crazy? That's not the way it's supposed to be, you know? That's not what I do. I'm not a snuggler like you. I've never wanted to snuggle with a woman. But I did with Aspyn." I sighed. "What does that mean? What's next, rubbing my asshole on her feet?"

He closed his eyes as I massaged his head.

I wanted to see her again. And I needed an excuse.

As I looked over at a pile of overripe bananas on my counter, I got an idea.

Just call me the paleo Betty *Cocker*.

• • •

I hoped I was doing the right thing. I'd told her I would leave without talking about what we did, but this was the next day, right? A whole new day was fair game. We didn't need to discuss anything either. It was breakfast.

Just breakfast.

I'd texted her that I was coming by. She seemed okay with it. Hopefully that was really the case.

I got to her doorstep and knocked.

A few seconds later, Aspyn opened the door.

Her long hair was still as messy as it had looked when I left last night, and she still wore the same short, silk robe that clung to her tits perfectly. Her nipples pierced the fabric, and I was thrilled that she still hadn't put a bra on.

"Hey," she said groggily.

"Hi." I smiled, my eyes falling to her neck. Aspyn had marks all over her skin from where I'd sucked on her last night. My dick stiffened with the realization that I'd marked her. It made me yearn for a repeat right this second. She must have noticed me gawking because she adjusted the robe.

Show over.

"I brought breakfast," I announced, holding out the Tupperware. "Your not-so-favorite cookies, since you said they're good with coffee in the morning."

"When the hell did you make them?"

"3 AM. Patrick helped."

"You didn't sleep?"

"I was a little wired. Had quite a night, but I'm not allowed to talk about it." I pretended to zip my lips. "Just here for an innocent breakfast."

Her eyes wandered all over me. "Breakfast is all you're here for, huh?"

I gulped. "Yep." My eyes lowered to her chest again as my mouth watered. "Aspyn, last night was incredible. The truth is, I couldn't sleep because I needed more."

"Why did you leave, then?"

"Because I was trying to give you space. I knew if I stayed, I'd fuck something up or cross some boundary. Not to mention, I didn't have any more condoms."

"Well, we might as well have been together. I was up all night, too."

That surprised me. "You were?"

"Yes."

She walked over to the coffeemaker and poured me a cup. "How do you take it?"

Even her simple question made me think dirty thoughts. *You bent over the damn counter with your ass cheeks spread apart sounds really good right about now.*

I cleared my throat. "You probably don't have cream or sugar, right?"

"I do keep sugar in the house for Kiki. I don't have cream, but I have milk?"

"That's perfect. One sugar and some milk will be great." *I want to fucking milk you.*

I watched as she prepared my coffee, tempted to hug her from behind, then flip her around and kiss her hard. Instead, I reluctantly kept my distance.

She handed me a mug. "Here you go."

I took it from her and sipped. "Thank you. I needed this."

Aspyn poured herself the usual black coffee and leaned against the counter across from me.

"What do you normally do on Sundays?" I asked.

"It's my catch-up day before Kiki comes home tonight. I usually clean, go food shopping, stuff like that. What about you?"

"Sometimes I bring Nonno donuts for breakfast. Not today, obviously. I work out at some point usually. Sundays are pretty lazy for me."

Aspyn opened the cookie container and took one out before dunking it into her coffee. She bit into it and chewed for a few seconds. "Mmm... These taste better than the last batch. Did you do something different?"

She noticed. "I added some coconut flakes my dad had in the cupboard," I said proudly.

"Ah. I could tell. Really nice addition."

"The bananas were even riper this time, too."

I watched as she continued to eat the cookie and her mind seemed to wander.

"What are you thinking, Aspyn?"

She let out a long sigh. "I'm thinking I don't know what to do with you."

"I have a few ideas."

175

"Yeah. That's the problem. I don't even know how to act around you right now." She took a sip of her coffee.

"Can I be honest?"

"Yes," she said with her mouth full of cookie.

"I don't know what the fuck I'm doing either. I'm just fairly certain I won't get to see you this week because you'll have Kiki. So I didn't want to stay away today. I missed you."

"It's only been seven hours." She chuckled.

"I think I might be addicted." I pointed my thumb toward the door. "I can totally leave if you'd rather I let you get going with your day."

"No." Her eyes moved over me. "I don't want you to go."

Her insistence that I stay gave me courage. "I can't stop thinking about doing you from behind."

She turned crimson as she put her coffee down.

I took a chance. "Turn around."

Things moved pretty fast from there. Aspyn leaned against the counter as I slipped her robe above her waist and undid my jeans. The thong she wore left little to the imagination. Despite last night, I hadn't gotten a good look at her beautiful ass in broad daylight until now.

"I need to see this ass jiggle while I'm fucking you. It's my ultimate fantasy."

Slipping my hand into the back pocket of my pants, I took out a condom and carefully ripped it open. After sheathing myself, I looped my fingers around her thong and pulled it down so her ass was fully on display. Within seconds, I pushed inside of her as she gasped. Aspyn felt even better than last night, if that was possible.

"This fucking ass is gonna be the end of me," I said as I watched my cock slide in and out of her.

Aspyn moaned, moving her hips faster as I continued to plow into her from behind.

She nearly undid me when she said, "Your dick feels so good right now."

Fuck. Me.

Egged on by her words, I pumped into her faster. "You have no idea what you do to me." Kissing behind her neck, I continued to thrust as she gripped the edge of the counter for stability. My body quaked. "I'm about to lose it. You make me come so fast, Aspyn. It's insane."

I exploded into the condom, but the feeling of euphoria was marred by the knowledge that she hadn't climaxed yet. As my movements slowed, I couldn't accept what I'd done. I needed to make sure she experienced as much pleasure as I had. After I came down from my orgasm, I slowly pulled out of her before removing the condom and discarding it in the garbage.

I reached for her hand. "Come on. We're going to finish you off, since I couldn't slow my roll."

Her eyes glimmered as she followed me back to her bedroom.

We undressed before I pushed her gently down on the bed. Spreading her legs apart, I lowered my face down to her wet pussy. She was so aroused, and I took great pleasure in the fact that I'd done that to her body.

Lowering my mouth to her mound, I flicked my tongue over her clit, surprised at how hungry I was to taste her pussy, despite the fact that I'd come just a couple of minutes ago. Savoring every bit of her sweet taste, I licked and sucked, applying just the right amount of pressure.

Her hips bucked as her breathing became labored. She swirled her pelvis, pressing her pussy into my mouth. She soon yelled out in pleasure.

Fuck if I wasn't hard again and needing to be inside of her a second time.

Aspyn came against my mouth, eventually slowing her movements and collapsing into the mattress. I lowered my body onto hers and kissed her neck.

Out of breath, she said, "That was so good, Troy."

Satisfaction washed over me, but honestly, anything she said might have affected me right now in this intoxicated state.

I moved over so I wasn't crushing her with the weight of my body.

We lay in silence for a while, and then I lifted my head to rest in my hand as I looked at her. "The right thing to do would be to go home and let you get your stuff done today. But all I want to do is lie here with you."

She didn't say anything to that. Instead, she nestled her body into mine. After getting no sleep last night, it felt so good to just rest here with her. I listened to the rhythm of her breathing as we both drifted off to sleep.

• • •

The sound of loud banging woke me. I looked at the alarm clock by Aspyn's bed. It was 5 PM! We'd fucking slept the entire day away.

"Shit!" She jumped up.

"What's wrong?"

"That's my mom and Kiki. She normally drops her off at five. I can't believe we slept that long. We have to get dressed. I don't want them to know...you know..."

Aspyn scurried around in search of her clothes as I grabbed my jeans and put them on as fast as humanly possible.

Shit. I'm not prepared to meet her mother.

We made our way out to the living room, and Aspyn answered the door.

Her mother's eyes landed on me almost immediately. "Oh, hello," she said, looking between us. "I didn't realize you had company."

Aspyn's niece offered a slight smile. "Hi, Troy."

I waved, trying to act as casual as possible. "Hey, Kiki. Good to see you again."

Mrs. Dumont smirked. "Oh...*this* is Troy."

Aspyn gnawed on her bottom lip.

Mrs. Dumont was an attractive woman, probably in her mid-fifties. She looked like an older version of Aspyn with the same light brown hair and almond-shaped eyes.

I cocked my head. "I take it Aspyn's mentioned me?"

"Once or twice," she said.

Aspyn turned to Kiki. "How was your weekend?"

"Fun. We went apple picking at Wright's Orchard."

"I remember going there as a kid," I said. "One of the few places my grandfather would take me when he wasn't working. We went to get apples to make pies for his bakery."

"Did the pies taste better than those cookies you made for Auntie Aspyn?"

"Definitely." I chuckled.

Aspyn's mother turned to me. "You're only here in Meadowbrook temporarily, from what I understand?"

Nodding, I cleared my throat. "That's correct. I'll go back to Seattle when my father returns from Europe." I looked over at Aspyn, but her stoic expression was hard to read.

"I see." Mrs. Dumont gave me a scrutinizing look. "Well, I'm heading home." She gave her granddaughter a hug before turning to me. "Enjoy your time back in Meadowbrook, Troy."

She didn't need to say anything else. Her message was clear: *You'd better not fuck around with my daughter in the short time you're here, assnuts.*

"Thank you," I said. "It was wonderful meeting you."

Unfortunately, before Mrs. Dumont had a chance to fully exit, Kiki looked down at my pants and pointed.

"Your fly is open." She covered her mouth and giggled.

Aspyn's mom turned back around to face us, and everyone now stared at me.

I looked down and quickly zipped. "Well, that's embarrassing. Thank you for noticing that."

"She notices everything," Aspyn said.

Mrs. Dumont gave me one more funny look before she left. Aspyn was still chewing on her lip, seeming tense after her mother very likely drew the correct conclusion about what had been going on here today.

"Did Troy bring any food with him this time?" Kiki asked. "I'm hungry."

Aspyn walked toward the kitchen. "He made some cookies again."

"The ones that taste like rocks?" Kiki said.

"They came out really good this time," Aspyn told her.

I laughed. "Tell you what, next time I come for a visit, I'll bring something especially for you, Kiki. I wasn't thinking I'd get to see you today."

"With real sugar?"

"Yes. With real sugar."

"What did you guys do today?" she asked Aspyn.

Aspyn glanced over at me. "We had breakfast together and just hung out."

Kiki's eyes moved between us. "You guys figured out how to be friends?"

I flashed Aspyn an amused grin. "I didn't realize this was a challenge we were having."

"Yeah…" she told her niece. "We've worked it out."

"I finally figured out what makes her tick, Kiki." My eyes darted over to Aspyn mischievously. "Rock cookies."

"Yuck." She giggled, then she darted off, headed to her room.

When the door closed behind her, I whispered, "Do you think your mother put two and two together?"

"Trust me, even if your fly hadn't been open, she's very perceptive. I'm certain she'd figured it out before she took one look at us." She sighed. "But yeah, your fly pretty much sealed the deal."

"I suspect you didn't exactly put in the greatest word for me before today."

"She knows about our history and that we've hung out. But my mother doesn't judge me for the decisions I make. She lets me live and make my own mistakes without interfering too much."

"Ah, so you're already calling me a mistake."

Her eyes widened. "I didn't mean it like that."

"I'm teasing." I smiled. "Anyway, I'm glad she's not judgmental. I'd hate for her to give you shit about sleeping with the Whoreannosaurus. I mean, you could do so much better."

"She doesn't know about that nickname."

I leaned against the counter and crossed my arms. "Speaking of which...are you gonna tell Jasmine what we did this weekend?"

She cringed. "I'm not looking forward to it, but I'll have to at some point."

I knew they were still friends, but from my perspective, we didn't owe her an explanation.

"It's really none of her business, you know."

"Yeah. But I can't lie to her. She knows we've been hanging out."

"She's gonna badmouth me when you tell her," I said, feeling defensive.

"Trust me, there's nothing she could say that I haven't already thought."

"Great. Thanks for the confidence."

Aspyn slapped her forehead. "Sorry. That came out wrong."

"No, no, no. Let's face it. It's the truth. I think we should always be real with each other. And right now you're being real with me." I inched closer and tucked a piece of her hair behind her ear. "When do I get to see you again?"

She looked over toward Kiki's bedroom door a moment. "Maybe we can figure out something for next weekend."

"*Maybe*? You've got to give me something better than that. I'm already practically hard again, and I'm not gonna see you for almost a week. I need better than a *maybe*."

"I thought this whole thing was supposed to be, in your words, *noncommittal*."

"That was before I was inside of you and got addicted," I said, leaning in to nuzzle her neck.

"Saturday?" she finally offered.

"Friday," I countered.

Aspyn pursed her lips. "Maybe."

"You're killing me. But I guess I'll take a maybe over a no."

Chapter Ten

Aspyn

On Tuesday, Shala and I were hanging out by the administration desk. She'd been home with a sick kid yesterday, so I hadn't seen her since our night out on Saturday.

She looked up from her flip chart. "This weekend was really fun. Thanks for coming out with me."

"It was."

"Despite your weird behavior about Troy," she added.

"Yeah, uh, about that..."

Curiosity gleamed in her eyes. "Did something happen after I left?"

"He..." I whispered. "Sort of...came home with me."

Her jaw dropped. I quickly summarized the weekend as best I could. I needed someone to talk to about what was happening with Troy, or I was going to explode. She was pretty much my closest friend here. It wasn't like I wanted to run and tell Jasmine.

"Damn. I had no idea how exciting your night became after I left you. Here I was thinking you'd gone home bummed because he was on a date with that girl."

I shook my head. "I didn't see it coming either."

She sighed. "He is so hot, Aspyn. Seriously, don't even think about it. Just enjoy it."

"That's what I'm trying to do. But I feel myself getting wrapped up in him anyway. It sucks. I know he's not right for me in the long run, and he's leaving on top of that. But it is what it is."

She grinned. "We don't always get to choose what makes us lose our mind."

I blew a breath up into my hair. "That's for damn sure."

"All that matters is that you're having fun. Life is too short not to have amazing hate-sex with hot men." Her eyes traveled beyond my shoulder. She raised her chin and whispered, "Speak of the devil."

I turned around to find Troy approaching from the other end of the hall. He looked so handsome in a burgundy Polo shirt and dark jeans.

He stopped in front of us with a huge smile on his face. "Hey, ladies."

I cleared my throat. "Here to take your grandfather out?"

"Yep." His eyes fell to my chest, and somehow I knew he was undressing me with his eyes.

My nipples stiffened as I began to perspire.

"You good?" he asked.

My cheeks burned. "Yep."

He stared through me as he continued down the hall. "It was nice seeing you, Shala," he called.

"You too." Shala turned to me. "Okay, if that little interaction didn't scream *we're having sex*, I don't know what does."

I walked away, needing a minute to decompress. I had to head outside to take a few of our residents on a shopping trip in a few minutes, but I decided to pop my head into Mr. Serrano's room before I left. You know, to check on *Mr. Serrano.*

Troy was sitting across from his granddad.

He smiled and acted all casual. "Well, hey there, Aspyn. Nice to see you."

"Hi, Troy. I thought I'd come say hello before I have to head out."

"Isn't that sweet of you..." He smirked.

"Too bad you can't come with us today, Aspyn," Mr. Serrano said. "I miss your company."

I walked over and placed my hand on his arm. "Aw, Mr. Serrano, I miss you, too. I can't tell you how much I wish I could continue to go out with you guys."

The old man had a plate of peeled oranges next to his chair on a TV tray.

Troy grabbed an orange wedge and placed it between his lips, sucking on it slowly with his tongue. The way he devoured it as he looked at me was more than suggestive. He was showing me *exactly* what he'd be doing to me right now if he could. Thankfully, Mr. Serrano didn't seem to notice.

But the muscles between my legs tightened. I needed to get out of here and fast.

Heading toward the door, I said, "Well, you guys have a nice time."

Looking over at Troy one last time, I felt my cheeks heat at the way he was still staring at me.

As I walked down the hall, my phone vibrated.

Troy: Boy, I've never seen you leave a room faster.

Aspyn: You knew what you were doing with that orange.

Troy: Did it remind you of something?

Aspyn: How would you like it if I'd walked in there eating a banana?

Troy: Do you even have to ask? I'd take anything I could get right now, even if it's torture. I can't wait till Friday.

I decided to tease him.

Aspyn: Who said we're getting together Friday? I never confirmed that.

Troy: Don't do me like that, Aspyn. I've been looking forward to it.

Aspyn: I'm kidding. I'm looking forward to it, too.

Troy: Your ass looks amazing in those Betty Boop scrubs, by the way.

Aspyn: Was she laughing, too?

Troy: She was. Nonno fucking caught me adjusting myself after you walked out of the room. He asked me why I was messing with my balls. I made up a story about jock itch.

Aspyn: LOL

Troy: Seriously. You look beautiful.

Damn him.

• • •

That night at dinner, Kiki studied me carefully. "Are you okay, Auntie Aspyn?"

I'd been staring into space. "Sure. Why do you ask?"

"Hang on." She ran to her room and returned with something in her hand. "I opened my lunch box at school today, and this was in it." She held out the TV remote.

My mouth hung open. "I put this in there?"

"You don't remember?"

I continued to stare at it incredulously. Come to think of it, I'd been watching the news this morning before getting ready to leave the house... I must've stuck it in there without thinking? Gosh, I needed to get a grip.

"Wow. I'm really sorry. A remote is not a very good snack, is it?"

She snickered. "It probably tastes better than Troy's cookies." She shrugged. "Anyway, my friends thought it was funny."

"I'm sure they did. Next time, tell them your crazy aunt has her head in the clouds sometimes."

"Next time? You're gonna put the remote in my lunch again?"

"Hopefully not."

"If you want, you can accidentally put some M&Ms in there tomorrow. I won't mind."

I rustled her hair. "Silly girl."

• • •

After a week that went by as slowly as molasses, Friday night finally arrived.

Troy and I had decided to eat dinner at the Japanese restaurant with my favorite sushi. I guess you could say it had become our place. We made easy conversation during the meal. But between Troy looking at me with hazy eyes like he wanted to devour me right there at the table, and my own urgent need to be touched by him—this dinner couldn't have been over fast enough.

As we finished the last of our food, Troy seemed to read my mind. "Let's go to my house tonight. It's closer."

I wasn't going to argue with that. Not only was his place closer, but I'd been curious to see where he was living.

Troy drove faster than the legal limit all the way home. You weren't going to hear me complain, though. At one point, he turned on some music—Frank Sinatra's "The Lady is a Tramp." I chuckled. *Yes. Yes, I am right now, and I don't need to be judged, Frank.* I was about to get laid so good with this man tonight.

Troy's dad's house was a narrow, brick structure on a fairly busy residential street. Troy used his key to open the door, and we were greeted by a beautiful cat.

"Hey, Patrick! We have a visitor," Troy announced.

"So *this* is the famous Patrick." I knelt down to pet the kitty between his ears. He closed his eyes and purred. Patrick's fur was multicolored with stripes. "He's cuter than I ever imagined."

"Don't stroke his ego. He'll never leave you alone tonight. And I sort of want you to myself."

Then Troy grabbed my hand and led me to his room—which turned out to be a virtual time capsule. There were trophies up on a shelf and photos on the wall of many people we went to high school with.

"Has this place changed at all in ten years?"

"Pretty pathetic, right? Like I told you, this isn't the house I grew up in, but my dad basically transferred all the crap from my old room to this one after he moved out of the house we shared with my grandparents. I wasn't living in Meadowbrook when he bought this place, so I have nothing to do with the décor or this shrine to me."

"I think it's adorable. It would only be strange if you lived here full time and kept it like this."

I walked over to one of the photos of Troy and rubbed my finger over the image of his youthful face.

"What are you thinking when you look at that guy?" he asked.

I sighed. "What an asshole." I placed my hand on his shoulder. "I'm kidding." But I shook my head as I turned back to the photo. "Looking at this makes it all seem like yesterday."

"Is that photo giving you PTSD?" He blew out his cheeks. "Maybe bringing you here was a bad idea."

I gripped his shirt and spoke in a seductive tone. "I'll get over it soon enough."

"Oh, I'll make sure of that."

I looked down. His erection was straining against his jeans. He was ready, but unfortunately my mind *had* taken a bit of a detour. I looked back over at the photo of young Troy and his beautiful, angular face.

"You know, I used to hate you, but I always thought you were hot. That was never up for debate. I definitely had an unwanted crush on you when you were dating Jasmine."

He stroked the small of my back. "I never had a crush on you. I thought you were weird and standoffish...and later, after everything happened, batshit crazy."

"Gee, thanks. Tell me how you really feel..."

"Hear me out." He wrapped his arms around me from behind. "Now? I have a *massive* crush on you. You're all I think about..."

I turned my head to look at him and saw that he was staring at the photo of himself. "I'm not that kid anymore, Aspyn. That kid...he was fucked up in the head. He'd felt abandoned his whole life. I acted out against others because I couldn't act out against my mother—because she wasn't around to receive any of my angst. In recent years, I've come to terms with the story of how I came to be, but back then? I was a mess."

I nodded. "You had a hard time in high school. My hard time was *after* high school," I admitted.

He turned me around to face him. "Because of Ashlyn..."

I looked down at his hardwood floor. "Not just that."

"Talk to me, Aspyn. You don't speak much about what happened after high school. I feel like you're holding back on me."

Feeling an anxious rush of adrenaline, I shook my head. "Not now. But I'll talk about it in due time, okay? I just want to enjoy being with you tonight."

"I can be down with that." He scratched his chin and headed to his closet. He took out a green football jersey. "Remember this?"

Meadowbrook's colors were green and white. He handed me the shirt, and I stared down at the shimmery material.

"I think you should put it on," he said.

"Seriously?"

"Yeah. I want to see you in it."

I took off my shirt and unsnapped my bra, letting it fall to the floor. "Serrano, what am I gonna do with you?"

"I'll tell you." He helped me adjust his shirt over my breasts. "I want you to ride me while you're wearing my jersey. It's a fantasy I didn't even know I had until this moment."

Troy ripped off his shirt to reveal his amazingly cut chest and stomach. He pressed his lips against mine before slipping his tongue inside my mouth. I swirled my tongue around his, savoring his delicious taste, which still held a hint of Sapporo beer. We hadn't kissed all night, and I'd been starving to taste him. It didn't matter what fleeting memories those photos had brought on just a moment ago. Right now? Nothing could have stopped me from giving every inch of myself to this man—and taking anything he would give me in return. I was totally and utterly intoxicated by him—and was starting not to give a shit how pathetic that made me. I'd worry about all of that later.

Troy undid my jeans and pushed them lower until I kicked them off. He dragged his finger through my drenched underwear.

"Holy shit." He stopped kissing me for a moment as he inserted two fingers into me and looked into my eyes. "Are you fucking kidding me? How did you get this wet already?"

"I get aroused whenever you look at me like you want to devour me. And it just kept building throughout the night."

His breath trembled. "You're gonna be the end of me, Aspyn. The thought of you getting wet when we were at dinner makes me crazy. Seriously, I am so pumped to feel you around my cock. I'm afraid I'll come in like two seconds if I fuck you right now. My track record in that regard has been terrible. I need to pace myself and taste you first." He fell to his knees and pushed my panties down. He began to devour me, flicking his tongue so hard over my clit that now I was the one in danger of coming too soon.

I pulled on his hair and yanked his head back. "Stop. It's too much."

He looked up at me with glassy eyes. "In a good way?"

"Fuck, yes."

With a look of sheer hunger on his face, Troy stood up and removed his belt before throwing it aside. He undid his pants, and when he dropped them, his big, beautiful cock sprang out, hitting me in the abdomen.

Licking my lips, I knelt down and wrapped my hand around his shaft, pumping slowly and swirling my thumb along the crown. He bent his head back in ecstasy. Since his eyes were closed, he had no warning when I wrapped my mouth around him before taking him down my throat.

He shuddered. "Fuck, Aspyn. Just…fuck."

I moved his cock in and out of my mouth as I stroked the veiny skin. He threaded his fingers through my hair.

He suddenly pulled away. "I was about to come down your throat. That was so freaking good."

After I stood up, Troy kissed me hard and took my hand, leading me to his bed. He laid back. "Will you ride me? I ain't too proud to beg."

There was nothing I wanted more than to be on top right now, looking at his face. "I would love to ride your cock, Serrano."

He made a guttural sound. "That's the dirtiest thing to ever come out of your mouth. And I'm here for it."

Troy stroked himself a few times before reaching into his bedside table for a condom. He sheathed himself in a flash.

Positioning myself over him, I sank slowly down until he was fully inside. Troy grabbed my sides as I bucked my hips.

He panted. "Look at you, riding me in my shirt. I want to burn this into my memory. Pretty sure this might be the best moment of my life." He smiled. "You are so fucking beautiful, Aspyn Dumont."

After a couple of minutes, I got hot, so I slipped the shirt over my head. My breasts bounced as Troy reached up to squeeze them.

"I've missed these beautiful tits." He groaned.

As I swayed my hips over him, I felt his balls at my ass. I gripped the hard muscles of his chest and dug my nails into his skin, the pleasure of him so deep inside me almost too much to bear. Troy began to thrust his hips upward to meet my movements, and he kept his gaze fixed on me. Then he pushed even deeper inside of me. My clit pressed harder against him, and I suddenly felt my orgasm ricochet through my body.

"I'm coming," I gasped.

"Yes, I know." He smiled. "I can feel it."

This was the first time I'd lost control before he did.

He shut his eyes tightly as his mouth dropped open. His body shook under me as we came together.

Wow.

Every time with Troy was better than the last.

Utterly sated, I collapsed onto him. He kissed my head softly. I almost wished he didn't do stuff like that, because whenever he was gentle with me, it made me want...more. And I knew I couldn't set that expectation.

He slipped out from under me to discard the condom before returning to the bed. He pulled me back over to lie on top of him again. Resting my head on his chest, I felt his heartbeat thundering against my cheek. I didn't want to leave. I had no idea whether he planned to take me home or what, but I knew I was happy here. And I wanted to stay the night. But I wasn't going to be the first person to suggest that.

A minute later, I felt something heavy land on my back. I flinched, and it took me a bit to realize it was Patrick.

"Shit. I'm sorry," Troy said. "I'll get him off."

"No." I laughed. "It's okay. He can stay."

"You're okay with him on your back? He might never get up, you know."

"Yeah, it's fine. It kind of feels...nice. The purring vibration. He's sort of like a weighted blanket."

He flashed a beautiful smile, and that was the last thing I remembered as I drifted off to sleep—on top of Troy with a cat on my back. Kind of an odd threesome, if you ask me.

. . .

The following day, after we'd finally rolled out of bed after all the sex we had again this morning, Troy and I went out for a nice breakfast in Meadowbrook Center. While we waited for our food, he showed me some photos his dad had sent from Europe. I vowed to save enough money to take my own trip overseas someday. Staying in Meadowbrook was one thing, but never getting to experience the world at all wasn't an option.

The cool September breeze was a welcome addition to our outdoor meal. It really didn't get any better than this.

After breakfast, he came back to my place, and we chilled for a bit in my yard. It was the epitome of a lazy Saturday. Neither one of us acknowledged that all this time we were spending together was a clear violation of the sex-with-no-strings precedent we'd discussed early on. And I certainly wasn't going to acknowledge that the way Troy looked at me all day today made my heart do crazy stuff.

At one point, I left the yard to go inside and make us coffees. Even though I'd told him to wait outside, Troy must have gotten antsy because he soon joined me in the kitchen.

He placed my phone next to me on the counter. "You got a message."

"I did?"

"Your phone lit up outside. I looked over at it because I thought it was mine. We have the same notification sound, apparently. You got a message through the app."

He was referring to the *dating* app. My stomach sank as I looked down and saw a message from a guy I'd chatted with earlier this week.

Sorry for the delay in responding. I was offline to take care of some family stuff. Would you want to meet up for drinks tonight?

Shit. I'd gotten a message this past Thursday from a guy I'd matched with before Troy and I first hooked up. I'd casually responded, though I had no intention of meeting up with him now. But I could understand how this looked—like I was actively pursuing someone else. Not that Troy and I had any kind of formal exclusivity agreement, but it was still sucky that he had to see this, especially when it didn't mean anything. I'd just responded to the guy so as not to be rude.

His tone was bitter. "Maybe you should meet him."

"I don't want to meet him."

"But you were chatting with him. Why would you be chatting with him if you didn't intend to meet him?" His nostrils flared. "What's the point?"

"He and I matched before you and I started this… thing. We messaged briefly this past week, but nothing came of it, nor had I planned for anything to happen with him."

Troy just kept nodding and looked away. "Wow."

"What?"

"I don't like how I reacted just now." He shook his head, seeming dazed. "Like a fucking jealous bastard." His expression was sincere. "I'm sorry. That wasn't fair. I don't know what came over me. I shouldn't have been upset at you. We're not exclusive, right? I have no right to question anything."

"It's okay," I assured him. "I would've felt the same way if the roles were reversed."

Troy blinked, not seeming to have absorbed what I'd just said. "You know what?" He walked over to the end table by the front door and grabbed his keys. "I'm gonna take a drive."

My eyes widened. "Where are you going?"

"Just for a ride." He opened the door. "I'll be back."

He exited faster than I could even think to try to stop him. When the door shut behind him, the silence was deafening.

Feeling terrible, I didn't quite know what to do with myself after he left. I kept wondering what the hell was going on in his head and what had compelled him to leave so suddenly. Was he that upset that I'd been chatting with another guy? Or was there something more to his reaction?

Two hours passed, and Troy still hadn't returned. I must have cleaned my house three times over in an attempt to calm my nerves. I wasn't sure if he was ever coming back.

At nearly 5 PM, I'd almost given up hope of his return when the doorbell rang.

I rushed to the door and opened it.

With his hands in his pockets, Troy flashed a hesitant smile. "Hey…"

"I was beginning to think you weren't coming back." I moved out of the way to let him in.

"I took a long drive," he said.

"For two hours?"

"Yup."

"Where did you go?"

"Nowhere really. I took back roads, traveling south. Listened to music."

I pulled at the material of his shirt. "Troy, look—"

"No…" he interrupted, placing his hand over mine. "You don't owe me any explanation, Aspyn. Forget anything you planned to say to me when I came back. I'm the one who needs to explain." He inched closer so that he was right in front of me. "I was caught off guard by my reaction to that guy texting you. It made me realize that my feelings for you are stronger than I'd thought. I was overwhelmed by that and didn't know how to express what I was feeling, so I left to clear my head."

My heart pounded against my chest. "Did it help?"

"Somewhat." He cupped my cheek. "Aspyn, I don't know what's going on between us or where it's leading. But I do know that the thought of you with someone else right now makes me sick to my stomach."

I swallowed. "Noted."

"I needed to make sure I understood myself before I came back here to explain. The more I drove, the clearer it became." He spoke over my lips. "I don't want to share."

His mouth enveloped mine. My legs felt weak as my body melted into his. He grabbed my ass and squeezed it hard, almost possessively, as our tongues collided. I reached up and ran my hands through his silky hair, relishing his taste, and once again wondering what the hell I was supposed to do about my undeniable feelings for this man.

He broke the kiss. "As long as we're doing this, no other people, okay?" He looked deeply into my eyes. "Unless that's not what you want?"

"I haven't thought about anyone else for a long time," I admitted. "Yes, I responded to that guy's message. I felt like I needed to keep my options open, even though I had no intention of meeting up with him while we were spending time together." I sighed. "But I'm confused, Troy. Because this is temporary, isn't it? That's been my understanding this entire time. You're leaving. I've been trying not to get my heart involved based on that assumption."

He leaned his forehead against mine. "That was my plan before I realized I had these feelings. Maybe we should just...see where things go? Not label it, but not close the door either. Right now I can't stand the thought of you with anyone else."

I stepped back. "So, you're saying this is more than just a physical thing for you?"

"Did today not prove that? I have genuine feelings for you, Aspyn. I don't only want to fuck you. I want to *date* you." He looked down at his feet. "But at the same time, I don't want to make promises when I don't have much experience with monogamous relationships."

"Have you *ever* been monogamous?"

He took my hand. "Let's sit." Troy led me to the couch. "I had one serious relationship after grad school when

I first moved out to Seattle," he began. "I never cheated on her, but I also didn't feel like she was the one. Sarah ended up getting a job out of state, and when I convinced her to take it without suggesting we try a long-distance relationship, things ended. But that relationship hadn't even lasted a year." He searched my eyes. "What about you? When was your last relationship?"

I twisted my ring. "I went through a rough patch after my sister died. So, it took me a while to be in the mental state for a commitment with someone. In the past seven years or so I've only had two boyfriends. But I was with one of them—the most recent one—for three years. It ended a year ago."

"Who was he?"

"His name is Holden. He admitted to me once that he'd almost cheated on me, but he stopped it before anything happened. I would rather someone break up with me than have to stop themselves from cheating. Because of what I've witnessed my whole life—with my mother continually taking my unfaithful father back—I didn't want to take that chance. So, I was the one who ended things with him before he could inevitably screw up again."

"That's fucked up that he admitted that, but I guess it's good that he did. What an asshole, though."

"What really stunk was that Kiki was pretty attached to him. I think she was one of the main reasons I kept him around as long as I did, despite my doubts."

He blew out a breath. "I hadn't even thought about how any relationship you have will inevitably affect her. You're amazing for all the responsibility you've taken on." Troy brushed his finger along my cheek. "I'm gonna be real with you, Aspyn. I don't feel worthy of your time."

I placed my hand over his. "Why would you say that?"

"I don't know. It just came out."

"Why don't you feel worthy?"

Troy stared off. "I think it goes back to childhood. When I was a teenager, my mommy issues translated into anger or acting out. But as I get older, I focus less on the fact that she left and more on the deeper meaning behind *why* she left. The only conclusion I ever come to is that...I wasn't enough. I wasn't worthy of her love. That feeling, whether true or not, makes me feel unworthy of almost anything that might bring joy to my life." He paused to look over at me. "Right now, the joy in my life is you."

Wrapping my hands around his face, I brought his lips into mine and kissed them firmly. I pulled back to look at him. "I don't know if you're right for me, Troy, or where this is going to lead. I don't even know if I should trust you. But one thing I can say with absolute certainty is that you are most definitely worthy of joy, love, and everything this life has to offer." I paused. "Your mother made a mistake. And I'm sure she died with regret, even if she never admitted it to you. I'm sorry that her decision makes you doubt everything. But never doubt that you're worthy."

He kissed my forehead and whispered, "Thank you."

Troy and I spent the rest of the weekend together. And this marked an unofficial shift in our relationship, when Troy Serrano somehow morphed from fuckboy to boyfriend.

Chapter Eleven

Troy

Another weekend gone, and the waiting game to see Aspyn began once again.

The past few days had gone nothing like I'd anticipated. I hadn't been prepared for my flood gates to open so easily at the first threat of a little competition. I might have been experienced when it came to sex, but I sure as hell wasn't experienced when it came to dealing with actual feelings for someone.

As much as that car ride had helped me hone in on what was really bothering me—that I didn't want to share her—I was still no closer to knowing if I was *right* for her, or whether I should continue to lead her on by messing with her feelings.

I didn't usually talk to my grandfather about my personal life in any great detail. But today I paid a special visit to ask him for some guidance.

Aspyn had mentioned that she was taking some of the residents shopping on Monday afternoon, so I stopped by on my lunch break when I knew she wouldn't be here. I didn't want to be distracted. As much as I wanted to see her beautiful face, that's not what this visit was about.

My grandfather was sitting up in bed watching *Dr. Phil* when I walked in.

"Hey, Nonno."

He straightened his back. "I was wondering if I was gonna see you today. You never brought me a donut yesterday."

"I'm sorry about that. I was a little distracted this weekend." I sat down in the chair across from him. "Actually, I was hoping to get your input on something."

"Is this about Aspyn?"

I couldn't help but smile. "Why would you think that?"

"Like I've told you before, I may be old, but I ain't blind yet. Every time she walks in the room, you light up. Then there was that little guitar performance of yours. Are you kidding me? Come on. Since when do you play the guitar in public? Who do you think you are, Eddie Van Halen? Looked to me like you were looking for any opportunity to be around her."

I picked some lint off my jeans. "Yeah. I guess it's obvious."

He smirked. "Might she be the reason I didn't see you this weekend?"

"She might."

"It's about time you see some action, Troy. I was beginning to think you and that cat had something going on."

Yawning, I rubbed my eyes. Good sleep had continued to evade me lately, at least whenever I wasn't lying next to her.

He shook his head. "You got it that bad, huh?"

"I'm really into her, yeah, but I don't know what to do about it."

"What's there to wonder about? You have to please her if you want her to keep you around. Keep her happy. Keep her satisfied. Your grandmother never wanted for anything, and I'm not talking about money."

I held my palms up. "I don't need to know about the various ways you pleased Nonna. Keep that shit to yourself, for Christ's sake."

"I'm not just talking about sex, ya pighead. I'm talking about making her feel like she's the most important person in the world, that she's safe with you. That's how you keep a woman."

"Therein lies the problem. She's *not* necessarily safe with me. I have a horrible track record with her, going back to high school. And a horrible track record with women, in general."

He smacked his hand against the side table. "Well, then I'd say you're due for a change."

"I'm only supposed to be passing through town. I wasn't planning on developing feelings for someone that would require me to stay in Meadowbrook."

"You just wanted to boink her and didn't expect things to develop? You're not a kid anymore, Troy. And I think you knew from the beginning that she's not the type of girl you boink once and forget about. She's special, that one. A real woman. Like your grandmother."

"Exactly. She's a real woman. And that's why I don't know if she should be wasting her time with me. I don't want to hurt her."

"Why do you need to hurt her? You're writing the ending to the story before it even really begins. Maybe take your time seeing where things go before you draw conclusions. You're living in the future, not the present."

"She's been nearly cheated on by an ex—possibly actually cheated on without her knowledge. And she knows I cheated on her friend back in high school. How the hell do I get her to trust me?"

"You become someone worthy of trust." Nonno adjusted his blanket over his legs. "Let me ask you something. Do you think you're still a cheater? If so, maybe you should leave this girl alone."

If I really looked inside myself, I knew I would never hurt Aspyn in that way. "I would never cheat on her, but how do I get her to believe that?"

"It takes work and time, son. But just as important as earning her trust is keeping a woman happy." He grinned like a Cheshire cat. "I have some secrets in that regard."

I arched a brow. "Really. And you've been holding out on me?"

"Get a pen and paper. There're five of 'em, and I want you to write them down."

Chuckling, I stood up and walked down the hall to the administration desk where I asked for some paper and a pen before returning to my grandfather's room.

Sitting back down, I said, "Okay…I'm ready."

He lowered the volume on the television. "Now, keep in mind, these tricks of the trade are not substitutes for the big, obvious things like loyalty. These are little things you can do to make her smile. These are the things that basically seal the deal on an already good thing."

"Alright..." I clicked the top of the pen and readied myself to take notes.

He cleared his throat. "Okay, first secret."

"Yeah?"

"Rub her feet."

I cackled. "That's a secret to a successful relationship? I was expecting something a bit more profound."

"I told you, these are little things... But they add up, and they matter. Rubbing feet is an intimate act that shows her you understand how hard she works, that you don't mind getting your hands a little dirty, and that you care about her well-being."

Feet, in general, kind of skeeve me out. I never understood foot fetishes. But for some reason, the thought of rubbing Aspyn's feet didn't bother me. But I still didn't understand this so-called secret.

I wrote down *Foot Rub*. "Okay, well, that's easy enough. I suppose if you think it works, I'll try it," I said, mostly to humor my grandfather.

He reached over to his side table and began to peel an orange. "Second secret, write her notes, even if they're short, to tell her you're thinking about her. A note is more heartfelt than this texting business. In my day, you wrote a note and folded it nice. Make it short, sweet, and to the point. Your Nonna had a whole collection of them from me. Not only does it prove you really care about her, it gives her something to refer back to in the times when you've gone and pissed her off."

I nodded. "That makes sense. I just have to figure out how to write her notes that aren't cheesy."

"If it's from your heart, it's never cheesy. That's the problem with most men today—they think they need to act tough. But the truth of the matter is, if you don't express your feelings from time to time, how the hell will she know how you feel? You're building an insurance policy to make sure she doesn't ever feel neglected and won't need to turn to someone else to fulfill her. Writing out your feelings can be the best way to communicate. But you should mail it to arrive when you're not with her."

"Why mail?"

"Because it will be a nice surprise and add to the effect. Everyone loves getting nice things in the mail."

"Alright." I jotted it down. "That one is definitely a bit more challenging than the foot rub. But I'll see what I can do."

He smiled as he placed a piece of orange into his mouth. "Secret three."

I leaned in. "Give it to me."

"Grab her suddenly and kiss her when she least expects it. Dip her in a dramatic fashion. That last part is a must."

"What purpose does that serve?" I reached over for a wedge of his orange.

"It's an act of spontaneity—shows her how easily you lose control around her, even in the most ordinary of moments. But don't forget the dip. That's the romantic part."

I popped the orange into my mouth. "How the hell did you become such an expert in romance?"

"I had a great father, your great grandad. He was a true romantic. I learned from watching him, and your Nonna reaped the benefits."

"Okay." I shook my head and laughed. "Next."

"Secret four is to put on some music and dance with her. Doesn't matter if it's just an ordinary day. We don't need a special occasion to dance. Put on some Sinatra and go for it."

I nodded. "Okay. Cheesy but easy."

"Ready for the last one? It's the most important."

"Lay it on me."

He finished chewing. "Tickle her."

My eyes widened. "What?"

"I'm telling you." He chuckled. "Laughter is good for the soul. Tickling can be a physical expression of love. I used to tickle Nonna at least once a week. It would always get her out of any bad mood she was in."

I squinted skeptically. "I'm not sure about that one."

"Have you ever seen a bad outcome from making someone laugh uncontrollably? It releases hormones of happiness."

I sighed. "I'm starting to wonder if you're setting me up. Some of these things sound ridiculous, particularly this last one."

He shook his head. "Try all of these, and you'll be golden."

• • •

That evening, after my work day wound down, I was surprised to receive a call from Aspyn. She didn't normally call me during the week.

"Hey, beautiful. To what do I owe this surprise?"

"I just wanted to say hello."

"Well, *hello*. I've been thinking about you all day."

209

"I heard you were at Horizons today," she said. "Sorry I missed you."

"Yeah. I decided to pay an impromptu visit to Nonno on my lunch break. We had a nice little talk."

"Does he...know about us?"

"I kind of had to tell him. He guessed something was up. I didn't deny it. I hope that's okay with you."

"Okay, good to know. It's okay. I didn't want to play dumb around him if he knew."

"I don't think he'll say anything to you. He knows you're a private person." I sighed into the phone. "I can't believe I have to wait until Friday to see you again."

She hesitated. "Not necessarily."

"You're not pulling that *maybe* shit again, are you? I can't make it until Saturday, Aspyn."

"That's not what I meant. I was actually wondering if you wanted to come over for dinner tonight. I know it's last minute, but—"

"Last minute? You think I care about that? As if there's anything else I'd rather do than come have dinner with you."

"I'm trying this gluten-free lasagna made with nut cheese. It's a new recipe. It might come out horrible, but my guess is that Kiki's not gonna like it, and I'll have a ton of leftovers."

"Ah. So, you're inviting me over to be your human garbage disposal?"

She paused. "No, Troy. I'm inviting you over because I want to see you."

Loving the sound of that, I shut my eyes. "I want to see you, too."

"We obviously can't...you know, because of Kiki, and you can't stay the night."

"I get it. That doesn't matter. I just want to see you."

"Okay...seven then?"

"What can I bring?"

"Just yourself."

"Damn. I feel like a kid who just found out he gets to stay up late on a school night. This is a treat."

She laughed. "See you soon."

"Okay, beautiful."

After I hung up the phone, I looked over at Patrick sitting on the couch. His eyes were drowsy, and he looked like he was about to fall asleep.

"Wake up, Pat! This is big news. She invited me over *during the week*. I might officially be moving away from fuckboy status."

He let out a big yawn.

"That's all you have to say?"

• • •

I arrived at Aspyn's house at 7 PM sharp. The smell of whatever she was making immediately hit me. It smelled like savory tomato sauce and...something that resembled cheese. I took a long whiff in. "Damn, something smells good."

"Yeah, we'll see how it tastes. Not sure it's gonna match up to the smell."

It was hard not to reach out and kiss her on the lips, but with Kiki in the room, I knew I couldn't. I kissed her on the cheek and made my way inside her house.

Aspyn looked down at the white box I was carrying. "You didn't have to bring anything."

"Yeah, well, I promised Kiki a real dessert." I turned to her niece. "Remember?"

"I forgot about that." Kiki grinned.

"I brought some brownies. They have real sugar and chocolate and everything. And the best part is, I didn't make them."

"I love brownies." Kiki rubbed her stomach.

"Phew. Okay. Good."

Aspyn took the box from me. "That was very sweet."

"It's my pleasure."

The three of us sat down to dinner in the dining room. The lasagna Aspyn had made looked edible, though I was certainly curious how nut cheese was going to taste.

Aspyn served us each a slice.

"It's made with rice noodles, and the cheese is made from cashews." She looked over at Kiki. "Give it a chance."

Kiki took a bite and immediately spit it out.

Aspyn glared at her. "Come on, really?"

"I hate it. That's *not* cheese."

"It's nut cheese," Aspyn insisted.

"Nut cheese?" Kiki scrunched her nose. "*Not* cheese."

I wanted to laugh, but I knew that would piss Aspyn off, so I refrained.

Aspyn threw her hands up. "Well, if you won't eat it, what are you gonna have for supper? I don't have anything else." She blew out a frustrated breath. "I normally make her something different, but I wanted one night where I could just make one meal for everyone."

God, it wasn't easy parenting an eight-year-old. I could barely open a can of food for Patrick, let alone meal plan for myself and another person every single night of the week.

There was no way in hell I was going to make her feel bad about the lasagna. I didn't give a shit how it tasted; I would pretend to enjoy it. I took a bite, and without even registering the taste, I pretended to love it. "Mmm... Kiki, I don't know what you're talking about. This is delicious." I moved it around in my mouth.

"You started talking before you even chewed," Kiki challenged. "I watched you."

She has a point. I chewed a bit more and then swallowed. Okay, it wasn't great. Still, I said, "See? Chewing and loving it."

"You're such a liar," Aspyn whispered. Then she took a bite herself before throwing the fork down. "Oh my God. It totally sucks! The cheese is inedible, and the noodles are hard." She looked over at her niece. "I'm sorry for yelling at you, Kiki. You were right."

I reached out and placed my hand over Aspyn's. "I'm here for the company?"

Aspyn moved her hand from under mine and rubbed her eyes in frustration. She was tired. I could tell. She'd worked a long day and come home to make a meal no one appreciated. I needed to do something.

Standing from my seat, I said, "I'm gonna go pick up a pizza for Kiki and me and some sushi for you. Just give me a half hour."

Aspyn looked up at me. "You don't have to."

Kiki chimed in. "Yes, he does."

"I want to." I rubbed Aspyn's shoulders. "Relax and chill. Pour yourself a glass of wine or something. I'll be back." I winked at Kiki. "Black olives, right?"

She jumped in her seat. "Thanks, Troy."

An hour later, I returned with the food, and we sat down and devoured the takeout—the failed not-cheese lasagna a mere memory.

Halfway through dinner, Kiki announced, "Troy, guess what Auntie Aspyn put in my lunch box last week?"

"Not one of my cookies, I hope?"

"No." She giggled. "You'll never guess."

I took a bite of my pizza. "Give me a hint."

"It's something you use to turn something on."

I squinted as I looked over at Aspyn. All my dirty mind could conjure was a vibrator.

"I'll just tell him, Kiki, and get this torture over with." Aspyn rolled her eyes. "I put the TV remote in her lunch box, okay? Cue the laughter."

My eyes went wide. "What would possess you to do that?"

"Clearly, it was unintentional. I must have been packing it so fast that I grabbed everything in sight."

"You said this was about a week ago, huh, Kiki?"

"Yup."

Looking back over at Aspyn, I smirked. "Something must have been distracting you."

She blushed. It gave me great pleasure to know I'd consumed her thoughts enough to make her lose her mind for a moment.

After Kiki left the table to head to her room, Aspyn turned to me. "Thank you for saving the night." She smiled. "I'll have to make it up to you."

Now I really wished we were alone. That made me want to take her right on this table. "Keep saying shit like that, and I'll bring you dinner every night."

Kiki came out again, holding a math workbook.

"Troy, can you help me with my homework?" she asked.

"Uh, yeah...sure, if it's okay with your aunt."

"Only if it's okay with you," Aspyn said.

"Of course it is. I'd love to help."

I got up and followed Kiki back to her room. Over the next several minutes, I helped her work through a few math problems.

After we finished, she whispered, "I didn't really need help with my homework. I have to ask you something."

"Oh, okay. What's up?"

She let out a long exhale. "There's this girl. She's the worst. So mean to me. Anyway, they're having a father-daughter dance at school in a week. Everyone knows I don't have parents. And Maisy was all like, 'Too bad you can't go to the dance because you don't have a father to take you.' I wasn't gonna go. But she made me mad when she said that. I was gonna ask my grandpa, but he's kind of embarrassing and smells like cigarette smoke. I don't know who else to ask." She paused and handed me a flyer. "Will you come with me?"

Her question hit me right in the gut, and I had no idea how to handle it. I looked down at the paper. "Is it only for fathers, or can anyone go? I mean, how would we explain me?"

"I don't know. But I want to show her I can still go even if I don't have a dad. I just can't show up alone. I need a guy to go with."

How can I say no? But I also couldn't say yes—not without clearing it with Aspyn.

"I'll tell you what, if it's okay with Aspyn, I would love to accompany you."

"I knew you were going to say that." She blew out a frustrated breath. "She's gonna say no. Because you're not my dad and because she told me things were complicated with you."

Of course she did. "I can't agree to take you without her approval. She's gonna have to know anyway. But I'll try to convince her, okay?"

Her shoulders slumped. She looked defeated, as if she never expected her aunt to say yes. "Okay. Thanks for trying."

My heart broke for her. I understood full well what it was like to feel left out because you didn't have a parent around. I knew Aspyn did everything she could for Kiki, but no one could replace her parents. Not to mention, it took courage to ask me—a virtual stranger—for a favor like that. It also angered me that some snotty-nosed kid would go out of her way to make Kiki feel bad about something she had absolutely no control over. Made me want to punch that kid's parents for raising a little asshole.

Aspyn immediately registered the serious expression on my face when I reappeared in the living room.

"Is everything okay? You look like she ran you ragged. Did you barely survive the math homework?" She laughed. "It always surprises me when elementary school math stumps me. Is it just me or has it gotten so much harder since we were in school?"

"It's not that. The homework was easy."

Her smile faded. "What happened?"

I sat down and lowered my voice. "Did you know about this father-daughter dance at her school?"

"She mentioned it, yeah. Told me some girl had made a comment that upset her."

"Yeah. It pissed her off pretty good." I paused. "She asked me if I would go with her. Would you be okay with that?"

Aspyn closed her eyes and sighed. "You're kidding..."

"No. She's very serious about it."

"She wants them to think you're her dad?"

"Not at all. She just wants to stick it to that girl—throw her off by showing up with me."

She shook her head. "I don't think that's a good idea, Troy."

I blew out a breath. "Kiki knew you'd say that."

"Do you think I'm wrong?"

She seemed a little angry. I didn't want that, but I'd promised Kiki I'd try.

"I can understand why you're hesitant. But I can also see why it might be important to let her show up with me."

Aspyn leaned her head on the back of the couch. "It's so hard sometimes. I don't always know how to handle things with her."

"I didn't give her an answer because I obviously can't overstep. But just know that I would be happy to take her, if you're okay with it. Absolutely no pressure from me. I'm not gonna say another word about it."

I could understand why Aspyn wasn't eager to have me go to the dance with Kiki. I didn't want to become the next guy to disappear from Kiki's life as fast as he'd entered it. I needed to tread lightly here. At the same time, I totally understood Kiki's need to stick it to that punk-ass kid.

"I'm gonna try to talk her out of wanting to go," Aspyn said. "But thank you for your willingness to take her. I do appreciate that."

"Of course."

As we continued to sit together on the couch, I reached out and began to massage her shoulder.

"I just wanna say one more thing," I said, unable to help myself.

"Okay…"

"I understand exactly how she feels. Kids can be cruel. I remember back in elementary school getting picked on for not having a mother. There are some people who wallow in the misfortunes of others just to feel better about themselves. Being around Kiki really brings back some of those old feelings—not in a bad way, more in a retrospective and self-compassionate way. The fact that she wants to go to that dance to prove she has just as much of a right to be there as anyone else shows how strong she is. And she gets that from you. I have nothing but respect for both of you, Aspyn."

I held my hand out, and she took it, looping our fingers together.

We sat in silence for a couple of minutes. "You want me to let you get ready for bed?"

Aspyn squeezed my hand. "Stay for a little while longer."

"Okay. You just say the word, and I'll get out of your hair."

Since she still seemed tense, I had the not-so-brilliant idea to implement one of Nonno's secrets. Reaching down and grabbing her foot, I started to remove her sock.

Aspyn immediately jerked away from me. "What are you doing?"

"You've had a long day. I want to give you a foot rub."

"You can't." She looked horrified.

"Why not?"

"Because my feet are...dirty. I haven't showered yet, and I worked all day."

I chuckled. "You ruined my romantic moment." *Strike one, Nonno.*

"Well, I'm sorry, but I'd rather have you do just about anything right now other than rub my feet."

"Hmm...now you're talking. If Kiki wasn't home, it would be on. For the record, I'd rub your dirty feet and put my mouth on anything else that was dirty, too, if you'd let me right now."

"Well, that's pretty gross, but I won't fault you for it."

I rubbed her thigh. "You clearly have some understanding of my level of desperation."

Chapter Twelve

Aspyn

How is it only Wednesday?

I needed to get out of here.

I never called out of work unless I had a good reason. In fact, I couldn't think of a time I'd pretended to be sick to play hooky. But today, in the middle of the work day, I just couldn't take being at Horizons anymore. Friday seemed forever away. I needed to see Troy before then. The only way I could do that was to leave work while Kiki was in school.

It had been a frustrating start to the week. After Troy left my house on Monday night, I had a heart-to-heart with Kiki and ultimately convinced her it was best not to go to the dance. But since then, I'd been second-guessing my decision, wondering if my fears about her getting attached to another man in my life had influenced my take on things.

I was stressed, and more than that, I was horny.

So, while it was unlike me, I popped my head into my supervisor's office. "Hey, Laura. I'm not feeling well," I lied.

"I think I'd better leave before I get anyone sick. Hopefully it's nothing, but I wouldn't want to take a chance."

She removed her glasses and tossed them aside on her desk. "Wow. You're never sick. Go get some rest. We can cancel the afternoon activities. No problem."

"Thank you. I appreciate you understanding."

A slight twinge of guilt followed me out to the parking lot and into my car. But as I drove off, mostly I was just aroused and filled with anticipation. I wanted to surprise Troy, because I knew he'd never expect me to show up at his door, particularly at this hour. That made me just as nervous as I was excited. He was in the middle of his workday, and I could very well be interrupting something important.

It took about twenty minutes to get to Troy's house from Horizons. When I got to his door, I knocked a few times. My palms started to sweat. *What if he's not home?*

When the door opened, Troy had a look of alarm on his face.

"Hey. Is everything okay? Did something happen to Nonno?"

I covered my chest with my hand, my heart beating rapidly. "Oh my God. He's fine. I'm sorry if I scared you. It hadn't occurred to me that you might think that. I just... left work early. I made up a story and said I was sick. I know it's bad to lie, but I wanted to see you."

"No shit?" A huge smile spread across his face. "Aspyn Dumont, did you just leave work to come over and fuck me?"

I exhaled. "Yes?"

Wow, he mouthed before moving aside to let me in.

I noticed his laptop on the coffee table, a bunch of papers strewn about, and a mug of coffee. Patrick entered the room and meowed, weaving in and out of my legs.

Troy turned me around to face him. "Have you ever done anything like this in your life?"

I shook my head. "Never."

"I'd better make it worth it then." He lifted me up as I wrapped my legs around him.

He kissed me so hard I thought my mouth might fall off. Our tongues collided as the kiss grew more frenzied by the second. *This*. This was what I'd so desperately needed all day. My panties were wet in a matter of seconds. I was so far gone when it came to this man, it wasn't even funny. I didn't care how desperate this all seemed. All that mattered was getting him inside of me.

I pulled on his shirt, our lips separating only long enough for me to lift it over his head. His hair was a tousled mess as he continued to hold me up. He pushed my pants down and shoved my panties to the side. I felt the burn of his cock entering me. It was a blissful several seconds of feeling him inside of me bare before he groaned and pulled out.

"I'm sorry. I lost control for a second. I have to get something."

Jesus. I hadn't been paying attention myself, but those few seconds were bliss.

He put me down and took me by the hand as we went to his room. He opened his side table drawer and fumbled to grab a condom before ripping it open. He sheathed himself and came back over to me.

Troy took my mouth again as he pressed his chest against mine, leading me toward the wall. He flipped me around so my ass faced him. With my hands up against the wall, I bit my bottom lip, bracing myself for what he was going to do next.

"I want to fuck you from behind like this for a little bit, then finish you off in my bed, okay?"

Through shallow breaths, I nodded.

With my work pants halfway down my legs, I widened my stance to make room for him as he slid himself slowly inside of me.

"You're so goddamn ready." He kissed the back of my neck and pulled my hair as he fucked me faster.

Unable to form words, I simply moaned in response as I used my fingers to massage my clit. My legs quivered as I felt my orgasm ready to roll through me at any moment.

He stopped suddenly, taking me by the hand and leading me to his bed. Troy tore off the remainder of his clothes and finished undressing me. We were both completely naked now as he pinned me under him. He spread my legs apart and lowered himself before sinking into me. His warm skin pressed against mine felt so good. His naked ass felt even better as I gripped it, guiding his movements.

But nothing could have prepared me for what it felt like when he slowed the rhythm of his thrusts and looked me straight in the eyes as he fucked me slower, his hips grinding in a circular motion, bringing me such intense pleasure I wanted to scream. But I didn't. I just continued to look at him intently.

He flashed a gentle smile, and I smiled back as we continued to watch each other.

"You don't hate me anymore," he whispered as he pulled out slowly and pushed inside of me again.

"I don't."

He smiled wider.

Feeling my muscles tighten, I started to come. He shut his eyes and let go in a series of hard thrusts as the heat of his cum filled the condom. It was the most intense orgasm I'd experienced with him yet.

Playing hooky was so worth it.

After we came down from our high, he got up to discard the condom before returning to his spot next to me on the bed.

Troy wrapped me in his arms and kissed the back of my neck. "How much longer do I get to have you here with me today?"

"A couple more hours." I turned to face him. "Unless you have to get back to work."

"I'll make up for the work tonight. That's one of the benefits of working remotely. I want you here as long as you can stay." He planted a firm kiss on my lips. "How did you know I was thinking about you all day and couldn't wait till Friday?"

"I didn't." I smiled, but when it faded, he gave me a scrutinizing look.

"What's on your mind?"

I ran my finger along his chin. "I don't know. I feel like I should have a lot on my mind, considering how out of control I felt this afternoon. But I just want to enjoy this moment and not analyze my crazy behavior."

"That sounds like a damn good plan. And you weren't out of control or crazy. You were simply adhering to the three Hs."

"The three Hs?"

"You're *human*, you were *horny*, and it's *hump* day." He grinned.

I shook with laughter. "Well, that explains it. Thanks for the insight."

He squeezed my side. "You knew exactly where to go, too. You have needs. And I'm so happy to be the person you chose to meet them."

Troy lowered his mouth to my breast and sucked my nipple. Bending my head back, I let out a sigh of pleasure, dumbfounded at how quickly I was ready for round two as I raked my fingers through his silky hair.

Troy spoke into my chest. "I'm sorry I slipped inside you with nothing when you first got here. That was irresponsible, even if it was only a few seconds."

"It's okay. I'm on the pill."

He looked up at me. "You never mentioned it."

"Yeah. I've wanted to be extra careful."

"Makes sense. But that's good to know. I don't have to worry anymore about the miniscule chance that I fucked up earlier."

His eyes bore into mine. It was hard to lie with him in this intimate place and not let my mind wander to all the what-if questions. My body hadn't been the only thing bursting with energy today. My heart had been working overtime, too.

"Okay, I can see the wheels turning in your head." He straightened up a little. "Talk to me, Aspyn."

"I feel like I've been kidding myself this whole time," I said.

A look of concern crossed his face. "In what way?"

"Convincing myself that I can just have some fun with you and not get attached."

"And you worry that getting attached is a bad idea."

"Yeah, but it's hard work trying not to get attached."

"Maybe you should get attached then."

I already am.

"You're not the only one feeling like this." He stared deeply into my eyes. "Give me something, Aspyn."

"What do you mean?"

"I mean...I feel like I've opened up to you a little, and you haven't done the same. Tell me what you've been keeping inside."

I sighed, not looking forward to this. "Maybe you should ask me what you want to know."

"I want to know about your life after high school before we reconnected. It's like a black hole you don't talk about."

"That's exactly what it feels like. A black hole. Mainly because I've blocked a lot of it out."

"Why?"

I brushed my finger along his chest. "After high school, things didn't go as planned. I ended up taking a couple of years off instead of starting college right away. I fell into the wrong crowd and partied a lot, which was the opposite of me in high school. It was like I was going backwards. I wasn't using drugs or anything, but there was a lot of drinking."

"We've all done shit we regret," he said. "Believe me, I had my share of drunken nights in my early twenties."

He has no idea where I'm going with this. "The night my sister died, she and her boyfriend had been on their way to pick me up from a party, because I was too drunk to drive myself home."

Troy pulled me closer. "I see…"

"Nothing was ever really the same again after that night. I stopped going out. I stopped everything. Everything just…stopped." A tear rolled down my cheek. "This is very difficult for me to talk about, Troy. Because I've never stopped blaming myself. The only time I don't blame myself is if I block it out. So, that's what I do."

He squeezed my side. "It wasn't your fault, Aspyn."

"On a rational level, I know I didn't cause the accident. It was a rainy night, and their car flipped. I have no idea how fast Toby was driving. But the fact remains that they wouldn't have been out in that rain in the first place if it weren't for me." I stared off. "I thank God every day that they didn't have Kiki with them. They'd left her with my parents that night." I shook my head. "It's so cruel that I get to see her grow up, and they can't. You talk about feeling unworthy—I feel the same, but for a different reason."

Troy's eyes glistened. "Life can be cruel. There's no doubt about that. Unimaginable shit happens. But no one deserves to blame herself for the rest of her life for something that isn't her fault. We don't understand why we're put here on this Earth or why some people are suddenly taken away. It could have been your sister's time to go, regardless of where she was headed that night. Maybe that sounds hokey, but what if it's true, and you've been blaming yourself? We can't know anything for certain. I realize that's not necessarily gonna make you feel better, but that's one truth in life—that we don't know anything. So why not assume it's okay to let go of the guilt because there's nothing you could have done?"

His perspective comforted me, at least momentarily. "Well, letting go is certainly easier said than done."

"I know." He sighed. "I just wish I could make you feel better." Troy leaned his forehead against mine. "And I'm sorry if I forced you to talk about it."

"You didn't force me, although this is the most I've said aloud about it in years. I do feel a little lighter, though, even if just for now." I pinched his cheek. "Life is strange..."

He took my hand and kissed it. "You mean this...us..."

"Yeah." I smiled. "I once hated you so much, and right now there's no place in the world I'd rather be."

"I feel the exact same way." He nuzzled my neck. "Except I'll take it a step further and say I'd rather be inside you again right now. That's the one place in the world I want to be."

I wrapped my hand around his rigid cock. Opening my legs, I placed his crown at my entrance.

He repositioned himself on top of me before pushing inside in one deep thrust.

"Are you sure this is okay? I can get something." He immediately shut his eyes in ecstasy.

"Yes. This is good."

He gasped and pushed himself deeper. As he began to move in and out, he said, "God, this feels so fucking incredible. I don't think I can ever go back to condoms with you now that I know what it's like."

I bucked my hips. "As long as you're with no one else, you don't have to."

"There's no one else," he whispered as he thrust deeper. "You're all I fucking want."

Today had certainly been the day of firsts. First time playing hooky. First time having sex with Troy without a condom. First time opening up to him. And I'd never felt closer to him than the moment he came inside of me. The fact that I'd let him proved that on some level—even if I hadn't admitted it—I did trust him.

A while later, as we lay in bed, fully satisfied, a small cloud of guilt returned. Not sure why I'd thought of it in this moment. Maybe it was my inclination to always feel undeserving of peace in the rare moments I experienced it.

"I think I need to tell Jasmine about us sooner rather than later," I said.

Troy nodded. "I agree, if that's been weighing on you. I don't think we owe her an explanation personally...but she's still your friend. So I get it."

I looked over at my phone. "I have about an hour left before I have to go pick up Kiki from my parents' house."

"Did you have lunch?"

"No. I left work before I had a chance to eat."

"Let me whip you up something. You can have eggs, so how about an omelet with veggies—no cheese?"

My stomach growled. "That sounds amazing."

After we put our clothes on, I followed him to the kitchen, and Troy prepared me a yummy late lunch. We sat at his counter and ate our omelets together while Patrick eagerly awaited any scraps by our feet.

When we were cleaning up, Troy randomly stopped what he was doing, wrapped his arms around me, and planted the longest kiss on my lips. To my surprise, he concluded by dipping me back in an exaggerated fashion, causing my head to hit the side of the center island.

"Ow!"

"Fuck. I'm sorry. That was supposed to be a dramatic dip." He swore under his breath as he rubbed the top of my head.

"It was dramatic alright."

"God, I'm a disaster." He pulled me close and kissed over the area that had been injured. "Damn Nonno and his secrets. I'm two for two in the failure zone."

"What are you talking about?"

He kissed the top of my head again. "Nothing."

• • •

Four days later, Troy and I were in the middle of yet another weekend together. Lazy Sundays had apparently become our thing.

We were napping in my bed after playing around all morning when a knock on the door caused us both to bolt upright.

"Are you expecting someone?" he asked.

I rubbed my eyes. "No?"

Totally naked and warm in my bed, I was in no condition to answer the door.

Troy moved to the edge of my bed, displaying his beautiful, carved back and the crack of his muscular backside. "It's not Kiki this early, is it?"

"No. She and my mother went to the harvest festival today."

The harvest festival was one of the biggest things to happen in Meadowbrook every year. It brought people all the way from neighboring states like New York and

Pennsylvania. I'd almost suggested Troy and I go, but I sort of preferred just hanging in with him today.

Then I remembered I'd ordered from my favorite organic market, and FedEx was scheduled to deliver it today.

"I think it's a delivery I'm expecting."

He turned around and kissed the tip of my nose. "Stay here. I'll go grab it."

"They probably just dropped it at the door," I said. "They usually knock to let me know I have a package, so it's not sitting out there."

As Troy slipped on his jeans, I enjoyed the brief glimpse of his sculpted ass.

A few seconds after he left the room, I could hear muffled talking. It sounded like more than one person. And then came the sound of baby babble.

I jumped out of bed.

What the hell?

Rushing to grab my silk robe from the closet, I wrapped it around myself before venturing out to the living room.

Then my heart nearly stopped.

Troy stood there with no shirt on as he faced Jasmine and her husband, Cole, who was carrying their baby, Hannah.

I gulped, tightening the closure on my robe as I felt adrenaline rush through my body. "Jasmine! What are you doing here?"

"We were in town for the harvest festival," she said, her eyes wide. "We drove right by here on our way home, so I figured we could pop in and say hello since I'm never in Meadowbrook."

I had called Jasmine this week and made plans to visit her next Saturday, specifically so I could tell her about Troy and me. This was certainly not the way I'd wanted her to find out.

Jasmine's face grew flushed. "Troy was telling me you guys have...hanging out."

Troy looked them straight in the eyes, making it clear he had nothing to hide. That was the opposite of how I felt—like I was going to lose my shit any second. His just-fucked hair sticking up only made the situation worse. I wasn't ashamed of what he and I had developed, just that I hadn't had a chance to properly explain it to her.

"I know what this looks like," I stupidly said. "Okay, not what it *looks* like—what it *is*. This is the reason I wanted to come see you next weekend, to explain that Troy and I have been seeing each other."

Jasmine looked between Troy and me. "You don't need to explain. If you remember, I sort of called this. So, it's not a total surprise. The way you kept rambling on about him that day you came to visit—I kind of suspected something would happen."

Troy snickered. "Rambling on about me, huh?"

Cole bopped the baby up and down awkwardly but didn't say anything.

Jasmine grabbed her husband's arm. "We should go. Clearly we're interrupting."

"No!" I insisted.

I couldn't let her go now. As embarrassed as I was, I needed to face the music, and letting her leave would only make things harder to explain later.

"You guys almost never come to Meadowbrook. Please don't go. Stay." I looked over at Troy. "We obviously have a lot to discuss." I pointed toward my kitchen. "I'll put on some coffee."

Troy held his palm up. "Actually, you know what? I think I should leave you to enjoy your friends in peace. I have to head home anyway because Patrick is getting a little low on food, and I've neglected him enough this weekend." He pointed his thumb back toward my bedroom. "Just gonna grab the rest of my stuff."

Hannah babbled. After a few seconds of awkward silence, I gestured to the sofa. "Sit. Please. Make yourself comfortable. I'll be right back."

I went to my room and put on a bra, top, and some pants while Troy went in search of his shirt.

"I'm fucking sorry this happened before you had a chance to tell her," he whispered as he pulled it over his head.

"It is what it is," I said in a low voice.

"I don't want you to think I'm leaving to throw you into the fire alone. But I figure it will only make it more awkward if I stay. And I assumed you weren't gonna tell me to leave. I made up that story about needing to feed Patrick, but if you want me to stick around, I will. Just say the word."

"No. That was a good call. I do think it would be more awkward if you were here."

"I'm sure she's gonna want to bitch about me in peace. She deserves to be able to do that, I guess."

"Yeah." I flashed a sympathetic smile.

We went together back out to the living room. After Troy bid them a quick adieu, I walked him to the door.

He pulled at the material of my shirt. "Call me when they leave, okay?"

"Yeah."

He gave me a quick peck on the lips before walking to his car.

When I reentered the house, Jasmine was sitting next to her husband on my couch. What made this all the more awkward? I didn't know what I could and couldn't say since I had no idea whether Cole knew Troy was his wife's ex-boyfriend.

The mystery was soon over when Jasmine blurted, "So that was the asshole who cheated on me in high school."

Okay. Way to ease into things.

"Say what?" His eyes narrowed as he bounced his daughter on his lap. "You *dated* that guy?"

"That's *Troy*. Remember me telling you about him? He cheated on me with Noel's wife, Samantha, back when we were cheerleaders together."

"Oh, that guy." He turned to me. "Didn't Aspyn make him shit himself or something?"

Clearing my throat, I nodded. "I tried...with a donut."

"Why the hell are you dating him, Aspyn? That's crazy."

"She's not dating him," Jasmine clarified. "She's *messing around* with him."

I swallowed. Troy had become quite a bit more to me than a convenient fuck, but no way was I getting into all that with them.

I rubbed my palms together. "Well, like you said that day at your house, Jasmine, he and I are both single. And we'd been spending a lot of time together anyway. It's not easy to meet people. Especially in Meadowbrook. So, one thing led to another. I figured there was no harm if we're both adults."

"Yeah, I mean, as long as you don't go getting attached to the guy," Cole said, placing his hand on his wife's thigh. "Because clearly he doesn't know how to treat a woman, if he cheated on this beautiful one."

That stung a little. Not only because it made me feel like Cole thought I was gullible, but because it also reminded me of Troy's past, something I'd been working hard to forget. Yes, Troy had cheated on a beautiful and kind girl. He was technically the same person who'd done terrible things. But more and more, I also felt like he'd changed. To what extent, I still couldn't be a hundred-percent sure. But he wasn't the same person he'd been back then. It didn't seem like the appropriate time to defend him, though, when I'd literally been caught with my pants down.

"Be right back," I said, needing a moment to breathe. "Gonna put on that coffee."

I fumbled with the coffee jar, practically forgetting how to complete this simple task. Vowing to put my big girl panties on, I needed to face this situation head on.

I returned to the living room carrying a tray with a carafe of coffee and three mugs. I poured each of us a cup and let them handle putting their own milk and sugar in. Embarrassingly, I didn't have anything in the house to serve alongside the coffee on such short notice. Food wasn't my priority these days, apparently. Perhaps I should've offered them a TV remote to munch on.

"I just don't want you to get hurt," Jasmine said as she stirred sugar into her drink. "You're good with Troy as long as you don't take it seriously. I wholeheartedly believe that guys like that don't change." She looked over at Cole. "I'm just so relieved I got one of the good ones."

I wanted to throw up a little. That was great for them, but hadn't she confessed that sex wasn't all that exciting anymore? Anyway, I digress. The real reason I felt so uneasy was this inexplicable need to defend Troy. It was killing me not to. And that, I suppose, said a lot about my feelings for him.

"I agree that you got a good one." I forced a smile. "But Troy is good for me right now. He's what I need in my life at the moment. And he may not have known how to be a proper boyfriend in the past, but he was practically a kid then and going through a lot. There's stuff I've learned that I didn't know then. Things you don't know either, Jasmine. I'm not saying he's perfect. But I wouldn't be spending my time with someone I believed was still an asshole—even for casual sex." I looked her in the eyes. "It's taken me some time to draw that conclusion about him. This was not something I jumped into."

Jasmine just stared at me for a few moments. "Are you serious? You're thinking he's boyfriend material?"

"Right now we're just seeing where things go. But the side of him I've experienced over the past few weeks isn't anything like I would have expected. He's been nothing but considerate, reliable, attentive—kind to Kiki. I understand where you're coming from as well, though. That's why I've had my guard up this entire time."

"Well," she said smugly. "I guess time will tell."

I could surmise from her tone that regardless of what I might say, she felt I was being naïve. But she was right about one thing: time would certainly tell.

"Honestly, I've been terrified to tell you. Because that night at your house, I never saw this coming, even if you say *you* did. And I knew you would reiterate that 'once a cheater, always a cheater.' Just know that I'm being cautious, and that I'm sorry for any awkwardness I've caused you because of this decision. You're handling it a heck of a lot better than I ever would."

"Don't worry about me. I'm fine." Her eyes lingered on mine. "Truly, Aspyn. Just look out for yourself."

I put down my coffee and walked over to hug her.

She rubbed my back. "I don't want to beat a dead horse. So let's talk about something else."

"After you're done with this tryst," Cole said, "I'm gonna make it my mission to find you a stand-up guy." He gave Hannah her sippy cup. "I've got a few single friends."

As we continued to sit and talk, Jasmine fidgeted a lot. She still seemed uncomfortable. Despite her encouraging me to go for Troy, I don't think she ever thought it would happen.

I certainly didn't.

Chapter Thirteen

Troy

I pulled on my hair. "Why am I so nervous, Pat? She's not gonna let what Jasmine says affect her, right? She's starting to trust me."

Meow.

"Thank you for agreeing with me even if you don't really mean it." I narrowed my eyes at him. "I sense your distrust sometimes, too."

Patrick purred.

My phone rang, causing me to jump. It wasn't like I'd been waiting with bated breath or anything. Trying to sound like I hadn't been shitting my pants for the past couple of hours, I picked up. "Hey, beautiful."

"Hi," she said.

"They left?"

"Yeah."

I swallowed. "How was it?"

"Well, I'd say it was a nice visit, but it was awkward as hell, as you might imagine."

"Yeah. I can imagine what was happening over there.

That was some bad luck. The first time I ever answer your door and *bam*."

"Without a shirt no less." She sighed. "Anyway, Kiki just got back, so I can't talk long. I have to make dinner. But I just wanted you to know that they left, and I handled it okay."

Rubbing my temple, I asked, "Did she…have anything interesting to say about you and me?"

"As you might expect, she did. She thinks you're safe for a good time, but that's about it. But can you blame her?"

"No, I can't. And it doesn't matter to me what she thinks, as long as what she says doesn't get in your head and make you second-guess everything. I only care what *you* think."

"I'm a big girl with a mind of my own. Believe it or not, I tried to defend you."

"Aspyn Dumont defending Troy Serrano. What's gotten into the water in Meadowbrook? I never thought I'd see the day."

"I guess good sex will mar one's judgment." She laughed.

"Whatever's working, I'll keep doing it."

"You know what the worst part of today was?"

"What?" I smiled, finally feeling my pulse come down.

"That you had to leave early, and we didn't get to spend the remainder of the weekend together."

"Well, if I'm on my best behavior, maybe I'll get another weeknight dinner invitation."

"I'll have to figure out how to not make dinner a science experiment next time."

The following Thursday evening, I was home alone in front of the television eating a dish of pasta, beans, and broccoli I'd thrown together. I hadn't had a chance to see Aspyn this week after all. She'd mentioned she was having some issues with Kiki and that it was probably best if we waited until Friday to get together. Although I couldn't be sure, I suspected part of it might have had something to do with that dance scheduled for Friday night at her school.

While Aspyn was busy dealing with life stuff, I took advantage of the free evenings to catch up on work and had dinner one night with Nonno. During the day today, he and I had gone to the mall since the weather was too crappy to do anything else. I always thought of Aspyn every time we went anywhere now, and it made me miss her company.

Just as I'd taken my dirty plate to the kitchen, my cell phone rang. I smiled when I saw her name pop up.

"How did you know I was thinking about you?" I asked when I answered.

"I didn't. But that's nice to know."

"How's everything going?"

She let out what sounded like a frustrated breath. "Not that great, actually."

My stomach sank. "Are you okay?"

"It's nothing bad. I didn't mean to alarm you."

Back in the living room, I sat down on the couch and kicked my feet up. "Talk to me. What's going on?"

After a moment's pause, she said, "Kiki is really upset that I haven't changed my mind about the dance. I'm starting to doubt whether I'm making the right decision in not letting her go."

"Let's talk it through then. What's the bottom line? Is it that you're worried she'll get the wrong idea if I go with her—get too attached to me or something? Or is there more to your apprehension?"

"It's not only my apprehension about her expectations when it comes to you." She paused. "That's part of it. But also, if she shows up, isn't it almost like...giving into bullying? I mean, what if you weren't willing to take her and she had no one to go with? She would have dealt with it. I don't want to teach her to have knee-jerk reactions every time someone is mean to her. She doesn't need to prove anything to anyone by showing up just to make a point. At the same time, I can see why that would be empowering, so I'm not sure whether I'm blowing everything out of proportion." She exhaled. "I'm just...tired."

The frustration in her voice was palpable.

"I wish I could hug you right now," I said.

She sighed.

"Okay. Wanna know what I think?"

"Yes," she immediately said.

"It's just one night. Not even that—just a couple of hours. It's not worth you stressing out about. It would be one thing if she didn't have anyone to go with, but she does. She has me. And I'm truly happy to take her."

"She doesn't even have a dress. I'd have to take her shopping right after school tomorrow. We won't have much time."

"You'll find one. Take a deep breath. Everything's gonna be fine."

"Some days I don't know if I'm cut out for this."

"You're always on the go, whether it's work or taking care of her. You can't even stop long enough to look at yourself and see that you're doing a damn good job. As someone who didn't have a mother growing up, I can assure you you're badly needed in her life. You're filling huge shoes, and I know you didn't choose this role, but you're doing the damn thing, Aspyn, and I'm proud of you."

There was a bit of silence. "Now I'm the one who wishes she could hug *you*. Thank you for taking her, Troy. I owe you big time."

"Even more of a reason to take her," I teased.

· · ·

Aspyn looked me up and down as she let me into her house on Friday night. "You look nice, Serrano."

"Why, thank you, beautiful."

She'd mentioned that the dress code wasn't specified, so I'd decided on a dark blue collared shirt and black dress pants. I hoped I wasn't underdressed, but I figured dressing down was safer than looking like a dork if I overdid it. I didn't want to embarrass Kiki.

She looked down at what I held in my hand. "Oh my God. You bought her a corsage?" Aspyn covered her mouth.

"Don't laugh. But yeah. I looked up what to do for a daddy-daughter dance on YouTube to make sure I wasn't missing something. I'm clueless about what I'm getting into here. As an example, it hadn't occurred to me that I might be actually *dancing*. Anyway, getting some sort of flower is a must, apparently. She can wear this one on her wrist, so it doesn't have to ruin her dress."

"That was really nice, thank you."

"Don't be too impressed. I have ulterior motives when it comes to her aunt." I wrapped my hands around her back to pull her into a brief kiss. Then I looked around. "Where is Kiki anyway?"

"She's taking her sweet time in there. I just helped her get her dress on, but she insisted on doing her own hair—wouldn't let me touch it. I'm praying she doesn't burn herself with the curling iron."

"So, you ended up finding a dress okay?"

"Yeah. We actually found a really nice one on clearance."

"Good. See? It all worked out." I looked down at my phone. "We'd better get going, though."

"Let me check on her." Aspyn rushed down the hall.

I stood in the living room waiting, looking out the window at the streetlights.

When I turned around, Kiki was walking toward me slowly. She wore a light blue dress with a big skirt and looked freaking adorable.

I held my hands out. "Wow. Look at you. What a dress!"

Kiki spun around. "Thank you."

"I've never seen you with your hair curly. It looks nice."

Kiki had the same light, sandy-brown hair color as Aspyn. For some reason, I hadn't noticed until now just how much they resembled each other.

"I didn't even burn myself like Auntie Aspyn thought." She looked down at the plastic container in my hand. "Is that a piece of cake?"

"No, silly. Look closer." I held it out.

She smiled. "You bought me a big flower?"

"Yeah. A corsage. It's even blue like your dress. I had no idea you were wearing that color, so it was meant to be. But you don't have to wear it if you don't want to."

"No, I like it. Thank you."

I took it out of the plastic container and placed it over her wrist. Aspyn had her hand on her chest, looking at us adoringly. She didn't seem like she had doubts about this anymore, which made me happy. I just wanted *her* to be happy. And Kiki, too. That's what this whole thing came down to.

Aspyn walked us to the door. "You two have fun. Kiki, make sure Troy behaves, okay?"

Kiki turned around. "I will."

I helped her into my Range Rover and ran around to the driver's side. Before I started the ignition, I turned to her. "You okay? Ready to do this?"

She shrugged, looking unsure of herself.

"Are you nervous?" I asked.

"A little," she admitted.

"Does that problem child know you're coming?"

"No. I never said anything."

"Good. I can't wait to see her face. Don't be nervous, okay? It's gonna be good. And if you're not happy there, we don't have to stay. There are plenty of other places we can go all dressed up tonight."

When we arrived at the dance, about twenty-five little girls were hopping around the dance floor while various men lingered around the edges, forcing themselves to talk to each other. Some of these dudes had tuxedos on. I might have been underdressed. *Good call on the flower, though.* Not a single girl didn't have some kind of flower pinned to her or around her wrist.

I knelt down and whispered in Kiki's ear, "Where's the bratty bully?"

She looked around. "I don't see her yet."

"Point her out to me when you do. I'll give her and her father the stink eye."

A few minutes later, Kiki and I were minding our business by the punch bowl when I heard a little voice from behind us.

"Did you rent a dad for the night?"

I turned around to find a brown-haired girl, who I could only assume was the little Cruella Deville.

Kiki's face turned red as she looked up at me. "He's not a dad," she said. "He's my boyfriend."

I winced. *Um...what the fuck?*

The girl's eyes widened. "Your boyfriend?"

Kiki nodded. "Ye—"

Grabbing her arm, I pulled her aside. "Kiki, you can't say I'm your boyfriend."

"Why not?"

"Because it's not appropriate. If someone believed you, I could get arrested."

"I'm sorry. It just came out."

"I know. She had you all tripped up. You can say I am anything else, just not your boyfriend, okay?"

She nodded. "Okay."

"I lied," she told the girl when we returned to our spot by the punch bowl. "He's not my boyfriend." She paused. "He's my aunt's boy toy."

I snorted. *Jesus.* She'd definitely taken me up on my offer to call me *anything* else.

"What's a boy toy?" the girl asked.

"It's a guy who comes over a lot, and then one day you don't see him ever again," Kiki answered matter-of-factly.

Shit.

"If he's not your dad, why is he here? This is for dads and daughters."

Not even a minute into meeting her, and this girl had already gotten on my last nerve.

I couldn't help but yell, "Who died and made you the daddy-daughter dance police?"

The girl blinked in confusion.

"Everything okay over here?" A man who I presumed was her father interrupted our conversation and began to size me up. "Troy Serrano?"

It took me a second to recognize him.

Christ. No wonder she's an asshole. "Albie Cummings. It's been a long time."

Albie was the older brother of my first girlfriend in junior high school, Larissa Cummings. He'd made my life miserable back then, bullying and threatening me until I eventually stopped seeing her. I should've known I might run into someone I knew here. Meadowbrook isn't all that big of a place.

He glanced down at Kiki. "This is your daughter?"

"No. She's my girlfriend's niece. I'm accompanying her tonight."

My use of the term *girlfriend* to describe Aspyn wasn't lost on me. It had come out naturally and felt right, given the current state of our relationship—even if I hadn't told her I saw her that way.

"He's her aunt's boy toy." The girl giggled.

He narrowed his eyes. "Oh. That makes more sense."

My fists tightened, but rather than respond, I reminded myself that this was Kiki's night. I needed to cool my jets.

I nodded. "Good seeing you." Placing my hand on Kiki's back, I said, "Come on, Kiki. Let's check out the photo booth."

As we walked away, she said, "You know Maisy's dad?"

"Yup. And let's just say the apple doesn't fall far from the tree. The reason that girl is a jerk is because she learned how to be one from her father. He used to bully me just like she bullies you."

To my surprise, Kiki looked like she was about to cry. "I think I want to go home."

I knelt so I was eye level with her. "What do you mean? We just got here."

Kiki looked around the room. "I don't want to be here anymore."

"I don't understand. You were so insistent about coming and proving that girl couldn't get to you. What happened?"

She shrugged. "She got to me."

I put my hands on her shoulders. "Kiki, you deserve to be here just as much as anyone else. *Don't* let her get to you. People like that, they feel better when they put others down because it makes them feel better about themselves. Usually if you look deeper, there's a reason behind their behavior, and it has nothing to do with the person they're targeting. I promise that as you get older, you'll understand that better." I looked out at the dance floor. "We can't leave. We haven't even danced yet—or gotten our picture taken in the booth."

How could I look Aspyn in the eye if I let Kiki go home all sad? There was no way I was bringing this kid back feeling worse than when she left.

"I don't know how to dance," she said.

"Sure, you do. You just move to the rhythm of the music and don't think about it too much."

Kiki fidgeted, looking like she was ready to run out the door. I figured maybe if we took part in an activity, she'd loosen up.

"Let's wait in line for the photo booth."

I led the way, and she reluctantly followed. There were all kinds of props on a table near the booth: feather boas, hats, masquerade masks, and pom-poms.

I put on a top hat, and Kiki chose a blue boa to match her dress. When it was our turn, we made our way inside the booth. Kiki pressed the button before I was ready, and the flashes started. While I stuck out my tongue, Kiki stuck her middle finger up. Maybe that was inappropriate, but I couldn't even be mad at her. It made me crack up, which proved I might not be cut out to parent children someday. All of the photos after that ended up being me laughing at her giving the finger. Such a sweet memento we'd be bringing back to Aspyn.

Kiki and I waited for our photo strips to develop, and then I tucked them into my pocket.

When the DJ started playing "Daughters" by John Mayer, he encouraged the girls to grab their dads and head out to the dance floor.

I nudged Kiki. "We should go, too."

She wrapped her hands around her arms and shook her head.

Damn. I had really hoped the night would go better than this. I thought once we got here, she'd feel better. I guess I was delusional in assuming I could hand her a flower and make everything better. But that Maisy girl really was an asshole—just like her father. And honestly, they were both just the way *I* used to be in school. It took one to know one.

While everyone else was dancing, Kiki and I watched from the sidelines. I needed to somehow save this night— either that, or give in and take her somewhere else. But I couldn't just stand here and do nothing.

"I'll be right back," I told her as I left her momentarily.

I walked over to the DJ booth and explained the situation to the teenager in charge of the music tonight. I slipped him a fifty, asking that he pick a song that would be appropriate for Kiki and me to dance to.

After the Mayer song ended, everyone dispersed.

The DJ took to the mic and said, "This next one is a special request. I'd like to call Troy and Kiki out to the dance floor. This song is for anyone here who thinks it's cool to bully someone just because they don't have a dad. I'm one of those kids whose dad isn't here, too. And let me just say..." He paused. "Well, I'll let the song say it. Keep your head up, Kiki."

Kiki's eyes widened. Pointing my head in the direction of the dance floor, I somehow managed to get her to take my hand and follow me.

At first, the song was just a pleasant and light melody, fast but easy to dance to. I began to clap my hands, shake my hips, and stomp my feet in an attempt to get Kiki to dance with me. Instead, she was stoic, refusing to move as I danced around her.

Then the lyrics of the song came in.

"Fuck you."

It was just those words, over and over again.

Kiki started to crack up, jumping up and down and getting into the music. She seemed to think this was the funniest thing ever.

Meanwhile, I froze and stopped dancing. *Shit. What have I done?*

I recognized the song now, the aptly named "Fuck You" by Lily Allen.

My eyes darted over to the teenager at the helm. I threw my hands up and mouthed, *What the fuck is wrong with you?*

He shrugged.

With each *fuck you* Lily belted out, Kiki laughed harder. It seemed she'd finally broken through her funk. So rather than demand he change the song, I let it roll. Whatever made her happy at this point.

I looked around to find the eyes of every guy and little girl in the room on me.

It might be time to go.

As the song wound down, I turned to Kiki. "Want to go grab a burger or something?"

"Yeah." She smiled, looking genuinely at ease for the first time tonight.

We ran out of there like two bats out of hell. We'd left our mark on the dance, just not the way I'd envisioned.

• • •

Kiki and I ended up at Wonder Diner, one of the oldest and greatest institutions in all of Meadowbrook. I texted Aspyn to tell her where we were and said I'd fill her in on the rest later but assured her all was well.

"Everyone's gonna be talking about that song next week," Kiki said.

"I would never have chosen that song. I only asked him to pick something that would send a message to Maisy."

"I'm not embarrassed. It was funny."

"Inappropriate, but I guess it was funny, yeah. If anyone gives you shit, you tell me. I'll go to your school on Monday and explain what happened." *Aspyn's going to kill me.*

"The look on Maisy's face made it worth it," Kiki said.

"No one has the right to bully you, Kiki." My stance on this was pretty ironic, given my behavior in high school. "Actually, I have a secret."

"Are you gay?"

I blinked. "No."

"My friend's brother told her the same thing, that he had a secret, and that's what he said after."

"No." I chuckled. "What I wanted to tell you is that...I wasn't the greatest kid when I was younger. I teased people and acted a lot like Maisy sometimes. When you're older, you understand better how important it is to be kind. But like I said earlier, most of the time when people act like that, there's a reason. In my case, I was an angry kid. Angry at my mom, mostly, for not being around. While some might have said I had a right to be angry, I didn't have the right to take it out on other people. No one ever has that right."

She took a sip of her milkshake. "I get angry too."

"But you're a good person. Even when that girl was being mean tonight, you held back from stooping to her level. That says a lot about you. Don't ever change."

Kiki took a bite of her burger. Her mouth was full when she asked, "When are you gonna stop coming around?"

I blinked. "What made you ask me that?"

"Because that's what Holden did. He just went away. And he doesn't call or anything. He disappeared."

I didn't respond right away, because I needed to be very careful not to make promises I wasn't a hundred-percent sure I could keep.

"I know it can be hard when you get used to someone being around and then you don't see them anymore," I said.

"I don't want to see my auntie cry again."

My body stiffened. "He made her cry?"

She nodded.

"After he left, you mean? Or while he was there?"

"After he left. She was sad." Kiki dipped her fry in some ketchup. "I was sad, too."

That made me feel both anger and, oddly, jealousy. Not because I wanted to be the one who made her cry, but

I now realized Aspyn had true feelings for that Holden guy, though she'd downplayed the breakup the one time she'd told me about him. If she'd cried when he left, there was a good chance she'd been in love with him.

Staring out at the neon lights from the diner sign, I felt a bit guilty for skirting the issue Kiki had brought up a second ago. When you choose to be a part of a child's life because you're involved with their caretaker, it's not fair to disappear just because things didn't work out with that relationship. That asshole Holden could've been an adult and at least made an effort to keep in touch with Kiki.

"No one who's ever meant anything to you should completely disappear from your life, Kiki. Aspyn and I are having a really good time together. And I would love for that never to change. I care about her a lot. But I think your aunt was right when she mentioned that things between guys and girls can be complicated. I would never want to make a promise to you that I can't keep. But what I can tell you is no matter what happens, you can always count on me if you need a friend. I'll give you my number and email, if you ever want to talk."

She licked some ketchup off the side of her mouth as she looked up at me in surprise. "Thanks."

"In fact, let me give you my info right now, okay? That way you have it."

I walked to the front and asked a waitress for some paper and a pen so I could jot down my email and cell phone number.

"Can I email you now or only if you disappear?"

I chuckled. "You can email me anytime."

She took the piece of paper. "Thanks. Auntie Aspyn just let me create an email account."

"Well, perfect timing then."

· · ·

Our bellies were full, and thankfully Kiki was still in good spirits by the time we returned home.

Aspyn's eyes immediately found the massive ketchup stain on Kiki's dress. "How was it?" she asked.

Kiki was practically speed-talking. "Maisy was mean, I gave the middle finger in the photo booth, we danced to the eff you song, then we had burgers, and Troy gave me his email."

My shoulders shook in laughter.

Aspyn narrowed her eyes. "Okay... It's gonna take me a little bit to decipher all of that."

Kiki yawned. "Can we talk about it in the morning? I'm tired."

"Of course. But jump in the shower, please, before you hit the sack, okay?"

Kiki started to run off, but suddenly turned around and headed back my direction. To my surprise, she reached up to hug me. I knelt and took her into my arms, closing my eyes at the sweetness of it all. I could smell French fries in her hair. She didn't say anything. She didn't have to.

After Kiki left, Aspyn gaped. "Wow."

"We had a good time." I smiled.

"She doesn't give hugs very easily."

"Well, she's a tough customer...like her aunt."

I spent the next several minutes elaborating on the brief details Kiki had spat out about our night.

Aspyn shook her head incredulously. "What was the DJ thinking playing that song? But I'm happy it brought her out of her shell."

"I knew if I didn't do something drastic, she was going to continue to let that girl get to her. That song wasn't what I intended, but it definitely broke the somber mood."

"I'm really glad I let her go tonight. It was good practice for *me* in letting go, too."

"I personally love it when you let go." I squeezed her thigh. "There's something else I need to tell you."

She raised her brow. "Okay..."

"When we were at the diner, Kiki and I got on the subject of your ex. She mentioned how she never heard from him again after you guys broke up. She feels like the same thing is going to happen with me someday. So I sort of made her a promise. And I hope you're okay with it."

Aspyn's forehead creased. "What did you say?"

"I told her that no matter what happens between you and me, I'd keep in touch with her—that she can always count on me if she needs to talk to someone. I gave her my email and phone number. Hopefully that's okay with you. I know I probably should've checked first."

Aspyn nodded, taking it all in. "That's a pretty big promise. But if you're okay with that responsibility, I am too. It's all on you to follow through."

"I am." I straightened my back. "And I know that. I won't take it lightly."

I was tempted to ask her why she cried after her ex left when she had supposedly initiated the breakup. But ultimately, it wasn't any of my business. I also didn't want her getting mad at Kiki for mentioning it.

"The night is still young," I said. "What do you want to do?"

She fiddled with the button on my shirt. "You wanna watch a movie?"

"Sounds good to me."

We chose a film at the top spot on Netflix. Aspyn grabbed a massive, furry blanket from the loveseat and placed it over us. I wrapped my arms around her and took in a long whiff of her flowery scent. Ending the night on this note made anything that came before this moment worth it. There was no way in hell I felt like going back to my lonely house tonight. (Sorry, Patrick.) Everything I needed was right here on this couch, under this blanket.

Aspyn nestled into my chest. At one point in the middle of the movie, she arched her neck and turned to look at me. She didn't say anything, but I knew she wanted a kiss. I gladly obliged, lowering my lips and taking her mouth in mine. Then she flipped her body around so she was facing me. Adjusting the blanket over us, I deepened the kiss.

"I want you," she whispered.

My dick stiffened.

"Does Kiki ever get up once she's asleep?" I asked.

"Rarely."

"I can be discreet, if you can."

I'd expected her to give me a reason having sex on this couch was a bad idea, but instead, with hazy eyes, she nodded, apparently giving me full permission to go all in under this blanket.

I unzipped my jeans just enough to take my cock out as she lowered her leggings. I adjusted the blanket to cover us, and she sat on top of me as I sank into her. I didn't know what it was about this—that we were forced to be quiet, or just that I'd missed her so damn much this week—but being inside of her felt even more incredible than usual. We both came quickly, which was probably a good thing, considering the circumstances.

I kissed the top of her head. "What time can I come over tomorrow?"

"You're still inside of me, and you're wondering when you can do it again?"

"Is it just me?"

"No. It's not."

My laughter shook against her. "So, what time?"

"My mother is picking her up at noon."

"So, a minute past twelve?"

"That works."

After, she disappeared to the bathroom to wash up. When she returned to the couch, she leaned her body against mine as we watched what was left of the movie.

When the credits rolled, I could sense her staring at me. I smiled. "What are you thinking right now?"

"How did I go from hating you to this, Serrano?"

"Define *this*."

"I can't, really. It's indescribable. Like I'm outside of my own body, watching it all. It's a phenomenal feeling, though."

"Oh, *that*. Yeah. I've had that feeling for weeks. Pretty sure I'm ten steps ahead of you. It only gets more intense, by the way. Like, don't be surprised if you put the TV itself in her lunch box next."

"That bad, huh?" She laughed.

I held her tighter. "Yeah...in a good way."

Chapter Fourteen

Aspyn

The following Tuesday at work, I made a point to pop into Mr. Serrano's room to say hello. I wanted to make sure I wasn't subconsciously ignoring him to avoid having to address my relationship with Troy. When I entered, the usual scent of Love Spell body spray lingered in the air.

"I feel like I haven't seen you in a while," I said.

"Well, from what I hear you've been busy." He grinned.

I was still formulating my response to that when he saved me.

"I'm teasing," he said.

"I know your grandson has filled you in." I took a seat across from him.

He nodded seriously. "He's a good boy, Aspyn. He's made some mistakes in the past. But I believe he's changed. And I also know he really likes you. I've never seen Troy talk about anyone the way he talks about you. But you didn't hear that from me."

A pathetic level of butterflies developed in my stomach

upon hearing that news. I smiled. "My lips are sealed, but thank you for letting me know."

"He told me he took your niece to that dance."

"He did. Kiki has really taken a liking to him. She is a handful but a blessing in my life."

"Troy feels like he can relate to her situation, I think. It wasn't easy for him, growing up without a mother and all. We were so busy all the time. We did the best we could, but we certainly made our mistakes. He didn't have the happiest childhood."

I patted his arm. "Well, if there's one thing I know, it's that you can try your hardest and still have an unhappy kid at times."

Mr. Serrano turned down the volume of *Judge Judy*. "I had no idea when I met you that you had so much on your plate. And you still manage to have a nice smile on your face all the time."

"Well, it doesn't help anything to be miserable. I try to look on the bright side, even if I'm having a bad day."

He cleared his throat. "I'm just going to say one more quick thing, because I know what's going on with you and Troy isn't my business..."

"It's okay." I smiled. "I value your opinion."

"I hope it works out for you two. Because he deserves a girl as nice as you."

That warmed my heart. I didn't always feel like a nice girl, but the fact that he saw me that way made me happy.

"Thank you for saying that," I told him. "We're taking it one day at a time. A lot is still up in the air. But he does make me happy, Mr. Serrano. Between you and me, I haven't been this happy in a very long time."

"Well, that makes *me* happy." He smiled.

I hadn't even admitted that to Troy. For some reason, it was easier to open up to the old man instead.

"I realize how ironic all of this is, given the way things started between us."

He nodded. "Life can be funny. If there's one thing I've learned, it's that life has an amazing sense of humor."

• • •

That evening, I was sorting through the mail when I noticed a small envelope addressed to me. The return address was Troy's. Oddly, my first reaction was panic. Was this a Dear John letter? Why the hell did he mail me something when he could have just given it to me the next time we were together?

I opened it as fast as I could. Inside was a simple piece of off-white, lined paper with a handwritten note in blue ink.

Dear Aspyn,

I've been trying to figure something out for a while, and I think I finally have.

Lately, my coffee tastes better. At first, I thought maybe I'd bought a different brand by mistake, but no. It's the same brand I've always used.

Then I noticed that the leaves on the trees seem so much more colorful than I remember. I don't think I'd ever stopped to appreciate fall in Meadowbrook. Why am I noticing it all of a sudden?

The answer is, it's not the coffee or the leaves. It's you, Aspyn. You make me happy. And everything is better, more vibrant, when you're happy. You're the first woman to ever make me feel this way.

I hope you realize how special you are.

XO Troy

I couldn't believe he'd sent me this. My heart beat rapidly as I held my hand to my chest. At first, I wondered whether he'd written this because of what I'd told his grandfather. I thought maybe Mr. Serrano had told him about my confession. But that conversation was only earlier today. And this had been mailed before then.

I picked up the phone and dialed Troy.

He answered on the third ring. "Hey…"

I breathed into the phone. "You know, if there were such a thing as death by swoon, I would be lying on the floor with no pulse in a pile of mush right now."

"You got my note?"

"Yeah. It was very sweet and profound and amazing—and damn, you're good, Serrano. I don't even know what to say."

"You don't need to say anything. The purpose wasn't to garner a response. It was just to tell you how I'm feeling. Every word of that is the truth. I'm not the most romantic when it comes to words. But that was the only way I could describe what I've felt like lately."

"What possessed you to mail it instead of giving it to me?"

"I wanted to let you know I was thinking of you while we couldn't be together during the week. Also, my romance guru told me that would be a nice gesture."

My cheeks practically hurt from smiling. "Romance guru? What's gotten into you? And who is your romance guru, anyway?"

"My grandfather."

"Really? He told you to send me that?"

"This was the first of his tips that actually worked."

Something clicked. "Wait a minute...does this have anything to do with the foot-rub attempt?"

He chuckled. "Maybe."

"Oh my God. The dip! When I hit my head."

"Maybe." He laughed. "But it's important to note that even though he gave me the suggestion to write you a letter and mail it, everything in it was all me."

"Well, thank you again. You made my night."

"Thank you for giving me a reason to write it, beautiful."

I let out a long sigh into the phone.

"Tell me what that was about—that sigh," he said.

"I guess I keep waiting for the other shoe to drop with you. Is it horrible to admit that?"

He didn't respond for a few seconds. "No, because I always want you to be honest with me."

"You've given me no reason to feel this way," I said.

"I think the way I've acted in the past is ingrained in your mind."

"Maybe on a subconscious level, but it's not just you. It's *me* as well, Troy. I have major trust issues. I know I haven't opened up much about my last relationship. I *was* devastated when it ended, even if I was the one who technically broke up with him. Once he told me he'd considered cheating on me, I knew it was over. He might as well have done it. It was a huge blow because I had trusted him before that."

"Did you end things immediately?"

"It took me a month or so before I ripped the Band-Aid off. I kept thinking about Kiki. And how much she loved him. He begged me not to end it. He said he felt so guilty he had to confess what he'd almost done, but he tried to get me to believe that the fact that he *hadn't* cheated meant he loved me. I knew that wasn't true." I sighed. "I feel lucky that he admitted it to me. I can't imagine if I'd just continued to assume I was safe with him."

Troy sighed. "As someone who's cheated on a girlfriend in the past, maybe I have no right to offer my opinion here... But anyone who loves you is not going to consider cheating for even a second. You made the right call."

"I know that. Believing someone loved me one minute and then realizing I wasn't enough for him all along was a real wake-up call. It certainly didn't help my trust issues."

Troy was quiet for a moment. "I wasn't going to tell you this, but I feel like I need to in order to explain something."

"Okay..."

"The other night with Kiki, when we were at the diner, she mentioned that she didn't want to see you cry again. She was alluding to the time after your ex left. That sort of led to our conversation about my keeping in touch with her no matter what happened between you and me.

Anyway, that was the first time I realized how badly he'd hurt you."

"I wish she hadn't told you that..."

"I figured it wasn't something you wanted me to know. But it hit me hard. Before that, I'd viewed you as somewhat guarded, someone who kept her emotions inside. And to hear that he'd broken you like that... It made me not only angry, but weirdly jealous that you had experienced deep feelings for someone. It also made me wonder if what you had with him was more of an emotional connection, whereas with me it might be more...physical."

I nodded, even though he couldn't see me. "Things with you might have started out physical, but my feelings for you have evolved." I closed my eyes to gather my thoughts. "I think I should better explain. It wasn't that I thought Holden was *the one*. While I definitely believed I loved him at the time, I think the reason behind my tears had more to do with how his confession reflected on *me*, what it meant about my ability to be enough for someone. And of course, it reminded me of my parents, how my dad always claims to love my mother, even though he cheats on her. I'm telling you, Troy, I'd rather be alone than lie next to someone at night who would do that."

He paused. "Anyone who would cheat on you is an absolute, fucking fool. You are the smartest, sexiest woman I have ever met."

I looked up at the ceiling and shook my head. "Troy Serrano, my brain has been in the clouds for weeks. And it's all your damn fault. It's a wonder I haven't packed the vacuum in Kiki's lunch yet. I don't know what I'm going to do with you."

"You ask that a lot, but now I have a specific answer. I know what you can do with me. Call out sick in the middle of the day again. Come over and sit on my face tomorrow."

"Well, that's one idea."

• • •

The next day, Troy's suggestion about calling out sick ran through my head on repeat the entire morning at work. I was a lost cause. Rather than make up a story about being ill this time, I created a fictitious appointment. So while I would have far less time with him as a result, I would take what I would get.

As I left work in the middle of the day, feeling like I was getting away with murder, I couldn't wait to surprise him. But when I pulled up in front of his house, I saw another car next to his Range Rover. My stomach sank as I realized Troy had a visitor. My pulse began to race as I exited my car and approached his front door.

He'd denounced my ex for cheating last night on the phone, so why was my first inclination to pray that his guest wasn't a woman? Why was I so damn distrusting right off the bat? I could only chalk it up to the trauma of my dad's cheating and Holden's almost-cheating.

My heart fluttered as I knocked on the door. My hands shook.

Stop.

The door opened, but it wasn't Troy who answered. It was an older man.

"Can I help you?" he asked.

"Hi. I'm here to see Troy?"

He smiled. "Are you Aspyn?"

My pulse immediately calmed a bit. "Yes."

He held out his hand. "I'm Giovanni Serrano. Troy's dad."

What? "Oh...wow. You're back from Europe?"

"Yeah. Unfortunately, my girlfriend's mother had a heart attack. It looks like she's going to be okay, but we cut our trip short and rushed back last night."

"I'm so sorry to hear that."

"Thank you." He waved me inside. "Anyway, come in. Come in. Troy just got into the shower. I've been going on and on all morning about my trip. This was the first chance he managed to break away from me. He didn't mention he was expecting you, though?"

Troy's dad had jet black hair, darker than Troy's chestnut brown. While they were both tall and handsome, I suspected Troy must have looked more like his mother. He and his dad didn't resemble each other much in the face. On the other hand, Giovanni definitely looked a lot like his dad, Louie.

Licking my lips nervously, I said, "I, uh, didn't tell him I was coming. I just decided to pop in and say hello."

"Don't you work at Horizons at this time?"

Busted.

"Yes." I squirmed. "But I had an appointment today. I got out of that a bit early, so I decided to stop by here and say hello before I have to return to work."

"Ah. Gotcha. Well, I'm sure he'll be happy to see you when he gets out. Shall I peek my head in and tell him you're here?"

"Sure. That would be great. I don't want to catch him off guard."

266

As he walked backwards toward the bathroom, he said, "Can I get you something? Some tea or coffee?"

"No, thank you."

It must have been only two minutes later that Troy appeared, wrapped in a towel with his hair dripping wet. Water droplets streamed down his beautiful, hard chest.

Even with my nerves shot, I still wanted to jump him right now.

He slicked his wet hair back. "You didn't tell me you were coming."

"I know. I wanted to surprise you."

"Must have been my suggestion yesterday on the phone." He smirked.

I cleared my throat. "I had an appointment that finished early."

"Right." His eyes twinkled. "I see you met my dad."

"Yes." I let out a shaky breath. "He knew who I was."

"That's because after he talked my ear off about Europe this morning, I talked his ear off about you."

"And I'm very happy you dropped by," his father said. "Because who knows how long it would have taken Troy to properly introduce us."

Troy turned to him. "Not with this one. You would have met her soon."

Heat rushed through my body.

"Well, alright, then." His dad beamed. "Listen, I have to stock up on some real food, since my son has almost nothing in the fridge. So I'll let you two be for a while. I'll be gone for at least an hour, if that information is of any use." He glanced over at Troy, and then nodded in my direction. "If I don't see you when I get back, Aspyn, it was an absolute pleasure. I can see now why Troy wouldn't shut up about you."

"Thanks, Mr. Serrano."

"Mr. Serrano is my dad, the old man you know and love. Please call me Giovanni." He grinned.

"Okay." I smiled. "Nice meeting you, Giovanni."

After he exited the house, Troy and I just looked at each other.

He moved his head slowly from side to side. "You naughty girl. You came over to sit on my face and got a rude awakening, didn't ya?"

"I certainly wasn't expecting to meet your dad, no. And I'm pretty sure he knew *exactly* why I came over."

"Yeah. He probably did. But so what?"

Maybe it should have made me uncomfortable that Troy's father knew what we were about to do in his absence, but I guess I was too horny to care. I shrugged.

"I love that you're making a habit of lying through your teeth to be with me," Troy said.

"This addiction is probably going to be the end of me."

"I'd better make it worth your while."

After I followed him into his room, he dropped his towel.

"Come here and get on your knees. I want to feel that beautiful mouth around my cock for a few minutes."

I got down and wrapped my hand around his engorged shaft. I closed my eyes as I took him into my mouth and sucked hard.

Troy let out an unintelligible sound, and I looked up as he bent his head back, his chest rising and falling.

"Fuck, you give good head, Aspyn."

I stopped for a moment, and his eyes sparkled as he looked down at me with a wicked grin. Licking my lips, I opened my mouth wide and began going to town. I'd never enjoyed giving blowjobs until Troy. I couldn't say whether it was my level of attraction to him or the way he so loudly expressed his enjoyment that turned me on so much, but I absolutely loved doing this to him.

He pulled out of my mouth with a pop and said, "Let's get you naked."

Troy helped me strip my clothes off until I was totally bare. A shiver ran down my spine as I anticipated what was coming next. I lay back on his bed, and my knees trembled as he spread my legs apart. He lowered himself, and there was no easing into it. He immediately began lapping at my clit as I guided every movement with my hands around his head.

"I love how you use me," he rasped.

He kept going until he'd almost made me come, but then he suddenly stopped. "I need to fuck you now. We don't have all that much time."

Spreading my knees wider to make room for him, I waited for the moment he entered me. It happened in one hard thrust, causing me to gasp so loudly that Patrick freaked and ran out of the room. I hadn't even realized the poor cat was in here.

The bed shook as Troy pounded into me, his balls slapping against my ass. I loved the way it felt when we were skin to skin. Even more, I loved the way he fucked me even harder right before he was about to come.

"You close?" he panted.

I nodded, letting myself go and knowing he would know exactly when to release. Sure enough, the moment my muscles began to contract, I felt the heat of his cum spilling inside of me. He continued to move in and out until there was nothing left.

"Sorry. I was particularly revved up today. Pretty sure I left a hazmat situation inside of you." He panted. "Goddamn, that was good."

I chuckled. "Can I take a quick shower in your bathroom?"

"Go right ahead." He slowly pulled out.

After I washed up, I felt so relaxed. This was just what I'd needed, even if this booty call had an embarrassing start.

The moment I emerged from the bathroom, Troy pulled me into his arms and whispered in my ear, "I'm so glad you made that *appointment* today. What was it, by the way?"

"I like to think it was something like…acupuncture." I joked. "Nothing too scary, like a pap smear."

"Well, I hope it went well."

"It went *very* well."

I looked at my phone. "Shit. I have to get going."

He pressed his lips to mine. "Thank you for this wonderful surprise."

On my way out of his room, my eyes landed on a sparkling gold ring on the top of his bureau.

"Is that your class ring from Meadowbrook?"

"Yeah. Did you have one?"

"No, I could never have afforded it at the time. They were like four-hundred dollars."

"I don't think I've even worn it once. I bet it would look nice around your neck." He wrapped his arms around me and unclasped the chain I had on, which held a small, bean-shaped pendant. He looped the bulky ring onto the chain and locked the clasp. I immediately felt the weight of the gold.

"It looks way better on you than it would on me."

I ran my fingers along the stone. "I can't take this."

"Why not?"

"It's a special memento, the only one of its kind."

He stared into my eyes. "Aspyn, *you're* my most special memento from high school. The fact that I've been gifted this second chance, this time with you, is everything to me. I want you to have it. Especially since you said you didn't get one yourself." He tugged lightly on the chain. "Now you have one." He kissed my forehead. "And you have *me*."

Feeling ready to melt, I said, "Thank you. It's beautiful. Emerald is my birthstone, too."

"Well, see? It was meant to be."

On the drive back to work that day, I felt so many different emotions. The heavy ring now hanging from my neck wasn't the only thing weighing on me. With Troy's father back in town, he no longer had to stay in Meadowbrook. The only thing keeping him here was... me. That felt like a lot of pressure. I wanted him here, of course. I wanted it to work out so badly. I'd been worried about his ability to be a partner, but now I felt like it was *me* who needed to work on myself even more than him. I had trust issues that had nothing to do with Troy. And if I let them ruin this, he had no reason not to return to Seattle for good.

Chapter Fifteen

Aspyn

Four days later, Troy invited Kiki and me over to his dad's house for Sunday dinner. Giovanni made his famous spaghetti sauce, which Troy had always raved about. It was nice to sit down to a home-cooked meal prepared by someone other than me. Giovanni even bought special gluten-free pasta so I could eat with everyone.

As dinner wound down, Giovanni wiped his mouth and asked, "When are you leaving, son?"

"I haven't decided yet. Tuesday or Wednesday, probably. But I haven't had a chance yet to discuss it with Aspyn."

"Oh, I didn't realize that," his father said. "I'm sorry for bringing it up."

My eyes widened. "You're going somewhere?"

"Yeah. I only just found out about it. I was waiting to tell you tonight before he opened his big mouth."

Giovanni winced. "Sorry, son."

"I'm heading back to Seattle," Troy explained. "It's just for a couple of weeks."

My heart sank, despite knowing that this was inevitable.

"My office needs me to come in for an in-person event," he continued. "I figured I'd use the time to get some stuff from my apartment there and bring it back here, tie up some loose ends while I'm out there."

Kiki bit into her roll. "That stinks that you have to leave."

"It won't be for long," Troy said.

"Do you miss your friends there?" she asked.

"I do sometimes, but not enough to make me want to be there and not here."

Trying to appear outwardly calm while inwardly freaking out, I cleared my throat. "What's the status on your apartment there?"

"I'm not sure yet. I've been paying my rent this whole time, but my lease is up in a couple of months. I guess I need to figure it out, right?"

The room felt like it was spinning a little. I grabbed the red wine in front of me and took a long sip. *You're overreacting.*

Giovanni must have sensed the tension in the air. He turned to Kiki. "Kiki, have you ever played bocce?"

"What's that?"

"It's an Italian bowling game. I have it set up in the yard. Why don't you come let me show you how to play?"

She turned to me, her eyes sparkling. "Can I?"

"Of course." I forced a smile.

Kiki took her plate to the sink without having to be asked and followed Giovanni out to the backyard.

Once we were alone, Troy reached for my hand. "What's on your mind?"

I played with the remnants of my pasta. "Nothing... I had kind of been bracing for this, I guess—you heading back to Seattle."

He frowned. "I'm coming back, Aspyn. You know that, right?"

I stared off. "Yeah, I just..."

He squeezed my hand. "What's going on? Talk to me."

I looked up at him. "We really haven't talked about where we go from here, Troy. Now that your dad is back, there's nothing keeping you here in Meadowbrook—except me. That freaks me out a little. I mean, you wouldn't be here otherwise, right?"

"Honestly, no. I wouldn't be. You *are* the only thing keeping me here. But you've become a big part of my life. Which means I'd rather be here right now than there. That's really all there is to it."

"Right now." Am I reading too much into every word that comes out of his mouth?

"I'm not used to anyone adjusting their life for me, I guess."

"Well, I'm not used to adjusting my life for anyone. But I haven't felt the way I feel about you with anyone else." He pushed his chair closer to mine and locked my legs in with his. "Look, this is all new for me. That's no secret. Ever since the beginning, my biggest fear has been doing something to hurt you, even if it wasn't my intention. I'm not gonna lie, I still have my doubts sometimes—but not about my feelings for you. More about my ability to be the man you need long term. I desperately want to be that man. But some days, this feels like imposter syndrome. Am I really good enough for you to trust me with your heart? All I know is I *want* to be."

I appreciated his honesty, but it wasn't exactly making me feel better, even if I trusted that his insecurities didn't stem from his feelings for me. I suspected his issues were deep-rooted, just as my trust issues were.

Our discussion was unfortunately cut short when Kiki and Troy's dad came back inside.

"Auntie Aspyn, you have to come outside and play bocce with us. It's so much fun! It'll be even better with two teams of two."

Troy rubbed my arm and flashed a crooked smile. "Wanna play?"

Still feeling unsettled, I nodded and followed them outside.

•••

Back at my house later that night, after Kiki went to bed, Troy and I finally had an opportunity to be alone again.

We were sitting in the living room when out of nowhere, he pulled up a song on his phone. He put the volume on low and took me by the hand.

"What are you doing?"

He brought me to his chest. "Let's dance."

I listened a moment and recognized "The Way You Look Tonight" by Frank Sinatra. I raised an eyebrow. "Wait, Sinatra? This was another suggestion from your romance guru, wasn't it?"

He winked. "Maybe."

Troy held me close as we danced. With my head on his shoulder, I closed my eyes and breathed in his scent as we rocked back and forth. I didn't know if it was the way he held me, the music, or the fact that I knew he was leaving for a little while—maybe a combination of everything—but I just lost it.

When he looked down and noticed I was crying, he pulled back. "What have I done?"

I wiped my eyes. "Nothing. I'm sorry. It's nothing you did."

"I swear, almost every time I try one of Nonno's secrets, it backfires."

"It's not the dancing, Troy. That was beautiful." I sniffled. "Just hold me for a little bit."

He pulled me close as the music continued to play.

When the song ended, he led me over to the couch. "I hate to see you cry."

I sniffled again. "I'm sorry. This is so unlike me. I'm not even sure where all this is coming from."

"Don't apologize. I just want to make it better." Concern filled his beautiful eyes.

All the doubts and fears inside me seemed to be rising to the surface. And I couldn't hold them in any longer. I needed to be crystal clear with him.

"Can I ask you a favor?" I said.

He looped his fingers with mine. "Of course."

"If there's any doubt in your mind about settling here in Meadowbrook, if you feel like you're unsure of this—of us—in any way, will you tell me as soon as you know?" I looked down at our joined hands. "I don't want to be caught off guard. There's nothing worse than feeling like you're safe with someone and then realizing you aren't... that you never were."

"You think I'm gonna decide not to come back or something? Why is all of this coming out now?"

"Your leaving is what prompted this, but the truth is… things have been weighing on me for a while. And this isn't only about you, Troy."

He blinked several times. "I'm sorry. I'm lost."

"All this time, you've been feeling like you have something to prove to me, but I'm the one who needs work. I'm so afraid of getting hurt that I can't even seem to enjoy the moment."

"Knowing you're so afraid of getting hurt makes me all that much more afraid to hurt you." He tightened his grip on my hand. "Fuck, Aspyn, that's my biggest fear."

I sighed. "I'm making things harder than they should be by overthinking everything. But I can't seem to help it." Shaking my head, I muttered, "I have a tendency to sabotage things that are important to me."

Troy frowned. "What are you talking about?"

"There's still so much I haven't told you." Letting go of his hand, I settled into my seat. "I don't know if you knew this, but I was pretty smart in high school. I always got good grades and was ranked toward the top of the class."

"That doesn't surprise me, but no, I didn't know that because my head was stuck in my ass back then."

I placed a pillow on my lap and squeezed it for support. "Have you ever heard of the Kauffman Scholarship?"

He chewed his lip. "Yeah. It rings a bell—the name, at least."

"Only two students in the entire high school get chosen, but they narrow it down to ten finalists initially. And I was one of them."

His mouth dropped. "That's amazing."

"Around the time I found out about the scholarship possibility, I also got an early acceptance to Princeton."

"Wow. But you ended up going to state college, right?"

I nodded. "I'm leading up to that. We were told the scholarship would come down to the highest GPA at the end of the year—the top two."

"Damn, that's a lot of pressure. No wonder you were so mean to me," he teased.

"This was *after* all that stuff happened with you."

"I'm kidding, of course."

"Anyway, I wasn't sure if I could afford Princeton without the scholarship, and the stress was too much. Ironically, it started affecting my grades." I cringed. "And I made a really poor decision."

He moved closer and placed his hand on my knee. "What was it?"

Blowing out a breath, I hugged the throw pillow tighter. "I cheated on an important exam. I'd excelled in every subject except AP Calculus, and a friend of mine found it so easy. So I copied her answers." I shook my head. "I really thought I'd gotten away with it—but I got caught. That led to both the scholarship and the acceptance to Princeton getting reneged. Everything I'd worked so hard for was gone. And it was all my fault, because I'd let the stress of winning influence me to act out of character. I'd never cheated a day in my life before that."

Troy's mouth fell open, and the color drained from his face. He looked absolutely devastated. "Holy shit," he finally said. "I'm...I'm so sorry, Aspyn."

Shrugging, I said, "I couldn't be mad at anyone but myself. I knew what I was doing when I made that decision to cheat, and I had to pay the price. That's all there is to it."

He shook his head. "I don't know if that's true." He looked away. "I had no idea you lost all that."

"Anyway, that was a catalyst for a lot of my issues in the years that followed. I fell into a depression and decided to take time off before starting college. That was the biggest mistake I could've made. I had too much time on my hands and started hanging out with the wrong crowd—wasting my life away."

He scratched his chin. "What were you doing?"

I laughed angrily. "A whole lot of nothing, really. I didn't work for a while. It was like I fell into a hole and couldn't get out. I became ambivalent about life and really very self-centered. Around that time, my parents were going through a rough patch in their marriage, and my sister was the only person in the family with her head screwed on straight. She'd graduated from college with a nursing degree and was happy and in love. Toby and Ashlyn were already planning to get married when she got pregnant with Kiki. Even though the pregnancy was a surprise, she was over the moon to have a baby." I stared off toward Kiki's closed bedroom door. "They loved her so much."

Troy rubbed his thumb gently along my knee.

"When I found out my sister was pregnant, I was happy for her, but so miserable about my own life. I wanted what she had—not necessarily the boyfriend and baby on the way, but a *purpose*." I shut my eyes. "The night they died on their way to pick me up was the last night I acted selfishly. That was the end of my years-long pity party. I had to pick myself up and figure out how to be a better person for my niece. It was the biggest wake-up call I could've had."

Troy sighed deeply, still seeming a little shaken. "I can't imagine what that must have been like—being in a tough place to begin with and then to have that tragedy happen... How did you manage to cope?"

"I didn't, really. I just went through the motions. When Ashlyn died, I still lived with my parents. I started going to state college full time. We all just did the best we could. I graduated with a degree in general studies and took odd jobs, but I never found anything I was passionate about. My priority became helping take care of Kiki and trying in some way to right the wrong I'd caused. In many ways, it all seemed to stem from the one bad decision I'd made to cheat on that test. It's amazing how one choice can change the entire course of your life—but also the lives of others." I whispered, "A domino effect."

Troy closed his eyes.

The choice to focus on this dark, depressing stuff tonight was unfortunately a waste of our time together before he had to leave. But it had all needed to come out.

"How did you end up at Horizons?" he finally asked.

"At the time I was hired, I'd been working in retail. My mother and Nancy have a mutual friend. I got the position even though I had no real work experience even remotely connected to being an activities director. I didn't deserve the job, and I've always looked at it as a gift. I learned as I went along. But for the first time in my life, I do feel fulfilled in this career. I'm good at what I do, even if I started like a fish out of water."

He nodded. "That's why when we first took Nonno out, you said you fell into the job."

"Yeah. That's what it felt like, as if I'd stumbled upon it accidentally. But it's been one of the best things for me." Stroking his cheek, I added, "You have been, too, Troy. I'm sorry I haven't opened up to you more. It hadn't felt right until now."

He placed his hand over mine. "I'm glad you did. I never wanted to push you because I figured it was difficult to talk about."

"The ironic thing is, only in my sister's death did I find my true purpose, which is to take care of Kiki, to be a role model for her. That's not the way things should've been, of course. But it's the way things are. I became a better person after losing my sister. I was forced to grow up."

"I'm sure she's proud of you. I know I am." Troy looked down at the floor for a while.

Eventually I moved the subject back to us. "I feel like we've reached a crossroads, Troy. I've realized I want so much more than a casual relationship with you. But I don't want to get further attached unless you're a hundred-percent sure you want to continue building something. We have so much fun together. It's seemed effortless until now, but a relationship with me won't always be easy. I need you to take time while you're away to think about whether you see a future with me here in Meadowbrook. Really think it through before making any promises, okay?"

Troy placed his head on my lap and just lay there for a while. I could feel his hot breath on my stomach.

When he looked back up at me, his eyes were glassy and held an intensity I'd never seen before. "How I feel about you is not in question," he said. "The only thing in doubt is whether I can be the man you need. And I *do* think I need to take a step back and think about that."

My stomach sank. For some reason, I hadn't expected him to go along with my request so *easily*. I'd spoken out of fear tonight, and to hear that he agreed with me and felt like *taking a step back* was a good idea made me freak out a little.

"I never want you to look at me with hate or distrust again," he said. "I'll do whatever it takes to make sure that doesn't happen, even if it means letting you go."

Again, his choice of words alarmed me. Where was this coming from? But I'd *asked* him to scrutinize our relationship. Yet another example of how I tended to sabotage things.

He wrapped his arms around my waist. "I promise to use my time away to think about everything you've said. As much as I don't want to leave Meadowbrook yet, I think it will be good to put some distance between us while we think about what's best. Things got intense between us fast. And I agree that we're at a point of no return—we're both setting ourselves up to get hurt if we're not on the same page. I need to be sure that what I want and what I can deliver are one and the same." He pulled me into a tight hug. "You've changed me and made me want things I've never wanted before. But at the same time, I recognize what an incredible honor and responsibility it would be to own your heart. And I will *not* toy with it."

Dread overtook me as I pulled away. "It's late. I should get to bed. Will I see you again before you leave?"

"I would love that, if I can come by on a weeknight."

I swallowed. "Of course."

After he left, my stomach was in knots. I'd made myself clear to Troy, but I guess I'd wanted him to tell me I was nuts for thinking we might not work out. He hadn't exactly done that.

• • •

The following day at work, I'd just finished a singalong when I decided to stop in at Ruby Blandford's room. Ruby was eighty-seven and loved romance novels and Blue Moon beer. She was also a distant relative on my mother's side, so she always referred to me as *cousin* or *cuz*. Whenever I felt down, I'd stop into Ruby's room, which let more sun in than any of the other units at Horizons. Framed photos of her grandchildren covered the walls.

I helped her with her laundry for a few minutes, but she finally put down the item she'd been knitting. "Something on your mind, cuz?"

"Why do you say that?"

"You seem a little distracted. You just put your phone in my drawer along with the shirts you helped me fold."

Jesus. I was dangerous when I was distracted. "I did? I'm sorry." I opened the drawer and sure enough, my phone was sitting there on top of one of her blouses.

"Don't apologize. Tell me what's wrong. You look a bit down."

I hadn't shed a tear over the situation with Troy since our talk last night, and I'd vowed not to, especially in front of Kiki.

But Ruby's simple question caused my eyes to well up.

She noticed right away. "Oh, dear."

Wiping a lone tear, I sniffled. "I'm not supposed to be doing this at work."

"You're not at work. You're technically in my house— or at least the only house I have. See that sign?" She pointed to an embroidered wall hanging. "Home sweet home? I make the rules in this space. So, tell me what has you so sad."

The words that came out of my mouth were a surprise. "I think I'm in love."

There was no other explanation for how sick to my stomach I felt at the first real threat of losing what I had with Troy.

"Well, that's a beautiful thing. Why are you crying?"

"Because I don't think I realized it until I felt like I was about to lose him. I *am* about to lose him. And it's partly my fault."

"Why are you losing him?"

I took a seat across from her. "I sort of gave him an ultimatum—not in so many words, but I asked him to assess whether a long-term relationship with me was what he really wanted before we took things any further. You see, he's never been the monogamous type. So, I think we're gonna be on a break while he goes back to Seattle to take care of some business. He technically lives there. The whole thing was my suggestion, but almost the second he agreed with me, I felt devastated. I think I wanted him to try to talk me out of it. The fear I felt when he didn't made me realize how strong my feelings are. I already miss him, and he hasn't even left yet."

Ruby snapped her fingers. "Wait, this is Louie's grandson, isn't it?"

I'd never said anything to her about dating Troy. "How did you know?"

"When you said Seattle, it hit me. He's a nice kid. I've spoken to him, and I knew he was from out of town.

Plus, I remember that little duet you did at The Carpenters singalong."

"Yeah, you got me. It's Troy Serrano."

"No secrets among family, you hear?" She winked. "You can tell me anything. It's safe with me."

"Thank you, Ruby."

"You've heard the term *absence makes the heart grow fonder*, of course?"

"Yeah..."

"Well, sometimes absence takes out the trash." She chuckled. "Trust me, if he doesn't come back to you, you never had him to begin with. This little separation will be good. It will prove once and for all whether you mean something to him."

Is it really that black and white? "What if he cares about me, but doesn't think he's cut out for a long-term relationship?"

She shook her head. "No such thing. Either you love someone enough to take the chance on yourself or you don't. End of story."

• • •

Later that afternoon, I was shocked to find Troy pacing in the hallway in front of his grandfather's room.

"Hey, I didn't know you were coming today," I called as I approached.

He breathed out a sigh of relief. "There you are. They said they didn't know where you were." Despite the worried expression on his face, Troy looked amazingly handsome in a black wool coat and scarf, as if he'd just walked out of a men's clothing catalog. His thick, gorgeous hair was wind-blown.

"I was talking to one of the residents. Is everything okay?"

"The meeting I have to attend for work got pushed up to early tomorrow morning. That means I have to take the next flight out. I'm headed to the airport."

My heart dropped to my stomach. "We won't get to spend time together before you leave?"

His forehead wrinkled. "No. I'm afraid not. But I couldn't leave without seeing you. So I came to say goodbye."

The whole thing didn't sit right with me, even if he had no control over the situation.

He looked devastated. "I'm so sorry, Aspyn."

My throat tightened. Was he sorry for leaving early or in anticipation of something else? I shoved my concerns aside. "You can't help it, right? There's nothing to be sorry for." My entire body tensed in an attempt to fight the feelings of sadness and longing.

"Do you think you could sneak outside for a couple of minutes so we can have a moment alone?" he asked.

I checked my phone. We had a trip to the outlet mall scheduled, and the van would be boarding soon. "I have just a few minutes before we have to leave for a trip."

Troy followed me out a side door. It was chilly out, and I hadn't put on a jacket. The cold air seeped through the thin material of my scrubs.

Troy looked down at me. "Of course you have to be wearing my favorite scrubs right now. As if leaving wasn't painful enough." He forced a smile.

I rubbed my arms. "Did you have something to say to me in private? Is that why you wanted to be alone?"

"No. I just want to hold you without any prying eyes. Because I'm gonna miss you."

Maybe I was reading into things too much *again*, but I wondered why he was going to miss me so much if he was coming back in a couple of weeks. I didn't want to sound paranoid, so I didn't ask. Instead, I let the question fester inside of me with all the other uncertainties floating around.

He took his jacket off and wrapped it around my shoulders, then used it to pull me to him. The warmth felt painfully good. In his arms, it was a lot harder to bury my emotions, and I felt them rising to the surface.

"You're the most beautiful woman in the world, you know that?" he whispered.

I didn't say anything, afraid that if I uttered a word, my insecurities would come flooding out or I'd blurt a question I didn't really want the answer to. I needed to trust that if this was meant to work out, it would. *He'll be back.*

Troy pulled away and placed his hand on my chin, prompting me to look up at him. His smile faded, presumably because he saw the sadness in my eyes.

He leaned in and kissed my lips. It tasted bittersweet as the stubble on his chin scratched my face. I took a long breath of his scent, knowing it would be some time before I would smell it again.

My phone buzzed. I looked down to find a text from Nancy, asking where I was because the van was waiting.

"I have to go."

Troy wrapped his hands around my face and planted one last kiss on my forehead.

"Let me know when you arrive safely," I said.

"I will," he whispered against my skin.

I removed his coat and handed it to him before walking back inside. Even though I wanted to cry again, I wouldn't let myself.

Only time would tell if Troy was worth the tears.

Chapter Sixteen

Aspyn

Four weeks later, things hadn't turned out the way I'd hoped.

It was now early December, and Troy's supposed two-week trip back to Seattle had already lasted a month and counting. According to him, they'd given him a new project that required he stay out west a bit longer. That didn't exactly make sense to me since he'd always told me he could work from anywhere.

We'd messaged back and forth, but he'd grown distant, opting to text rather than pick up the phone beyond a couple of calls when he first arrived. He kept saying work had him stressed and used that as the reason for his lack of communication. Since we couldn't seem to talk about much of anything, I avoided asking him questions about the state of things between us. I mean, also, *why should I have to ask?* I'd made my stance clear. The ball was in his court now. He was the one who left, not me.

Rather than wallow in my sadness over Troy's virtual disappearance from my life, I threw myself into my job and taking care of Kiki. Deep down, though, I felt empty. I just wasn't willing to admit that to anyone, least of all Troy.

In my fantasy world, Troy would've rushed home the first opportunity he had, maybe even flown home for the weekend and insisted he didn't want to live without me. But instead, he seemed pretty accepting of the fact that he'd have to stay out there a while. He never spoke of how hard it was to be away from me, and his silence sent me a loud and clear message—that things with us seemed to be *out of sight, out of mind.*

Perhaps the more time that passed, the more he discovered that what we had was just a phase, and he didn't want to come back to Meadowbrook. I suppose the worst part of Troy's silence was that it left me to draw my *own* conclusions. They may not have accurately described how he felt, but they suited my need to protect myself from getting hurt.

• • •

A couple more weeks passed, and before I knew it, the holiday season was in full swing. At least getting ready for Christmas—mostly shopping for Kiki—kept me busier than usual and my mind off of analyzing why Troy had stopped being a meaningful part of my life.

Jasmine had invited Kiki and me to a Christmas party she and Cole were throwing on a Saturday in mid-December. So, my niece and I bundled up and drove to New Hope. I wore a red turtleneck sweater dress that had little sparkles built into the material. Kiki dressed in a velour tartan plaid dress I'd recently bought her. She'd worn it for our yearly Christmas card picture.

I'd only seen Jasmine once since the awkward run-in at my house during the harvest festival, so this visit was long overdue. I'd decided to go to her house a little earlier in the afternoon to help her set up for her guests. I figured that would give us some time to catch up.

I was cutting vegetables for a veggie and dip plate while Jasmine rolled cold cut slices onto a platter. She'd poured us each a cup of Twinings Christmas tea. Kiki was in the next room playing with Hannah while Cole supervised.

"So, what's the latest with you and Troy?" Jasmine finally asked.

I sighed and sliced into a carrot. "He's actually back in Seattle."

She ceased the turkey rolling for a moment. "For good?"

I put my knife down. "I don't know. It was supposed to be for just a couple of weeks for work, but he's ended up having to stay out there longer. Now I don't know when or *if* he's coming back."

"You haven't asked him?"

"I'm trying to give him space to assess what he really wants, whether that's to stay in Seattle or otherwise. I don't want to manipulate things, nor do I feel I should have to."

She nodded and resumed arranging the cold cuts. "Well, this is probably for the best. That one day I observed you with him, it seemed like you were pretty attached, that he had you under some kind of spell. Quite frankly, I still don't think he's right for you, and it's probably a good thing he left."

Her words were a blow, despite the fact that I knew she felt that way, and with each day that passed, I was closer to believing she was right.

"I understand what you're saying," I told her. "My impression of the time I spent with him is different, but I don't expect you to understand. I don't really want to spend this day analyzing what happened between him and me, though. It is what it is, at this point."

She opened a package of pepperoni. "Well, it sounds like now might be a good time to keep your options open. That's certainly better than sulking while Troy is in Seattle having fun, partying it up with his friends, I'm sure."

"He's not having fun," Kiki chimed in.

I hadn't realized my niece had entered the kitchen until she said that.

I looked over at her. "What are you talking about?"

"I talked to him the other day."

My heart sped up. "You spoke to Troy?"

"I sent him an email."

"Why did you email him?"

"You told me I could, remember?"

That was true. In fact, the entire reason they'd exchanged information was so she could keep in touch with him if things between him and me went awry. And it seemed they had. Nevertheless, it certainly wasn't fair of me to use her to get information. So I resisted asking her anything. Although, anything she *happened* to offer was fair game.

Maybe just one question. "What do you mean, he's not having fun?"

"He told me he was really tired. But he said receiving my message cheered him up."

Jasmine looked between us, her eyes narrowed, seeming judgy about the fact that my niece had been corresponding with Troy.

Okay, I lied. I need to know one more thing. "What else did you talk about?"

Kiki shrugged. "I wrote to him to complain about Maisy because I know he understands. He told me I need to act like she doesn't bother me because she's only being mean to get a reaction."

"That's good advice."

"Then he said he was working a lot and that he missed Meadowbrook and told me again to write to him whenever I wanted."

Hmm... "Well, that's nice." I resisted the urge to ask whether he'd mentioned me.

After Kiki left the room again, Jasmine lowered her voice. "He's emailing with her?"

Here we go. "I know it seems weird. But they bonded pretty early on. They both grew up without moms, and she feels like he can relate to her in a way others can't."

She shrugged as she opened a jar of pepperoncini. "I guess that's kind of sweet."

On that note, it felt like a good time to move the conversation to other topics, so I asked Jasmine about her plans to go back to interior design part time.

Once her guests started arriving, the mood lightened considerably. Kiki and I spent a great deal of time playing with Hannah, allowing Jasmine and Cole time to enjoy their friends.

Jasmine's tree was spectacularly decorated with cream-colored ornaments and white lights. The entire house was lit up for the holidays, so warm and inviting. But being amidst all this Christmas cheer made me miss Troy. I could easily imagine him beside me, rubbing the small of my back and whispering in my ear, probably telling me what he planned to do to me after we got home. It was no surprise that my mind had wandered to sexual things when it came to him, since that had been such a huge part of our relationship. But the sex wasn't what I missed the most. I missed the feeling that someone had my back, his friendship, his encouragement, his jokes, his company, and just the way he'd hold me. I missed *him*. I missed the way things *were*.

My thoughts were interrupted when Cole walked over. He'd brought a friend with him.

"Aspyn, there's someone I want you to meet. This is my good friend, Christian Bartholomew. We work together at the agency."

"Nice to meet you," I said.

"You, too, Aspyn. What an interesting name." He tilted his head. "Were you born in Colorado?"

"No. The origin actually has something to do with trees and fluttering leaves—unrelated to Aspen, Colorado. It's spelled with a y-n at the end."

The next thing I knew, Cole had slipped away, leaving me alone with this guy. I don't know why it took me even that long to realize it was a setup.

• • •

Two evenings later, I'd just tucked my niece into bed on Monday night and sat down with a hot cup of tea. I'd opted not to put up a Christmas tree this year, much to Kiki's dismay. I'd told her my parents had such a large and beautiful tree that there was no way I could compete. Going to get a real tree was such a hassle, and I hadn't had the energy lately. I felt guilty about that decision, but not enough to change my mind. I'd tried to purchase a fake tree, but the only one I could find was too expensive. So, I put holiday candles in the windows, set out a few poinsettia plants, and left it at that. I was staring at the window lights when my cell phone rang.

When Troy's name showed on the screen, my heart began to race—not with excitement, but dread. The fact that he was calling all of a sudden after texting exclusively for several weeks set off an alarm.

My body tensed as I answered, "Hey…"

"Hey." He sounded tired. "How's it going?"

Hearing his voice made my chest tighten. Maybe that was my heart starting to break. "Good," I managed. "Kiki just went to sleep, and I'm sitting here drinking tea." I swallowed. "What's up?"

"I…just wanted to hear your voice and see how you're doing."

Not sure where to even begin, I stayed silent, letting him put two and two together.

He finally sighed. "I know I've been distant since I got out here. I'm trying to do what you asked of me, and at the same time, I'm…trying to come to terms with some of my own shit." After a long moment of silence, he added, "I don't want you to think I'm playing games with you."

The dread and sadness I'd felt a moment ago now morphed into pure anger and frustration. "I'm sorry, Troy. I don't speak cryptic. You'll have to speak English."

"Fuck," he muttered. "You know Kiki's been emailing me, right?"

"Well, she only mentioned it to me once."

"She emailed earlier today and mentioned that you guys went to a Christmas party at Jasmine's over the weekend."

"Yes, we did. It was a lot of fun," I lied.

"She said she heard some guy at the party ask you out on a date."

"This is why you're calling? Because you felt threatened?"

"No!" he insisted. He let out a long breath. "This is so hard for me," he whispered.

"Just say it, Troy. It's so obvious what's happening with us. What's *already* happened." My voice trembled. "Just fucking say it."

He didn't respond for several seconds, and when he finally did, it was a doozy—despite my bracing for it.

"I don't want you to wait around for me if I can't get my shit together and be what you need. You asked me to figure out if I was the right man for you, if I could be him." He hesitated. "I haven't been able to do that. And it's not fair for me to keep you in this limbo with no answers."

"You just gave me your answer," I spat. "Because you shouldn't have to think about it as hard as you have been. If you care about someone, you can't live without them. Whether you're the right man for me or not is irrelevant— it's about whether you're willing to take the risk. It shouldn't be this hard."

His breath shook. "You're right. You fucking deserve so much better, and you're better off without me."

I begged the damn tears to stay away, but they wouldn't obey. I wiped my eyes as they fell. "I don't understand what happened. It felt different with you. Different from Holden. Different from anyone who came before you."

"I fucking hate myself right now, Aspyn. You have no idea how much."

"I *wish* I could hate you again, Troy. That would make this so much easier. But I *don't* hate you. That's the problem."

I loved you.

I shook my head slowly, mustering some inner strength. "You do you. I don't regret our time together. I just regret that things didn't work out differently. You are who you are. And I should've never thought I could change you. That's on me. I can't even be mad at you because you've been up front with me from the beginning. If I think back, you never did make any promises. But…it was the way you looked at me. The way you made me feel. And you did say I was special to you."

His voice trembled. "You *are* special to me—fuck, you always will be."

I couldn't see his face, so I couldn't know if he was actually crying, but it sure as hell sounded like it, and that made me even more confused.

"I guess there are just some things in life that won't ever make sense," I said. "It's not the first time I've had to accept that."

I couldn't take this conversation anymore. I needed to go to bed and bury myself under the covers.

"I'm gonna let you go, Troy."

"Wait, are you okay?"

"I will be." Sniffling, I said, "Bye."

Before he could respond, I hung up.

It's over.

Chapter Seventeen

Troy

The weather in Boston was brisk as I made my way through the South End neighborhood. It was the morning of Christmas Eve, and the utility poles that lined the street were decked out in garland.

When I got to the address I'd written down, I stopped at the front steps and looked up. There was no point in knocking. She didn't live here anymore. I'd just wanted to see it.

A man came out of the townhouse. "Can I help you?"

I shook my head. "I don't think so."

"Troy?" He tilted his head. "Is that you?"

What? How does he know me? My eyes narrowed. "Who are you?"

"I'm Gregory Jones. I was Jennifer's boyfriend. I recognized your face—you look just like her. I was having some coffee in my kitchen and noticed you staring in the window."

"I didn't think anyone who knew her still lived here."

"We lived here together, and I never moved after she passed."

"I don't remember seeing you at the wake," I said.

"I was there. I just wasn't standing with the family. We didn't really get along. They never liked me, never thought I was good enough for her. They thought I was after her money. It didn't help when she left me her house." He chuckled. "Now they hate me even more."

"Well, that's one thing we have in common. Jennifer's parents hate me too."

"Were you just going to linger and not knock on the door?"

"I'm headed to New Jersey for Christmas, and I decided to stop here on the way. I've always been curious about where she lived. This is just a quick stop."

He gestured toward the black door where a holiday wreath with red ribbon hung. "Come in. Please."

He seemed nice enough. I guessed I had nothing to lose.

I followed him inside the high-end townhouse, which was warm, with an urban feel. A staircase framed in black wood with a mahogany handrail led to a second level. The walls were exposed brick painted white.

On the wall in the foyer was a huge piece of three-dimensional artwork.

"What is this?" I asked.

"I made it," he said. "It's metal that was thrown in the trash by people in this neighborhood, all welded together."

"Wow. That's cool."

I looked around, noticing the large windows that let in a lot of sun. "How long did she live here?"

"We moved here when she found out she was sick, actually. Jennifer did well for herself over the years, but for some reason she'd always rented, never wanting to commit to anything."

Never wanted to commit. The irony.

"She finally bit the bullet and bought a brownstone in the middle of the city, which was exactly where she wanted to be in her last days."

"Did you take care of her?"

He nodded. "Until the very end."

Should I thank him for that? I didn't know, so I said nothing, instead walking over to a corner of the room where a photo of my mother sat on a shelf. Lifting it, I said, "I'm the only one in my family who doesn't look like the Serrano side. It's because I look like her."

"You sure do. That's how I knew it was you standing outside."

I continued looking at the photo. Jennifer sure knew how to dress. Crisp white shirt. A string of pearls. Black blazer. She looked...powerful.

"I should feel something when I look at this, but I don't," I told him. "I guess that's better than feeling anger."

"I think she'd be happy with that. She didn't expect anything more from you."

I finally took my eyes off the photo and turned to him. "How do you know what she expected?"

"Because I knew her better than anyone. She was my entire life. After all these years, I still haven't been able to move on." He stood beside me and looked down at the photo. "I'd love to tell you about her, if you'll listen."

I put the frame back on the shelf. "Okay..."

"Can I make you some coffee or tea?" he asked.

"I could go for some coffee."

"How do you take it?"

"Black."

Since leaving Meadowbrook, I only drank my coffee that way. It reminded me of Aspyn.

"Easy enough." He smiled.

Gregory had longish, salt-and-pepper hair and a gray beard. He sort of reminded me of a scruffier George Clooney. His hipster style was the opposite of my mother's more formal vibe. Clearly, opposites attracted.

We moved into the kitchen, which had bright yellow cabinets.

"Did she pick that yellow color?"

"That was her appeasing me. Her taste was a bit more conservative. She let me handle the kitchen design, though." He chuckled. "Pretty sure she regretted that."

After Gregory poured me a coffee, we sat down together at the kitchen table, which had a lacquer top.

He took a sip from his mug. "I know you probably think you have her all figured out, that she was simply selfish for giving you up. But I can assure you, there's a lot you don't know."

"So enlighten me."

"I've thought about coming to find you over the years. But I was never quite sure if you'd want that." He rubbed his temple. "Anyway, I know Jennifer wanted to tell you a lot of this stuff herself, but she never had the chance."

"Okay..."

"Once it became clear that she wasn't going to make it, she started seeing her life in a different light. She had a lot of regrets—her biggest being never having a relationship with you. She had a tough time forgiving herself for that, and I have to say she took much of that regret with her when she died, never really achieving any peace with it."

It gave me no satisfaction to know that. No matter her mistakes, she deserved to die in peace.

"When we're younger," he continued, "sometimes we make decisions that haunt us for the rest of our lives. Your mother was a people pleaser, particularly when it came to her parents. They put a lot of pressure on her from a very young age to be successful. In that sense, I suppose they were progressive for their generation. They also put a tremendous amount of pressure on her to give you up. She couldn't blame them entirely—after all, she had free will. She could've run away or defied them. But she made the decision she felt was best at the time. She never doubted that your father would love you and take good care of you, because he fought her so hard to keep you. What she underestimated was the level of regret that would build up for her over the years at having missed seeing you grow up. With each year that passed, though, she felt like she had less and less right to a place in your life."

"Why didn't she ever have other kids?"

"She always felt that if she wasn't able to be a good mother to you, she shouldn't get a second chance." Gregory looked out the window for a moment. "But we all make mistakes. Some are so big you never come out from the shadow of them. She really did hope to make things right with you before she died. She knew it was too little too late, but she never gave up hope. I encouraged her to tell you she was sick and ask you to come, even though she suspected you might be hesitant."

"She thought I didn't want to come see her?"

"She mentioned that the first meeting with you hadn't gone as well as she'd hoped. She sensed your anger—and she didn't want to upset you again."

I nodded. "When she and I first met, I was an angry fifteen-year-old who wasn't ready in any way, shape, or form to forgive her. Things would have been different if I'd had the chance to see her at the end."

"Anyway..." he said. "I know you'd planned to come, even if you didn't make it in time. And she appreciated that."

Taking a sip of my coffee, I stared out the window a moment. "What was she going to tell me that day?"

"That she loved you. It was the one thing she was too cowardly to say when she met you the first time."

I shook my head as I contemplated that. "I spent so much of my younger years angry at her. It was a waste of energy."

"You couldn't help that."

"She died thinking I didn't love her. She didn't realize that most of my anger stemmed from the fact that I *did*. I didn't understand how I could love someone I also hated. Someone I didn't even know. But the truth is...her love was all I ever wanted. The only thing," I whispered.

Gregory's eyes shone with unshed tears. "You had it all along. You may think what she did was unforgivable, but she did love you, Troy." He paused. "You said all you wanted was her love. All *she* wanted was your forgiveness."

"I would have told her I forgave her if I'd made it in time."

He nodded. "Well, I do believe that wherever she is, she knows that." He looked down into his coffee cup. "I loved her. And it pained me to watch her die, but to know she wasn't going in peace? It's a lesson that as long as we're alive, it's never too late to make amends. But if we wait too long, we can lose the chance."

Snowflakes had started to fly outside, and I took a moment to let what Gregory had said sink in.

"What made you want to come see her now?" he asked. "I mean, I know you said you just wanted to see where she lived, but in a sense weren't you coming to see *her*?"

There was only one answer.

"I fell in love," I confessed.

"What's her name?"

"Aspyn."

He nodded with a smile.

"We're not together anymore, though."

"What happened?"

"I'm keeping something from her. And instead of dealing with it head on, I ran away. I can't face her again unless I tell her. She'll have to forgive me in order for us to be together. But who am I to think I deserve that? How can I expect her to forgive me if I couldn't forgive my mother while she was alive? If I can't forgive myself? I guess I came here today because I need hope...or a sign or something. I thought maybe I'd feel closer to Jennifer here, that I'd find the answers I've been looking for."

"Instead, you found me, an old, washed-up artist," he joked.

"I guess." I laughed. "Well, your story about Jennifer helped me see that I don't have forever to make things right in my current situation. And even if Aspyn can't forgive me, at least I'll know I tried. Talking about my mother definitely helped me see that it's never too late to try, as long as I'm alive."

He stood from his seat. "Come here. I want to show you something."

I followed him into a bedroom. He took a framed photo off the nightstand and handed it to me. It took me all of two seconds to recognize the person in the picture.

"That's me."

I must have been about six or seven. My hair was shaped into that ridiculous bowl cut my grandmother used to give me, because they were all too cheap to send me to a normal hairdresser.

"She kept that photo next to her bedside. I've never had the heart to move it. She loved how happy you looked. It made her feel like she'd done something right in letting your father raise you. She had nothing but wonderful things to say about him. She was very grateful to him for being there for you."

I placed it back on the nightstand, emotions twisting inside of me.

"Thank you for sharing that with me."

Gregory walked over to a wooden bureau and opened one of the drawers. "I want to give you something of hers."

He reached into a jewelry box. "This was one of Jennifer's favorite pins."

It was silver or white gold. Upon closer look, I realized it was a dragonfly.

"She liked dragonflies?"

"I'm not sure. I just know she always wore this on her jackets, so I presume she did."

The dragonfly's eyes were tiny emeralds. *Aspyn's birthstone.*

"It's beautiful," I said, rubbing my thumb over it. "Thank you."

I spent about another hour with Gregory, listening to his stories about life with my mother. They seemed to have had a strong mutual respect for one another and made each other happy—the kind of comfortable happiness I had with Aspyn before I fucked everything up.

While I can't say my time with Gregory magically erased twenty-nine years of pain, this was by far the most meaningful day of my life when it came to understanding my mother and what she might've been thinking.

Unlike my so-called grandparents on my mother's side, Gregory was definitely someone I'd be keeping in touch with. Moreover, I walked out of that brownstone truly understanding how dangerous it is to leave things unsaid. Today left me with a lot to think about in terms of my next move when I got back to Meadowbrook.

• • •

After my visit with Gregory, I went straight to the airport. Since I had a half hour before boarding, I opened my laptop to catch up on work. Before I could get started, though, I saw an email from Kiki in my inbox that had come in yesterday.

Hi, Troy,

Guess what? I tried what you said with Maisy, and I think it worked! She was teasing me at recess, and instead of getting upset, I started laughing. I didn't mean to laugh, but I got nervous. She looked at me like I was crazy, but then she just walked away! It was magic. So, I think I'm gonna laugh in her face all the time now.

What do people your age want for Christmas? I want to buy something for Auntie Aspyn but don't know what to get her. I only have ten dollars, and it's the day before Christmas Eve, so I don't know what to do!

Are you still feeling sad? Are you ever coming back?

Bye!

Kiki

Her emails always made me smile—particularly the abrupt way they ended. I hit reply.

Hey, Kiki!

I'm proud of you for being strong when it came to Maisy. I'm glad you can see that if you're not bothered by her, she's no longer interested in bullying you. It is like magic, isn't it? If only everyone realized this sooner, they could save themselves a lot of trouble.

I'm sorry I don't have a quick answer for you in terms of what Aspyn might like for Christmas. What I'm finding, the older I get, is that it's the thought that counts. Just knowing someone thought about you enough to make something or to pick something out is what matters.

I'm sorry if I gave you the impression I was sad the last time we spoke. When I said I was down and missing

Meadowbrook, I was just having a bad day. Like you, I have good days and bad days. And you know what? Today was a good day. I'll tell you about it some time, but I'm still kind of letting everything sink in.

I wasn't sure whether to tell her I was coming back to New Jersey for Christmas if I wouldn't be seeing her. So, I kept it generic:

I hope to be home very soon.
Keep up the good work with Maisy. I'll be rooting for you. And if I don't get to talk to you again before Christmas, I hope you have an amazing one. Please give Aspyn a big hug for me.

Talk to you soon,

Troy

• • •

I just needed a little tree. Unfortunately, all of the ones left were huge. This sucked. Nonno was going to be pissed.

He was already mad enough because I'd arrived back in Meadowbrook later than usual. It was the first year I hadn't brought him a fresh tree to put in his room ahead of Christmas. He said he hadn't asked my father to set one up because it was *my* job. He'd intentionally waited until the last minute, after I arrived in town, so I could do the honors.

Currently, I was at the only place still open and selling Christmas trees this late in the game on Christmas

Eve. After I'd gotten here this afternoon, I'd barely had time to unpack before my grandfather started blowing up my phone. *He's lucky I love him.* Unfortunately, love wasn't enough to save this night, and at this point, I was debating pulling a bush out of the ground somewhere. Nonno insisted on a real tree because he liked the fresh-pine smell. Like many things, he said it reminded him of my grandmother. My grandparents wouldn't have been caught dead with a fake tree when I was growing up.

My search for a tiny tree was further derailed the moment I spotted her: Kiki. I immediately hid behind the nearest evergreen. Peeking through the branches, I could see she was with Aspyn's mother and a man I assumed was Aspyn's dad. My chest tightened. The sight of her made me yearn to see Aspyn tonight. But that wasn't possible. I couldn't let her know I was in town until the day *after* Christmas, because we needed to talk, and I didn't want to ruin her holiday by upsetting her. But beyond December 26, it wouldn't be able to wait.

If Kiki saw me tonight, Aspyn would know I was back in New Jersey and hadn't told her I was coming home for Christmas. She would be unhappy, and that would spill over to Kiki. I might've done a lot of crappy things in my life, but up until now, shitting on a kid's Christmas wasn't one of them. I wanted to keep it that way.

Kiki and her grandparents had their backs to me as I made a beeline past them, headed to the parking lot. I'd get my ass handed to me by Nonno for coming back empty-handed, but I had no choice but to leave.

In my rush to exit the premises, I didn't watch where I was going, and I bumped right into someone. "I'm sorry, I—"

I lost my words the moment I realized I was staring into Aspyn's shocked eyes.

Chapter Eighteen

Aspyn

"Aspyn..." he whispered.

Cold air billowed from my mouth. "What are you doing here?"

"I...came to get my grandfather a tree. But they don't have one small enough." He fumbled on his words. "I was...gonna call you the day after Christmas."

I crossed my arms. "You don't owe me a call."

"The fuck I don't." He exhaled. "Look, nothing is what it seems like, okay? We really need to talk. But it's not going to be an easy conversation. I don't want to ruin your Christmas. So I chose not to tell you I was home until the twenty-sixth."

"You think I'm gonna be able to focus on anything else besides you now that I know you're back, and you just said that to me? You haven't wanted to have a real conversation with me in weeks. I don't even know what happened. You've already ruined my Christmas, Serrano. You might as well just say what you have to say now."

"Fuck," he muttered, looking down at the snow-covered ground.

A long moment of silence ensued as passersby moved around us, carrying their last-minute trees through the parking lot.

"I'm sorry. That was harsh," I said. "I'm shocked to see you, that's all."

"I know." He looked up. "I, uh, saw Kiki and your parents. They didn't see me."

"My parents' furnace isn't working. So we have to do Christmas at my place instead of theirs. Stupid me didn't want to get a tree this year, so I wasn't prepared. That's what I get. We have no choice but to bring home one of these gargantuan trees at the last minute that they have left over. I don't even know if it will fit in my house. The ceilings are pretty low."

"Troy!" Kiki came running toward us.

He forced a huge smile, pretending to be surprised to see her. "Kiki! Hey!"

My poor niece looked so damn happy. "I can't believe you're back!"

"Yeah. I came home to see my grandad for Christmas."

Her smile faded. "Not to see us?"

His mouth opened and closed a time or two before he finally said, "I was gonna come see you *after* Christmas, actually. I didn't want to interrupt your family time."

"Oh." She looked over at me. "We think we found a tree that might fit."

My father appeared. "It's gonna be a bitch getting it on the top of my car." He nodded toward Troy. "Who's this?"

"This is *Troy*," my mother answered from behind him.

My father's eyes widened. "The guy who broke up with you?"

"No!" Troy blurted.

I arched my brow. "No?"

"No," Troy whispered, his eyes searing into mine.

Confused, I turned to my dad. "He was always supposed to move back to Seattle. It was never permanent. It's all good."

The five of us stood in awkward silence until Troy pointed to his Range Rover. "Listen, I have a roof rack. I'd be happy to throw that thing on top of my car and drive it back for you."

My father looked skeptical. "Only if it's okay with my daughter."

We'd be here all night trying to secure that tree to my dad's car, so I agreed. "That would be great. Thank you."

Troy followed my dad back over to the trees, and Kiki ran after them, leaving me alone with my mother.

"He just happened to be here?" she asked.

"Yeah. He came to find a small tree for his granddad, apparently. He wasn't even going to tell me he was in town."

"We don't have to go along with this, you know."

"No. It's fine." I sighed. "We need to get this tree home. I owe it to Kiki after being so damn stubborn about not having one."

Since I'd met them here, I followed my dad's car back to my house. Troy's Range Rover drove behind me with the tree affixed to the top. We were in separate cars, not speaking, yet the weight of everything unsaid felt overpowering. I had so many questions, but no words to articulate any of them.

It was only 5 PM, but it was already dark, and light snowflakes had begun to fall.

After we got to my place, Troy and my dad carried the tree inside, but to everyone's dismay, it was indeed too tall to fit.

"What are we gonna do?" Kiki cried.

Troy turned to me. "You don't happen to have a saw, do you?"

I shook my head.

My dad scratched his chin. "I'm not sure I have anything appropriate at home, either."

"My father has every tool known to man," Troy said. "Let me run home and get something to cut it down."

Troy disappeared a few seconds later. This would definitely go down as one of the most bizarre Christmas Eves on record. As we waited for him to return, I decided to just roll with this, putting on some Christmas music and getting out stuff to make cookies with Kiki. My plan was to do everything in my power to pretend like the guy who'd broken my heart wasn't about to come back here and cut our freaking tree.

About a half hour later, Troy returned with a mix of large knives and saws. From my spot in the kitchen, I couldn't see whatever he was doing, but by the time Kiki and I returned to the living room, Troy had successfully trimmed the tree down. It didn't even look that warped. The fresh, woody scent was all I could smell.

My parents and Kiki began pulling ornaments and tinsel out of the box I'd had in storage. Troy gathered the pieces of tree scattered around the living room.

Some time later, he found me in the kitchen.

"Who knew you were a lumberjack?" I teased.

"A lumberjackass is what you really want to say, right?"

I took a tray of cookies out of the oven. "Actually, that *is* more fitting."

"Well, I think I can use those tree parts to put something together for my grandfather. I can throw them in a pot, tie them together somehow, and put some lights around it. At least he'll have the fresh smell he wanted. And better than going back there empty-handed."

"Is he not going to your dad's tonight?"

"He's coming over tomorrow. He wanted to stay at Horizons tonight with his friends because so many of them aren't gonna be with their families. They're having their own little party."

"Yeah, I heard. That's sweet."

Troy looked down at a tag of some sort in his hands.

"What's that?" I asked.

"It was hanging off the tree. It says Douglas fir. That's the type of tree it is." He paused. "My mother's last name was Douglas. I've been thinking a lot about her today, so it shook me a little."

"Wow," I whispered.

The muffled sounds of my family in the next room seemed to fade as Troy moved closer and looked into my eyes. His gaze moved down to my lips, causing goosebumps to pepper my skin. And I never dreamed he would say what came out of his mouth next.

"I love you, Aspyn."

I blinked. "What?"

His stare burned into mine. "I thought I could wait to tell you that. I wanted to get the tough conversation over with first, but I can't hold it in anymore. I fucking love you, and at the very least, I need you to know that."

"I don't understand." My chest heaved. "Why don't you just say what you need to say?"

"I just did. The rest can wait until the day after Christmas. What I need you to understand as you go to sleep tonight is that I love you—and I have for some time. Pretty sure the day I stormed out of here in jealousy and took that long ride, I already knew it then."

I shook my head. As much as I'd felt the same way about him, I couldn't return the sentiment right now without understanding the full picture.

Kiki came running into the kitchen and over to the stovetop where the cookies were cooling.

"Troy, you want a cookie?"

It took a few seconds before he moved his eyes off of me and over to her. "I would love a cookie."

"Aspyn can't have one," she said. "They have sugar."

"Damn, I should've made her some of mine." He winked.

Kiki took a bite out of the sugar cookie shaped like a gingerbread man. "On Christmas Eve, we get to have cookies before dinner." She handed him one.

"Lucky girl." Troy smiled.

"Are you staying for dinner?" she asked.

"Well, I have tree parts to get back to my granddad..." He looked over at me.

Despite my hesitation, I felt like I should at least offer him the opportunity to have dinner with us, given his hard work on the tree tonight.

"You should stay for dinner, if you want," I said.

He placed his hand on my shoulder, sending shockwaves of awareness through me. "No. You enjoy your evening with your family. Just make some time for me the day after tomorrow, okay?"

Still feeling almost outside my own body after his proclamation of love, I accompanied him to the door and watched as he disappeared into the cold winter night.

Needless to say, I spent most of that Christmas Eve and the day after totally preoccupied. I couldn't even look at the tree without thinking of Troy. His behavior had me completely baffled, but I couldn't help but be buoyed by hope. *He loves me.* I just hoped our conversation would make all the other pieces fall into place.

Chapter Nineteen

Troy

Nervous was too mild a word to describe how I felt as I stood at Aspyn's door the day after Christmas. My holiday had been filled with anticipatory anxiety. Nonno, my father, and I had eaten a nice dinner together yesterday, but while my body was there, my head wasn't.

Aspyn had agreed to let me come over at noon. And when she opened the door, she was dressed up a bit more than usual for just hanging around the house. She wore a lavender sweater and short black skirt with leather boots up to her knees. She looked incredibly hot, but I couldn't even allow myself to enjoy it until I knew the direction things would be heading today.

I wiped the snow off my feet before entering. "Thank you for making time for me. I assume Kiki is with your parents since it's a Saturday?"

"Yeah. She's not here, so we have privacy." Aspyn headed toward the kitchen. "You want some coffee? I just brewed a new pot."

"Sure."

"Milk and sugar, right?"

"No, actually I've been drinking it black."

"Really…"

"Yeah." I smiled, neglecting to admit the sappy reason why.

Aspyn quietly prepared our coffees before handing me a mug.

"Should we sit?" I asked, feeling jittery.

She shook her head. "No. I'm too antsy to sit still. Just tell me what this is all about. I don't understand anything that's happened since you went to Seattle."

I gave myself a mental push to start talking. All I was doing was wasting time. "So…I stopped in Boston on my way back to Meadowbrook."

Aspyn paused mid-sip. "You did?"

"Yeah. I decided to go see where my mother lived. I'd been doing a lot of self-reflection in Seattle, and part of that was needing to understand the things that were supposedly so important to Jennifer—more important than me." I inhaled and blew out some air. "Anyway, I ran into her boyfriend, Gregory, the man who'd taken care of her before she died."

"Wow. Okay…"

"He told me a lot of things I didn't know. My mother lived with more regret when it came to me than I'd ever imagined. I'll tell you more about that someday, if you want, but now's not the time." I reached into my pocket. "Look what he gave me." I held out the dragonfly. "He said it was one of her favorite pins."

Aspyn took it from me. "It's so pretty."

"He wasn't sure if she loved dragonflies or what the story was behind it. I decided to look up what dragonflies symbolize. Apparently, they represent change, transformation, and self-realization. Those are the things I've felt happening to me over these past four months. It took me coming home and connecting with you to realize that all the things I thought I wanted in life—money, independence—they mean shit. Just like they meant shit to my mother in the end. All she wanted on her deathbed was for me to know she loved me. I just didn't get there in time to find out."

Aspyn nodded sympathetically. After a long moment of silence she finally said, "I still don't understand. What's going on, Troy? What do you need to say to me that you couldn't before Christmas?"

I put my mug down. "The night I first told you I was going back to Seattle for a couple of weeks, the night you opened up to me about what happened to you senior year— you mentioned how one decision could change the entire course of your life. You said you believed your cheating on that exam ultimately led to all the things that came after, including what happened to your sister and the life you live now. Do you still believe that?"

She looked away. "Well, I'll never know for certain what my life would be like if that hadn't happened. But it's safe to assume things would be different if I'd gotten that scholarship and gone to Princeton. I'll never be able to say for certain that my sister would still be here if I hadn't made that one choice, but I do believe she would."

I took a long, slow breath in and exhaled. "If you believe getting caught cheating changed everything for you, I have to let you know that *I'm* the reason for that."

Her eyes widened. "What are you talking about?"

"I didn't remember what I'd done until you told me that story. I did and said so many shitty things back in high school, never anticipating that any of them could have dire consequences."

Her mouth slowly opened. "What are you saying?"

My heart pummeled my chest. "I was the one who ratted you out for cheating."

Aspyn took a few steps back, her face turning redder by the second. "What?"

"I was in that class, too. You probably didn't remember, because who the hell remembers who was in what class in high school. I was sitting behind you, and I saw you and that girl passing notes during the exam. I passed my own note to the teacher, and that was what tipped her off. I was so proud of myself for getting back at you. I had no freaking clue what was at stake, no clue that you were up for any scholarship, or that you were already accepted into Princeton. I just thought it was...funny." I laughed angrily. "Can you imagine? I actually got pleasure out of something that ended up ruining your life."

Aspyn dropped her head into her hands. "Oh my God."

Pain shot through my body. I wanted to reach out and hug her, but feared I'd make this worse if I touched her.

"When you told me the story and I remembered what I'd done, I wasn't sure if I could *ever* admit this to you. I couldn't bear to risk you hating me forever. I've spent my entire time out in Seattle debating the right choice—and until I knew what to do, I didn't know how to talk to you. It felt wrong to try to stay in your life, even though I missed you terribly. I kept going round and round: would

I rather not tell you, living without you but knowing you didn't hate me for ruining your life? Or risk telling you, in the hopes that you'd forgive me and still want to be with me?" My voice shook. "Ultimately, I knew I couldn't face you again unless I told you the truth. It's just taken me this long to build up the courage."

I'd wondered if maybe she'd cry when I told her, but Aspyn just seemed numb. Or maybe it was strength.

She looked up at me. "I don't know what to say," she whispered.

"You don't have to say anything. You owe me nothing."

She shook her head. "I'm just trying to understand the timeline. So...this wasn't the reason you initially were going to leave? But once you found out, you decided to go early?"

"Yes. After I left the night you told me about the scholarship, my panic over the possible repercussions grew. I knew I needed to work things out away from you. I really did have to go back to Seattle for a work meeting, and I never intended to leave you for more than those two weeks. But once you opened up to me, and I realized my part in it, that sent me into a tailspin. I didn't know how to handle it. It wasn't until I went to Boston and learned the lesson my mother had indirectly taught me that I decided to take the risk. I *had* to take the risk that you might hate me, in order to have a chance to love you."

Aspyn remained silent.

"It's more important to me that you know I love you, even if you hate me. I'm so sorry I disappeared, but know that every second of it was torture. Also know that I will fully understand if you can't find it in your heart to get past what I did. If there is anything I could take back in this life, it would be that decision—more than any other decision I've ever made."

She swallowed. "I can understand now why you didn't want to tell me before Christmas."

As the tension in the air lingered, I didn't know whether to go or stay. "Tell me what you need from me right now."

She took what felt like a full minute to answer, and when she did, it wasn't what I wanted to hear.

"I need to be alone for a while."

While that hurt, I understood. "Okay." I nodded. "I'll leave."

I walked out of there filled with fear over losing her forever, but I was at peace after having told her the truth. Life was too short to live a lie. I'd spend the next several hours, maybe days, praying she decided to forgive me.

• • •

Two days passed, and I'd still heard nothing from Aspyn. But I vowed to continue giving her space. In the meantime, I had some business to take care of.

There was probably one person who hated me more than I hated myself right now. So why not pay her a visit? Things couldn't get any worse anyway.

"What are you doing here?" she asked, looking completely shocked to see me at her door.

You know how you can just *feel* it when someone despises you? It emanates off of them? Well, that's the vibe I was getting right now.

"I'm sorry if I'm interrupting something," I told her. "I was hoping we could talk."

"I just put my daughter down for a nap."

"Can I come in?"

Jasmine moved aside as I wiped my feet on the welcome mat.

"May I sit?"

She gestured to the couch, and I walked over and took a seat.

I rubbed my palms on my pants. "I never apologized for hurting you back in high school. And I feel like it's long overdue."

"Now?" Jasmine crossed her arms. "That's really not necessary."

"Maybe you don't feel that it is, but it's necessary for me." Taking a breath in, I said, "I was a dick back then, with no regard for your feelings. I was going through a lot of shit, and even though that's no excuse for my behavior, just know that my actions were in no way a reflection on you."

She sighed. "I never took it personally, especially given the person you cheated on me with." She rolled her eyes. "This apology is obviously not about me, though, is it? It's about Aspyn."

"Have you spoken to her?"

"Not since the holiday party I had before Christmas."

For some reason, I'd feared Aspyn had called Jasmine to lament in the couple of days since I dropped that bomb on her. But I should've known better. Aspyn was private, and something told me that despite everything, she was still protecting my reputation.

"It's important to me that you know I'm not toying with her feelings. I love her, Jasmine. You have every right to your opinion about me. But if you think I'm trying to take her for a ride, you're wrong."

I spent the next several minutes admitting to Jasmine why I'd lied to her about my mother when she and I dated, trying my best to explain my actions during high school. I ended with an explanation of the current situation.

"So, you don't know if she's going to forgive you?" Jasmine asked.

"I don't. But I'd appreciate it if you can find it in your heart not to make things worse, if she talks to you about it. You're entitled to your opinion about me. I'm just asking that you not feed her unsolicited advice based on your old, preconceived notions. None of those are true anymore. And no matter what you think, it doesn't change the fact that I love her. Only I can know the truth about that."

I heard crying from down the hall.

"I have to tend to her." Jasmine stood up. "Look, I won't interfere. And I respect you for coming over to apologize to me, even if it was only out of fear that I'd fuck things up for you. You're right. I would've told her to ditch you otherwise. So I appreciate the explanation. And we won't have a problem if you're being genuine."

She saw me to the door.

Before I walked away, I turned around. "Thank you, Jasmine. Truly."

"Just for the record, I still think you're a dick. And I always will. But if you don't hurt her again, I won't interfere."

I cracked my first smile since arriving at her house. "I think we have a deal."

• • •

When I pulled up to my father's house a little while later, the last thing I expected was to see Aspyn outside.

I parked and rushed out of my car. "How long have you been waiting here?"

She pulled her brown peacoat closed. "About ten minutes. I know you went to see Jasmine. She called me after you left New Hope."

"Yeah. I just got back from there. What are you doing, waiting out in the cold?"

Her teeth chattered. "The cold air calms my nerves for some reason."

"What are you nervous about?" I waved my hand toward the door. "Come on. Let's go in the house."

As she stepped inside, she rubbed her hands together. "I'm surprised you went to see Jasmine."

Her cheeks were rosy from the wind. I'd missed her so damn much.

"I had some things I needed to say," I told her. "And I thought it would be nice if, after all these years, I finally apologized for treating her poorly. I know she's skeptical about me, and I needed her to understand that my feelings for you are genuine and I'd greatly appreciate her not interfering."

"I'm surprised you felt the urgent need to do that."

"Well, I needed to do something productive while I was giving you space. I guess when something matters to someone as much as you matter to me, you want to make sure there's nothing standing in your way. Although in this case, I realize the biggest thing standing in my way has been my own damn self."

Her eyes traveled over me. "I thought I might hear from you over the past couple of days."

"Really? I've been dying to contact you, but I thought you needed space to process what I unloaded."

Aspyn looked down at her feet, and then back up at me. "I figured you might've been thinking that, which is why I decided to come over."

I felt like my entire future was dependent on the next words to come out of her mouth. My heart felt ready to fly out of my chest.

"Do you know what the lifespan of a dragonfly is?" she asked.

My brows knitted. "No."

"Five weeks or less. And some only last a few days. I was surprised to learn that." She exhaled. "We're not guaranteed any more than that ourselves, even though we go through life thinking we have all this time. I could spend the rest of my life angry at you for what you did—for yet another bad choice you made in high school." She took a few steps toward me. "Or I can choose to forgive you."

Hope filled me. "And?"

"I was the one who made the decision to cheat. Ultimately, I'm responsible for that, no matter what happened after. And you didn't know the repercussions of ratting me out. Just like I didn't know my going out drinking that night would lead to my sister and her boyfriend dying in a car accident." Aspyn sucked in some air. "Holding grudges is a choice. I don't want to hold this grudge. I'm choosing not to. I value this life too much to do that to myself or you. And I know in your heart you're not that person anymore. No more than I'm the person who binge drinks and...keys cars." She inched closer. "We've both made mistakes, mistakes with unintentionally serious consequences. But they happened. And holding onto them isn't going to change anything."

It finally felt safe to touch her. I held out my hand.

She took it and squeezed. "We both fucked up. But we also *grew* up. And somehow, in the end we found each other—as much as it might have seemed like an odd pairing in the beginning. We had more in common than we knew, and in a strange way, I feel like you're the only person who relates to me. Now I can't imagine myself with anyone else." She let go of my hand to wrap her arms around my neck. "If I don't forgive you, I don't get to love you. And that's not an option. Because I *do* love you, Troy Serrano. But you can't disappear on me like that again."

Burying my face in her neck, I felt like I could breathe for the first time in weeks. I expelled a long breath onto her skin. "I love you so much, Aspyn." I pulled back to look at her. "The moment I returned to Seattle, I knew that was no longer home for me. It didn't feel right anymore, and that's because you weren't there. Meadowbrook never felt like home until I realized that home is not about the place. It's where the person you love the most is. I love you the most, Aspyn. More than anything or anyone. I don't want to be away from you. I want to be part of your life."

Her eyes watered as she reached up to kiss me. As our tongues collided, I knew this was probably the happiest moment of my life—the start of a new beginning in Meadowbrook. And I couldn't wait to find out what the future held.

"I'll never feel like I deserve you, Dumont," I said after we broke the kiss.

"You're not perfect, Serrano. Not by a longshot. Neither am I. But I think we're perfect for each other."

That night, I went home with her. On a *weeknight*. And I never really left.

· · ·

A few weeks later, Kiki, Aspyn, and I were at the table having breakfast on a Thursday morning when Kiki turned to me and asked, "Do you live here now?"

I cleared my throat, nearly choking on my Cheerios. "Why do you ask?"

"It just seems like it."

Dressed for work in her Goofy scrubs, Aspyn smiled behind her coffee mug.

Aspyn and I had talked about officially moving in together. I'd told her that was what I wanted, but only when she was ready. Nothing was official yet. We were sort of just living life and seeing where it took us. And honestly? It was freaking awesome.

I still spent a good portion of the day at my dad's house, and I didn't join Aspyn and Kiki for dinner *every* night. But I hadn't missed one night in Aspyn's bed since the day she officially forgave me. Each night, I'd sneak over after Kiki was asleep and make sure I got up at the crack of dawn to avoid her catching us in bed together. Kiki never really knew whether I'd been there the night before or just showed up for breakfast. By some miracle, she hadn't questioned it, either—until now.

"I really like it here," I said, finally answering her. "In fact, I like it better than any other place in the world. So

I've been spending more time here, yeah. Maybe someday I'll officially move in, if your aunt lets me—and if it's okay with you, of course." I gulped.

She looked over at Aspyn. "That would be cool if Troy moved in, wouldn't it? We could have dinner with him more often, and he wouldn't have to sneak over late at night so I don't see him." Kiki giggled.

My eyes widened. *Shit.*

Aspyn sighed. "Well, alrighty then."

"I guess I wasn't as quiet as I thought, huh?" I scratched my chin.

Kiki shook her head. "Those leather shoes you sometimes wear make a squeaky sound."

"Damn. Outed by my shoes."

Aspyn cleared her throat. "I wasn't sure how you would feel about him fully moving in with us."

Kiki drank the last of her cereal milk. She set the bowl on the table and wiped her mouth with the back of her hand. "I do want him to move in. Because he makes you happy." She shrugged. "And he makes *me* happy, too."

My chest constricted—in a good way. "I know you've had a bad experience in the past, that you trusted someone else who moved into this place. So just know I don't take your invitation lightly."

"Are you sure, Kiki?" Aspyn asked.

She nodded. "Troy's different. I can just tell. I don't know how, but when I look at him..." She turned to me. "I feel like he's...forever."

Wow.

Aspyn reached for my hand. "Yeah, I know what you mean." She placed her other hand on Kiki's arm.

"Well, maybe we should ask him now. You want to do the honors?"

Kiki beamed. "Would you want to move in with us, Troy?"

I answered without hesitation. "There's nothing I want more. *Forever* is a good way to describe the gut feeling I have about this, too. I can have my stuff here tonight."

"There's no rush, you know." Aspyn chuckled.

"I guess I'm just excited."

Kiki bounced. "Can we have a movie night tonight since Troy can stay after dinner and doesn't have to pretend like he doesn't live here?"

"Yeah, sure we can." Aspyn smiled.

"Cool!"

A couple of minutes later, Kiki ran off to finish getting ready for school, and Aspyn disappeared to finish getting ready for work.

After I cleaned up our mess from breakfast, I found Aspyn in her bedroom—our bedroom now—as she brushed her hair in front of the mirror. She'd be leaving any minute to drop Kiki off at school on the way to Horizons.

"So...that went differently than I expected," I said.

She put her brush on the bureau. "I should've known she was too smart not to know what was going on. I'm glad it's out in the open, and you're finally moving in." She flipped around to face me. "I feel lucky to be able to spend more time with you."

Lucky was an understatement of how I felt. I got the sudden urge to lift her up and spin her around, so that's what I did. And after that, I plopped her down on the bed and began to tickle her.

"Oh my God. What are you doing?" she shrieked.

Moving my fingertips over her sides, I said, "What do you think I'm doing?"

Her laughter echoed throughout the room. "Stop!"

Tickling her faster, I spoke over her giggles. "It's an expression of love."

"Says who?" She kicked her legs.

"My grandfather."

"Uh! Of course. I should've known."

Kiki appeared at the doorway and started to crack up.

I was just about to put Aspyn out of her misery when I heard what sounded like material ripping. I abruptly stopped.

She hopped up and ran over to look at her butt in the mirror. "My work pants ripped."

"Crap! I'm sorry."

She pointed to her ass. "Look what you did to your favorite scrubs!"

"Damn it. Split right down the middle of Goofy's face." I wrapped my arms around her from behind and kissed the back of her neck. "He'll never laugh again."

Epilogue

Aspyn

Two years later

"Cut the cake! I'm dying for a piece!" someone shouted.

"Cut the cake, or I'll cut the cheese!" ninety-five-year-old Frank Romo yelled from around the corner, prompting laughter from the group of people gathered in Mr. Serrano's room and spilling out into the hallway.

It wasn't the type of wedding I'd imagined, and somehow that made it all the more perfect. For one, I'd never imagined getting married in a nursing home. And let's face it, I'd also never imagined marrying my high school nemesis, Troy Serrano.

We were waiting for the photograher to return from the bathroom so we could cut into our three-tiered wedding cake. It had a topper featuring a bride and groom holding knives as they prepared to stab each other. Troy and I had thought that was fitting, considering the history of our relationship.

Dressed in my lace, A-line gown, I looked around at all of the happy faces in the room, many of them over the age of eighty-five. An overwhelming feeling of gratitude came over me—for this day, and mostly for the handsome man standing next to me.

"Have I mentioned how amazing your tits look in that dress?" Troy whispered.

"Yeah. A few times, actually."

"I guess I'm excited for the honeymoon."

Troy and I would be flying to Europe for a three-week trip tomorrow, my first time overseas.

Mr. Serrano—whom I, too, now affectionately called Nonno—hadn't been doing well as of late. At ninety-two and in failing health, it wasn't easy for him to venture out anymore. In fact, he was pretty much confined to his bed. There was no way in hell we were going to accept him missing out on our wedding, though, since he'd technically brought Troy and me together. So the only option was to have the ceremony and reception at Horizons.

We'd decided to do a small ceremony and cake cutting right in his room, with some additional dancing and catered fare out in the dining room. We'd decorated Nonno's room with yellow roses, in honor of Troy's grandmother. In attendance were family, a few friends, including Jasmine, and *all* of the residents and staff of Horizons.

"Where the hell is the photographer?" Troy asked, holding the knife as we waited to cut the cake.

"I know. She's taking forever."

In the meantime, Nonno lifted his hand to get my attention.

"I'll be right back," I told Troy before walking over to his grandfather. "Is everything okay, Nonno?"

In a groggy voice, he said, "I just want to tell you how lovely you look."

"Thank you. That's very sweet."

"And also how thankful I am that you decided to have the wedding here."

"There was nowhere else we'd rather have it."

He attempted to lean in. "I saved the last secret for you, beautiful Aspyn."

I blinked. "Secret?"

"Yes. The secret to a happy relationship. I gave Troy five."

"Oh, those! Yup."

"The first five were all the happy stuff, the little things. But there are actually six, and this one is for you, because I suspect Troy is more likely to screw up than you are."

I rested my hand over his. "What is it?"

"Never go to bed angry, no matter what my knucklehead grandson says or does. Always kiss and make up before your head hits the pillow. Okay? Troy's Nonna and I rarely fought, but we had a squabble the night before she died in her sleep. Nothing major—just a fight about the temperature in the house. But if there's one thing I could change, it would be going to bed mad that night and not giving her a kiss before bed. Going to bed angry isn't worth it. Life is too short. And you never know if you're gonna have the chance to make it right."

I smiled. That was advice I would hold close to my heart. "Okay, Nonno. Got it."

Troy appeared beside me, looking so dapper in his beige suit jacket. "Hey, you holding my wife hostage over here or something?" He kissed me on the cheek. "The photographer just got back. Ready to cut the cake?"

Because it was my wedding day, I'd opted to taste a tiny bit of the cake and deal with any potential side effects from the ingredients later. Amidst the camera flashes and laughter, Troy and I pretended to get ready to smash the cake in each other's faces. But neither of us had the heart to follow through as "Love and Marriage" by—who else?— Frank Sinatra played in the background.

After the cake cutting and more photos with family, we moved out into the dining room where a catered dinner was served for all the guests. After, Troy and I danced to "We've Only Just Begun" by The Carpenters, one of the songs we'd sung together when he crashed my singalong with his guitar.

After the song ended, Kiki came running toward us, her long skirt nearly tripping her. Pinned to the front of her dress was the dragonfly that had belonged to Troy's mother, Jennifer. Troy had given it to her when he proposed to me. That day, he'd also told Kiki of his intention to adopt her once he and I were married. That was the happiest day of my life—until today. I'd be legally adopting her as well, and we'd be starting the process soon.

"Can I have some money for the vending machine?" Kiki asked. "We want to get M&Ms."

"Are you sure? You're gonna have cake in a bit."

"Please?"

I walked over to my purse and handed her a few dollars.

"Thanks, Mrs. Serrano," her friend Maisy said.

Yup. Maisy. *That* Maisy. Maisy Cummings, the girl who used to bully her. Turns out, Troy and I weren't the only ones who'd grown up and learned to forgive mistakes of the past.

Troy put his arm around me. "Everything with Kiki okay?"

"Yeah. She just wanted money."

"Ah. What else is new?" He chuckled.

The sound of silverware clanking drew my attention away from Troy and out toward the tables.

"I guess they want us to kiss," Troy said.

"Is that what it's all about? How did you know that?"

"I know all the romantic stuff," he teased.

Troy placed a long kiss on my lips that was rated PG for the audience.

We then held hands and walked around the dining room, making sure we gave every table some attention.

Framed for public viewing on a table in the corner of the room was the newspaper clipping Troy had used to propose to me. He'd actually paid the local newspaper in Meadowbrook to print...his obituary.

"I didn't know you were gonna put this on display," he said.

"It was too good not to share." I smiled.

It was a lot different from the one he'd written for the dating app.

Troy Serrano, 31, of Meadowbrook

Between his grandfather and great-grandfather, financial advisor Troy Serrano came from a line of true romantics. But despite his Nonno Louie's best efforts to share the secrets to a woman's

heart, Troy didn't always execute those gestures seamlessly. It's a good thing that didn't matter to the love of his life. Aspyn was very forgiving of Troy's lack of romantic finesse. What she instead appreciated was his undying love and loyalty, despite the many imperfections that made him who he was.

Born in Meadowbrook, New Jersey, to a single father, Troy spent most of his childhood believing he wasn't worthy of love because his mother had abandoned him. It wasn't until after she died, years later, that he learned of the regret she held in her heart over the decision she'd made. Troy vowed to use his mother's experience as a reason to never leave anything unsaid. Like his mother's beloved dragonfly, which represents transformation, Troy came to pride himself on being open to change. As such, he learned to forgive many mistakes of the past, especially his own. He also learned to spend less time feeling sorry for himself, and instead to appreciate the things he did have—like a hardworking father and grandparents who did the best they could to support him.

Despite a successful career crunching numbers for virtual strangers, by his late twenties, Troy realized that much was missing from his life. It wasn't until he reconnected with a girl from high school who'd once tried to poison him that he learned how ironic the world can be. After falling in love with her (the aforementioned Aspyn),

Troy finally experienced true happiness. And for the first time in his life, he felt worthy of love.

He also realized, through the eyes of Aspyn's young niece, Kiki, that he wasn't alone in the plight to achieve a feeling of belonging in this world. Together, as kindred spirits who grew up without their birth mothers, Troy and Kiki bonded in a way he hadn't been able to with anyone else. Troy remained convinced that they were always meant to find each other.

So, you see, if this obituary were real and Troy really had passed away at the ripe age of thirty-one, he would've died a happy and enlightened man. But he's very much alive, and there's so much more he needs to achieve. Namely, he wants to marry Aspyn, adopt Kiki, and someday expand their family.

Thus, this particular obituary isn't an obituary at all. It's a proposal. It's not the end to a story. It's just the beginning—but only if she says yes.

Other Books by

PENELOPE WARD

The Aristocrat

The Anti-Boyfriend

RoomHate

The Crush

The Day He Came Back

Just One Year

When August Ends

Love Online

Gentleman Nine

Drunk Dial

Mack Daddy

Stepbrother Dearest

Neighbor Dearest

Jaded and Tyed (A novelette)

Sins of Sevin

Jake Undone (Jake #1)

Jake Understood (Jake #2)

My Skylar

Gemini

Well Played (Co-written with Vi Keeland)

Not Pretending Anymore (Co-written with Vi Keeland)

Cocky Bastard (Co-written with Vi Keeland)

Playboy Pilot (Co-written with Vi Keeland)

Mister Moneybags (Co-written with Vi Keeland)

British Bedmate (Co-written with Vi Keeland)

Park Avenue Player (Co-written with Vi Keeland)

Stuck-Up Suit (Co-written with Vi Keeland)

Rebel Heir (Co-written with Vi Keeland)

Rebel Heart (Co-written with Vi Keeland)

Hate Notes (Co-written with Vi Keeland)

Dirty Letters (Co-written with Vi Keeland)

My Favorite Souvenir (Co-written with Vi Keeland)

Happily Letter After (Co-written with Vi Keeland)

Acknowledgements

The acknowledgements are always the hardest part of the book to write. There are simply too many people that contribute to the success of a book, and it's impossible to properly thank each and every one.

First and foremost, I need to thank the readers all over the world who continue to support and promote my books. Your support and encouragement are my reasons for continuing this journey. And to all of the book bloggers/bookstagrammers/TikTokers who work tirelessly to support me book after book, please know how much I appreciate you.

To Vi – I would undoubtedly not be sane without you! You're the best friend and partner in crime that I could ask for. Not to mention, you're the GOAT.

To Julie – Thank you for your friendship, your amazing writing, outlook, and for always being just a click away. This year more than any, you inspire me!

To Luna – Getting to see you over the holidays is always a highlight of my year! Thank you for your love, support, and friendship and for being one of my biggest cheerleaders.

To Erika –I am so thankful for your love, humor, and summer visits. Thank you for always brightening my days with your messages of encouragement and nostalgic spirit. It's an E thing!

To Cheri – An amazing friend and supporter. Thanks for always looking out for me. Your Wednesday messages mean everything.

To Darlene – I am so grateful to have met you, and it has nothing to do with the delicious Medjool dates you send me, but rather your valued friendship.

To my Facebook reader group, Penelope's Peeps – I adore you all. You are my home and favorite place to be.

To my agent extraordinaire, Kimberly Brower – Thank you for everything you do and for getting my books out into the world.

To my editor Jessica Royer Ocken – It's always a pleasure working with you. I look forward to many more experiences to come.

To Elaine of Allusion Publishing – Thank you for being the best proofreader, formatter, and friend a girl could ask for.

To Julia Griffis of The Romance Bibliophile – Your eagle eye is amazing. Thank you for being so wonderful to work with.

To my assistant Brooke – Thank you for hard work in handling all of the things Vi and I can't seem to ever get to. We appreciate you so much!

To Kylie and Jo at Give Me Books – You guys are truly the best out there! Thank you for your tireless promotional work. I would be lost without you.

To Letitia Hasser of RBA Designs – My awesome cover designer. Thank you for always working with me until the finished product is exactly perfect.

To my husband – Thank you for always taking on so much more than you should have to so that I am able to write. I love you so much.

To the best parents in the world – I'm so lucky to have you! Thank you for everything you have ever done for me and for always being there.

Last but not least, to my daughter and son – Mommy loves you. You are my motivation and inspiration!

About the Author

Penelope Ward is a *New York Times, USA Today* and *#1 Wall Street Journal* bestselling author.

She grew up in Boston with five older brothers and spent most of her twenties as a television news anchor. Penelope resides in Rhode Island with her husband, son and beautiful daughter with autism.

With over two million books sold, she is a 21-time *New York Times* bestseller and the author of over twenty novels.

Penelope's books have been translated into over a dozen languages and can be found in bookstores around the world.

Made in United States
Orlando, FL
14 May 2022

17852781R00209